DOLPHIN CH

By James Carmo

For Margreet

1

Chapter One

Lucy Parr sat perched on a large boulder. She rested her elbows on her knees with her feet half immersed in the rocky pool below. She was wearing a black wet-suit, cut off at her elbows and knees. The exposed skin of her lower arms and legs was pink with cold from where she had been in the sea. Her dark hair dripped water down her back. The sun was still low in the sky and the light that dappled the water half dazzled her. She squinted as she stared back out to sea, scanning the horizon.

Lucy felt a pleasant sense of tiredness as she rested on the rock. Only twenty minutes before she had been swimming in the sea, free amongst the swirls and eddies of the cold waves that beat rhythmically at the base of the cliffs. She knew the waters well and was quite aware of the dangers that they held. The tidal currents could pull an unsuspecting swimmer out to sea before they knew it. Even a strong swimmer like Lucy was no match for the treacherous seas around this part of the coast. She shouldn't really be there, but Lucy had got up early and slipped out before her aunt Bethany had a chance to stop her. The sea exerted an irresistible pull on her and she could not keep away. Bethany knew that was part of who Lucy was and that although the seas

2

were dangerous her niece would be safe. She knew that Lucy would not be swimming alone.

Twenty metres behind her, half way up the cliff path, a boy crouched behind another rock, looking down upon her. He didn't want to be seen and peered out around the rock cautiously. He'd been watching her for some while as she swum with confident powerful strokes through the sea, diving and dipping in the sea like a seal, close by and further out. He'd seen who she had been swimming with too.

The boy was thin, a year or two younger than Lucy, with curly hair, and a narrow face. He looked smaller than other children of his own age. He was wearing a baggy tee-shirt and jeans and shivered slightly in the early morning breeze. The girl in the wetsuit had climbed back out of the sea some minutes before and was sitting still, as though she were rooted to the rock that she was sitting on. The boy was cramped behind the boulder and thought it safe enough to stretch out his legs, but doing so he accidentally kicked a pebble that skittered down the steep path to the shore. Lucy glanced up and the boy rapidly pulled in his legs so that she would not see him. Lucy sensed that someone was looking down at her and felt the hairs on the back of her neck prickle uncomfortably. She turned and stood up, taking a step or two towards the path that led up the cliff from the cove. The boy glanced nervously round the boulder and saw the girl coming towards him. He turned and ran away up the path.

Lucy watched the slight figure run off. The slope was steep and he was soon out of breath. As the boy slowed, Lucy had a clear sight of him as he turned the bend and disappeared. 'Just a kid' she thought. She sighed. It would have been nice to have someone to talk to.

There was an overhanging ledge of rock in one corner of the beach where Lucy had left her normal clothes. If the small cove was empty, she could change out of her wet-suit in seclusion without being overlooked. She peeled the wetsuit off and quickly dried herself with a large towel. Once dressed, she stuffed all her things into her rucksack and hoisted it onto her back. She walked over the pebbles towards the steep path that led out of Old Man's cove. Her legs felt heavy with tiredness and her feet sank into the pebbles as she walked. Small waves broke rhythmically on the pebble shoreline. The tide was coming in and had obscured the thin crescent of sand that was exposed when the tide was out. The smell of salt and seaweed on the air was particularly strong.

Lucy glanced back towards the sea again. Could she see them? No, no they were gone. Once or twice as she clambered up the steep path out of the cove Lucy had to hang on to clumps of grass to help pull herself up. She wasn't surprised the boy had exhausted himself trying to run up the path. She wondered who he was. They were a couple of miles out of Merwater. Maybe he was staying in one of the holiday cottages, she thought.

Once she cleared the top of the cliff, the path came out into an open field. Sometimes there were sheep grazing but there were

4

none there today. In the early morning light, the rabbits would emerge from their burrows under the hawthorn bushes and graze on the dew covered stems of grass. She could see their neat droppings on the grassy mound where they liked to sit. Lucy glanced back out at the sea. It was so great to be here in Cornwall. She wished she could stay here forever.

Lucy climbed over the stile to the road and pulled the old bike that Mary at the farmhouse had lent her out of the ditch where she had hidden it. It was all downhill from here and Lucy was happy to free-wheel gently down the lane. She clattered over the cattle grid into the farmyard, got off and propped the bike up. Bethany's studio was a converted outbuilding. Its iron-framed windows looked south down the valley and let in plenty of light all day. Lucy pushed open the door of the studio and walked in. Although it was still early, Bethany was already at work at her painting. She had a brush in hand and was standing back from it, regarding her work critically. A short bald man was staring out of the picture with a distant, almost angry expression on his face, while a group of sheep clustered around him, breathing steamily in the cold early morning air. Lucy thought the painting was a bit weird, but Bethany explained that she wanted to catch the faces of ordinary local people and didn't want to romanticise their lives.

'Hey Kiddo.' Bethany turned and smiled at Lucy. 'Or should I say early bird. I was still snoring when you got up.'

'Yes you were!' laughed Lucy.

'Oi, cheeky! You must be famished. I held off from breakfast till you got back. How does fried egg on toast sound?'

'Sounds pretty good to me' replied Lucy, 'Make it two.' Bethany's studio was divided into the work area, where Bethany did her painting, a kitchen area and a raised platform with a bed and sofa where Bethany could relax in the evening. Lucy slept on a camp bed at the foot of Bethany's own when she stayed there.

They went through to the kitchen and Lucy sat down at the table. Bethany put on the kettle, dropped bread into the toaster and put the frying pan on the hob.

'I'm guessing you took another early morning dip in the sea, Kiddo?' Bethany asked, regarding Lucy from under her fringe of curly blond hair.

'You know me' Lucy replied smiling, 'Gotta take a swim in the morning.'

'Ordinary people just have a shower you know. I still worry about you every time you go out. You know how dangerous those waters are. Goodness knows what your Dad would say if he knew what you were up to.'

Lucy knew the best tactic when Bethany started worrying again was not to say much in response and hope that she'd start talking about something else instead. She propped her head in her hands and stared dreamily out of the window. A sheep stood in the field ruminatively staring back at her. She glanced at Bethany.

Sometimes when she looked at Bethany, it felt as though Mum was looking back at her. Bethany was the younger sister by some six years and although their hair was completely different Bethany still had Mum's eyes and smile, sparkling with life. There was something about them both that was very similar. She still felt the pang of pain at the thought that she would never see Mum again. The feeling never seemed to get any better. She wondered how Dad felt. Maybe that was why he didn't get on with Bethany. Perhaps she just reminded him of Mum too much.

He didn't talk about Mum so much now, but Lucy wished that he did. She loved it when he told her about how they had met and what they used to do before Lucy had been born. Bethany said that people cope with grief in different ways. Dad just seemed to shut himself up in his work though.

It was the summer holidays now and he would be coming down to join them in a couple of weeks. She wondered how he felt back home all alone in the house. It'd be nice if he could have come down to Cornwall already, but on the other hand he'd give her much less freedom than Bethany did and she certainly wouldn't be able to go for early morning swims in the sea alone. Bethany let her do pretty much whatever she wanted. Sometimes Lucy wondered why.

'So tomorrow if you get up at the crack of dawn and want to go swimming in the sea, wake me up and I'll come too' continued Bethany, sliding a fried egg from the pan onto a plate. 'I love seeing you swim with them you know, and I can do some sketching as well while I keep an eye on you. I've got an idea for a picture I want to work on.'

'They're not always there when I swim in the sea. It's great when they are, but I don't always know.'

'Of course, but I don't even want you in the sea if you-know-who is not there to keep you safe' replied Bethany.

'I know, I know' said Lucy patiently. Bethany handed her a plate with fried egg on toast.

After breakfast Lucy went outside and wandered around the farmyard while Bethany continued to work on her painting. Her aunt had announced that they needed to go into Merwater to run a few errands later that morning and Lucy kicked her heels until they were ready to set off. Lucy saw Mary emerging from the farmhouse and walk briskly across the yard. Lucy's idea of a farmer's wife had been of a motherly lady baking endless loaves of bread and cakes in the kitchen. In fact Mary's husband worked in an office in Truro and she ran the farm pretty much single-handedly. She wore jeans and wellies and always seemed to be on the go.

'Hi there Lucy, you want to come and look at the Jerseys with me on the top field?'

'Yeah, why not?' replied Lucy. They strode companionably up to the top field a quarter of a mile away. 'What do you need to check them for anyway?' asked Lucy.

'Cows need more looking after than you might think' replied Mary. 'I want to check on the grazing in the pasture and look at the state of their trough. I might move them to the next field if the grass is getting low. They need milking twice a day, three hundred and sixty five days a year, Christmas and birthdays included. You don't get any lie-ins when you farm cattle.'

'So which one's called Daisy?' joked Lucy as they walked along. Mary shot her an amused glance and smiled back.

'Oh I've got nicknames for a few of them, but you're not really supposed to get close to them you know, or it's too hard when you have to send them off to market.'

'Do you get lots of money for them when you sell them?' Lucy asked.

'Hmm, not as much as I'd like' replied Mary. 'There wouldn't be much money in the pot if we lived by farming alone. Why do you think my Darren works for the council in Truro? We'd go broke otherwise. No, it's not easy, but there's something about it which hooks you in. I can't imagine myself behind a desk somewhere, can you?' Lucy smiled and shook her head.

Lucy wandered around the field as Mary tended to the cows. They were big animals and she wasn't really used to them. She kept her distance and tried to avoid walking in any cow-pats. Somewhere above them a light aircraft droned lazily. A song thrush burbled out its song from the hedgerow. When Mary was done with the cows, they started to walk back down the hill to the farmhouse.

'Do you go out on the sea much Mary?' she asked.

'Oh the sea's a beauty all right, but she doesn't like me much' laughed Mary. 'I go as green as this grass here when I'm on a boat', she said kicking a tuft to prove the point. 'I prefer to have my feet on firm ground. But then I'm not actually from round here you know' she went on, 'I'm a city girl that ran away to the country. My Darren's the local boy and he knows all about the tales of the fisher folk of Merwater. You should ask him sometime.'

When they got back Mary went through to her office to do some paperwork and Lucy strolled over to the studio to find Bethany.

'You ready to hit town?' asked her aunt. She'd been cleaning her brushes in turpentine and was wiping them dry with a cloth. Lucy hated the smell and pulled a bit of a face. 'Oh I know these turps do smell don't they?' Bethany added sympathetically, 'let's get on the road.'

They climbed into Bethany's Land Rover. It was an old, rusty and uncomfortable vehicle and had a bewildering number of gears. Until last week Bethany had had to prevent the exhaust from falling off by tying it on with a pair of old stockings. She grumbled about how much it was costing her in the garage but Lucy knew that Bethany loved the old car really.

Bethany would have preferred a studio overlooking the sea, but places with a sea-view were far too expensive to rent. Her studio on the farm was a bit basic and icy in the middle of winter, but it wasn't far from the sea and Bethany liked it there. She and Mary were now firm friends. They drove up the hedge-lined track that

Lucy had free-wheeled down on her bike barely an hour and a half before.

Up at the top of the lane, the main road was busy. It was high season now and there were plenty of tourists around at the moment. They soon got stuck behind a car pulling a caravan, but luckily it turned off down the road leading to a campsite just before Merwater.

Merwater had originally been a fishing village, with a small harbour built at the base of a steep hill that reared up from the sea. Its fishing cottages had mostly been bought up by rich city types as second homes and its shops turned into trendy cafes, boutiques and gift stores. There were only a few fishing boats left now and there were more boats taking tourists on tours of the harbour.

On a winter's day when there were no sight-seers around, the place looked half dead. Most of the local people were forced to live in the new part of town built over the ridge of the hill where houses were more affordable. They drove slowly down the main road of the town and pulled into the small car park just behind the harbour. They were lucky to find a parking space.

Lucy caught sight of the bus stop. A few months before she'd run away from Dad and turned up here on the bus unannounced at the beginning of half term. She hadn't even had Bethany's address and it had only been with luck that she'd found her aunt at all. Her life hadn't quite been the same since. In a way it seemed ages ago now, but in another sense it was as though she'd only just arrived on the bus.

Bethany said she needed to pop into one of the local galleries on the High Street. They'd sold one of her pictures and she was going to pick up the cheque and take it straight to the bank. Then she had some chores to do before she went to the grocers to get some food.

'It'll be pretty boring for you though. Maybe you'd rather hang out by the harbour instead. I'll catch up with you here in say forty five minutes?' She set off.

The sun was high in the sky now. It was going to be a hot day. Lucy idly kicked a pebble and looked out at the sea. If only she were in the cold salty water again, not just looking at it. It was great here in Cornwall, but sometimes Lucy wished her best friend Amy was here with her too. Lucy had lots to tell her and you could only fit so much onto a postcard. She hadn't really met any other kids of her own age down here and the children of Bethany's friends were all too young for her to really get on with.

Lucy walked over to the sea wall, just to the left of the small harbour. The tide was out now and she thought she might spot a crab or two scuttling along over the rocks below. She could hear the noise of chatter and as she looked over the sea wall she saw a group of children on the rocks below, messing around at the edge of the sea. Lucy felt shy but she kept looking. There was a group of about eight girls and boys. Some were her age and one or two were much younger. Probably someone's brother or sister she thought, hanging around with the big kids.

As she looked on, trying not to seem conspicuous, she realised the atmosphere amongst the group of children was turning ugly. It seemed that a couple of the older children were picking on a thin, younger boy with curly hair. With a start, Lucy realised that she recognised him. It was the boy she had seen running away from her up the path from Old Man's Cove earlier that morning. She thought that he had been a tourist from one of the nearby holiday cottages. Yet here he was in what looked like a group of local kids.

Lucy could hear one of the girls calling 'Liar!' at the boy and then another kid threw a slimy length of seaweed at him. It caught him with a wet slap across the face. She could see that the boy was upset and out of his depth amongst the group of aggressive children. His face turned red and Lucy thought he was going to start to cry. She felt anxious. The boy with the curly hair started moving away from the group as the children continued calling him names. Lucy had to crane over the sea wall to see where he was going. Another kid threw a wet length of seaweed at him and it stuck to the back of his head. The children laughed.

Lucy began to feel angry. She hated bullying. She had a strong sense of justice and simply could not just stand there and watch it happen. She called out but none of the children seemed to notice her. It looked like they were starting to chase the boy. She had to get down there. She glanced over the edge of the sea wall. There was a rusty old iron ladder fixed into the stones of the wall leading down to the stony beach below. Lucy straddled the wall and clambered down the ladder quickly.

Most of the children were still milling around but the boy with curly hair and a couple of the older kids seemed to have disappeared. Lucy suddenly felt shy again now she was near the group but strode across towards them anyway. A couple of the kids were shouting something and she turned to look at the direction they were shouting towards. To her surprise there was what looked like the opening to a tunnel in the sea wall which led back into the town. What seemed like a stream was trickling out of it over the rocks and into the sea. She guessed that the kids had disappeared into the tunnel and made her way quickly to the opening. She peered up into the tunnel's dark mouth nervously.

The tunnel ran a short way under a building and then opened up into the light again. The stream tumbled down over boulders and stones whilst old stone walls were built up on each side. Buildings lined the stream on each side at the top of the stone walls. Lucy could see the kids chasing the boy up the stream, jumping from rock to rock to avoid getting their feet wet. Lucy made her way after them, gingerly at first, trying to catch up and curious to know where they were going. They were still yelling insults at the boy who was running fast up the stream. He wasn't bothering about trying to keep his feet dry and was just running through the water, his trainers sodden with water. The other two kids were more careful and so was Lucy. Up ahead the stream went under the High Street and she could hear the rumble of traffic and see one or two people walking past at pavement level overhead and glancing down at them curiously.

Lucy kept going under the road. On the other side in the daylight again, she could see that the stream went up sharply, following the line of the hill. Then on the right there was a narrow channel where a smaller stream joined the main one. She paused. The two older kids had continued up along the main channel and disappeared around a bend, shouting as they went. Lucy had a feeling that the boy with curly hair might have slipped away up the smaller stream to shake them off. She decided to give it a go.

The stone walls built up on each side of the smaller channel got very narrow really quickly, barely wider than her shoulders. The stones Lucy was walking over were also very slippery, with green algae and slime growing over them. Fortunately the stream here was barely a trickle and so her feet did not get wet. She glanced up. There were no buildings above them now and grass was growing over the edge of each side of the walls. The stream and walls curved round to the left and Lucy thought she could hear the boy ahead of her, though she wasn't sure. Suddenly a stone hurtled past her head, banging noisily into the water at her feet.

'Go away and leave me alone!' the boy shouted down at her. Lucy looked up and could see him standing on the edge of the walled stream above her, with another stone held threateningly in his clenched fist.

'It's all right' called Lucy quickly. 'I'm not with them.' The boy lowered his fist and let the stone drop. She could see that he had recognised her.

'What are you doing here?' he asked warily.

'I didn't want those kids to get you' Lucy replied. 'What was that all about anyway?' She could see now where a stone wall on the left had tumbled down and she clambered up a steep grass bank to where the boy was standing. She was out of breath and sat down on the edge of the wall next to him, panting slightly.

The boy didn't answer but stared at her directly.

'You're a Dolphin-Child' he said after a long pause. It was more a statement than a question. Lucy was nonplussed. She hadn't expected him to say that. She'd never heard the term before and she could only guess what he meant by it.

'What's it to you anyway?' she replied guardedly.

'I saw you this morning. You were swimming with two dolphins. Only a Dolphin-Child can swim with them the way you did.'

'What about you then? Are you one too?' Lucy half hoped he was, but she didn't even know what a Dolphin-Child was supposed to be though, not really.

'No, well, I mean....' He became unsure of himself. 'I don't know.'

'Do you dream about them?' Lucy asked.

'Yes, yes I do' he replied hesitantly.

16

Chapter Two

It was a bright calm day. Sunlight sparkled on the surface of the windless sea. Spirit broke the surface of the water to breath through his air hole and could see that the sun had almost reached its highest point in the sky. He sliced back through the low waves and continued to swim just below the surface.

He was alone, returning from a pod of dolphins that lived beyond the islands to the south. Spirit felt a sense of independence and freedom at being away from the other members of his own pod for a while. A few moons ago, he had left the pod for his own coming of age swim in the same way that his best friend Dancer had a year before that. Unlike Dancer though, he had stolen away in the middle of the night because Storm, the oldest dolphin in their pod, had forbidden him from going. He'd got into trouble and he knew that he was lucky to be alive and well today. Spirit had got trapped in a loop of steel cable from a discarded sea buoy and had thought that he was going to die there. He could never have imagined how he would end up being saved. The wounds where the steel cable had cut into his tail had healed now, but he would carry the scars for the rest of his life.

Spirit used the be the smallest dolphin in the pod, but he was growing fast and soon he'd be bigger than Dancer he reckoned, though she joked that he'd have to catch himself a few more herring before that happened. Spirit had a small star-like mark on his chest and it was that identifying sign which Storm had said first hinted to them that he was in some way special and out of the ordinary. Spirit felt pretty normal really, but some extraordinary things had happened to him over the last few months and he knew that his life would never be the same again.

Since then Spirit had learned much more about the lore of the sea and was confident to swim alone, even if it was always safer with the rest of the pod. Spirit was careful to use his ability to echo-locate using clicking and monitor what was in the sea around him. He didn't want killer whales to ambush him like they had done once before when he was with Storm. Spirit like all dolphins was able to emit high-pitched clicks from his head without even opening his mouth. When water visibility was poor, which was often the case, the high-pitched clicks would bounce off any fish or rocks in the water and return to him, enabling him to construct a mental picture of what was in front of him, even when he could not actually see with his eyes. This echo-location was a valuable tool and he had learned to rely on it much more over the past few months.

Spirit listened as he swam. Across the vast expanse of ocean, he could hear whales calling to each other in the far distance, their eerie and haunting songs travelling tens of miles between the great mammals of the deep. Spirit could not yet hear the whistles and clicks of his own pod, but he knew that he soon would. His pod used to live much closer to islands but now, though they never stayed in one part of the sea for too long, they had moved nearer to the mainland and that suited Spirit well.

Spirit had been sent on what Storm had called a mission, though Chaser, another dolphin in the pod, had jokingly said that was too grand a term for what was really just a messenger errand. Spirit knew what he meant, but it had been an exciting trip nevertheless and he was eager to get back to the pod and tell them what had happened. Before long he could hear the calls of his own pod members and knew that he did not have far to go before he was back amongst them.

It was Dancer of course that was the first to swim up and greet him.

'Hey Spirit, it's so good to see you again' she called happily, swimming up and around him. He chased her and they leapt excitedly from the water before twisting tightly around each other. Eventually they rested on the surface and laughed.

'So were you successful?' asked Dancer curiously.

'I'm not sure. I hope so' he replied. The other dolphins in the pod swam up and greeted him, gently rubbing noses. Moonlight and Summer both nudged him affectionately while Storm, Chaser and Breeze looked on. Summer's newly born calf hung in the water next to his mother, not knowing what to do. Dolphins do not name their calves until three summers have passed, once the pod know the true character of the new addition. Until he was old enough to be named properly, the pod called any calves 'No-Name'. Yet already Summer said that she had a feeling that her calf might be called Shimmer, the same name as a wise old dolphin that had died a few months before.

'What of your trip Spirit?' asked Storm seriously. Though the pod did not have a leader, Storm was the oldest among them and carried most authority. Spirit had been sent on a special journey to try and restore peace among two neighbouring pods. A young dolphin called Blue, just a little older than Spirit himself, had argued with his own pod and run away to another without telling them. It reminded Spirit of the time that he himself had swum away in the dead of night to go on his 'coming of age' swim. Blue though was angry with his pod and did not want to go back. He had taken up with another group of dolphins further away from the islands and as a result the two pods had become estranged. They had clashed angrily, chasing the same shoals of fish and the council of dolphins had asked Storm to go and intervene. But Storm had sent Spirit instead, saying to everyone's surprise that the younger dolphin was better able to restore the peace than he was. Though Storm did not admit it, he was not entirely sure that he was right. Now he was anxious to find out.

'The trip went well I think Storm' replied Spirit cautiously. 'At first I could tell that Blue was really angry and that he did not want to listen to anything I would say. So I didn't say anything at all but stayed with the pod and got to know them all slowly. They'd heard a little of my story and wanted to know more. Eventually Blue realised that he was not so very different to me and we got to like each other.

I told him about what had happened to me. Then he opened up about why he had run away. I don't know, but I think that maybe he will go and see his own pod again. I hope they'll start talking again anyway. I thought I might go back and see Blue again soon.'

'You have done well Spirit' said Storm. 'Now rest awhile. You can tell us all more later.'

'Yes and all the gossip and stories' added Breeze. Spirit smiled.

'Of course' he said.

It felt good to be back. In a way his trip had not been so important, but he knew that Storm had put his trust in the young dolphin and Spirit hadn't wanted to let him down. Just a few months ago, he had been eager to prove that he was the equal of all the others in the pod. Now that he was accepted without question, he felt he truly had come of age. Yet there was an edge to his newly found respect. The others thought that he was different to them and apart from Dancer, he wondered whether at some level his connection to Lucy made them all a bit wary of him. The group spread out again and he and Dancer swam along together, talking quietly.

'What was it really like?' asked Dancer.

'I was so nervous' admitted Spirit 'At first no one would speak to me at all. I was ready just to turn around and come straight back again. But I was hungry and I needed to swim with them to hunt and feed. After the hunting trip the others seemed to warm to me a little, but Blue just ignored me. I can't say I liked him. It's no wonder that his home pod were angry with him. Like I said to Storm though, I did get through to him in the end, but you can't imagine how glad I am to get home to you all.' Dancer laughed appreciatively. She was just happy to have her friend back again.

Breeze called out to say that he had spotted a shoal of mackerel a league or so to the east and the dolphins set off to hunt. They swam round and round the shoal until it formed into a tight ball. Then one by one the dolphins plunged into the middle, each taking a fish or two before giving the next dolphin a turn. Though they could have eaten every fish, they were not like humans, who would scoop up every last one in their nets. They let the larger part of the shoal escape.

'That way' said Breeze, 'we will eat again another day.'

Spirit caught two fish and having eaten the first, took the second smaller fish to where Summer's calf was watching apprehensively. Not long ago, Spirit had been the youngster of the pod. Now No-Name was trying to find her way in the world, keeping close to her mother's side and calling out anxiously if she thought they might be separated. Spirit nudged the fish playfully towards the young calf, but she didn't really know what to do with it.

'She's still drinking milk you know Spirit' smiled Summer. 'I'll have that fish though' she laughed, snapping it up. 'I'm eating for two at the moment.' Spirit still marvelled at how small and vulnerable Summer's calf was. No-Name had not learnt to speak yet and Spirit could hardly remember ever having been that small.

It made him think of his own mother, Star-Gazer. She had disappeared in a storm fifteen moons ago. He had been much older than Summer's calf was now when Star-Gazer had disappeared, but he still felt her loss. It ached within him. He would never be able to tell his mother everything that had happened to him since she had disappeared and how his life had been transformed over the past few months. How he wished he could still speak to her. The wound of her loss was still raw and was all the more difficult because he didn't know what had happened to her.

'Star-Gazer was a good mother to you' said Summer, guessing at his thoughts. 'I hope I am as good a mother to this little one. Spirit smiled with his eyes, feeling emotional and then turned slightly to hide his feelings.

'I remember one time before you were born' Summer went on dreamily, 'when we were both looking up at the stars one night. Star-Gazer wouldn't let me sleep, though I was ready to. She said that something special was just about to happen and she was right. Five shooting stars streaked across the sky and seemed to hit the sea not far from where we were. Even though it was dark, Star-Gazer insisted that we chase after them. In stories it is said that it's the light from shooting stars that gives fish their iridescent silvery scales, but Star-Gazer told me that was nonsense. She hoped to find out what shooting stars were really made of. I was only interested if you could eat them, but she searched and searched with a passion all night long. We never did find those shooting stars in the water and when dawn came we slept for most of the next day.'

She looked back at Spirit. He was lost in thought.

'Get along now' she said. Summer understood how he felt. Spirit swam a short way off on his own. Dancer joined him.

'You okay?' she asked.

'I think so' he replied. Spirit glanced up. High above, he could see that a cloud had passed in front of the sun and the sea was in shadow. It would soon pass though, he thought.

'I know what you need' continued Dancer.

'More fish?' Spirit attempted a weak joke.

'No silly. You need time with Lucy. Has she come to you in the last couple of days?'

Lucy had a unique gift; a special technique of being able to use the power of her mind to pass from dry land to the watery world of dolphins. She had a particular connection with Spirit and it was him that she normally visited, but when Spirit had been trapped, Lucy had used her powers to transport herself and contact Dancer instead. Together they had been able to help save their friend's life. It had been so strange for Dancer to see this apparition, gliding along underwater effortlessly in a way that no human should be able to do, her hair floating out like the tentacles of a sea anemone. It was almost as though Lucy were a ghost.

24

Yet when they saved Spirit, Dancer had also seen the real Lucy in the water, stroking Spirit's flank, talking to him softly with words that she could not understand. It was then that Dancer had realised just how special the link between Spirit and Lucy actually was. They appeared to give each other a kind of energy. It seemed to Dancer that Lucy helped made Spirit feel complete.

Dancer couldn't explain it, but just accepted it. She didn't feel at all jealous. She understood that Spirit was different from most other dolphins, but it seemed a good thing to her, not a bad thing. Not everyone in the pod thought the same as Dancer though.

Spirit had been away on a challenging trip to another pod for a couple of days and though he would not admit it, Dancer could tell that he was tired. Being with Lucy again was just what he needed, she thought. It would re-energize him.

'Can you not just call to Lucy and get her to come to you somehow?' Dancer asked. Spirit gave a shake of his head.

'I haven't learned how to do that. Maybe I never will. I don't know. Somehow Lucy uses her mind to stretch out to me, but I cannot do the same when I want to' Spirit replied. 'I can't stretch out to her. I will have to wait until she is ready to come to me again.'

It seemed unfair to Dancer that humans could put their heads underwater and glimpse the world in which dolphins lived, but dolphins could not look up into the world of humans. Yes they could poke their heads into the air, or even leap high out of the water and see boats and such things, but they could never visit the places where humans lived. It was like looking into the night sky and trying to guess what it was like to live on the moon.

'She'll come to you soon, don't you worry' Dancer assured him.

The pod came together again and rested a while just under the surface while their stomachs digested their catch of fish. Dancer's words were truer than she thought. As they relaxed, Spirit suddenly found that Lucy was by his side. It always took him by surprise, no matter how often it happened.

'Hi Spirit' she said. 'How was your trip to the pod where Blue is staying? Did you bring him back to his own pod?' Spirit quickly explained to Lucy what had happened. He never knew how long she would be able stay with him. It was exhausting he knew for her to linger there with him for any length of time. She was more practiced now and though once or twice she had stayed with him for over half an hour, even now she might disappear after a minute or two, fading away in front of his eyes.

'I'd love to see you for real' he said. 'Will you come to the sea tomorrow morning?'

'Yes I can' replied Lucy with an excited grin. 'Down by Old Man's Cove at first light. You know the place.' When Lucy was with him for real, they could not talk together. It was only when Lucy came to him as a vision that they were able to communicate with each other, using neither human words nor dolphin clicks or whistles, but something different to pass thoughts between them.

Lucy stretched out her hand towards him. She could not truly touch him when she came to him as an apparition. That would

26

have to wait till the next morning. As she did so, Lucy faded and then disappeared into the water. Spirit was glad at the prospect of seeing Lucy for real again. He gave Dancer a gentle nudge and she woke up.

'You're coming with me to see Lucy tomorrow morning' he said.

Now that the pod stayed in the waters close to the mainland, it was much easier for Spirit to see Lucy. When he had stolen away for his coming of age journey, it had taken Spirit a whole day to swim from the waters near the islands to the mainland. It had been a long and arduous swim. Now, if he chose, Spirit could swim to the cliffs of the main body of land in less than an hour. The next morning the dawn broke red across the sky as the veil of darkness lifted. It used to be that Spirit would sleep through sunrise every day. Now it was his favourite time to be awake. He nudged Dancer until she opened her eyes and began to look around her.

'Come on sleepy head' he said to the groggy-headed Dancer. 'Let's go.' Dolphins are never fully asleep as humans are. One part of their mind has to stay awake so that they can stay alert to danger, keep their blow holes clear and breathe. Dancer yawned.

'I was having such a nice dream' she said. 'I was flying through the air with the gulls and swooping down over the heads of humans.'

'Well I was having a dream that you'd caught me some mackerel to eat' joked Spirit, 'but dreams like that never come true.'

'Cheeky!' exclaimed Dancer. They told Summer where they were going and headed off.

Spirit felt pleased at the thought of seeing Lucy again. A few months before when Lucy had saved him, an incredible energy had passed between them when she touched him. But three days afterwards, Lucy had had to return to her home far away from the sea. It was hard to imagine what the world above water must be like. Lucy had given him an idea, by using the power of her mind to project an image to him of what her home and school looked like. Spirit had been shocked at how small and cramped it had appeared. He was used to the wide open seas. The thought of walls horrified him.

It was painful for Spirit to realise that Lucy had to go home. He had only seen her for real two more times before she did and even then she had been with a fully grown adult on a boat, while he had been in the water. It was not the same as swimming with her.

Lucy had come to him using the power of her mind many times since, but to see her in real life still felt special, even though they could not speak when they did. Now she was back by the sea and he had seen her for real half a dozen times or more, carrying her on his back and feeling her warm skin against his own.

The two dolphins broke the waves happily as they sped along.

'I'm hungry' complained Dancer.

'We'll eat soon enough' replied Spirit. 'You can wait a while yet for your breakfast' he joked.

They neared the high grey cliffs which sheered up above them. They were the tallest things that Spirit had ever seen. Gulls wheeled lazily above them in the updrafts from the sea. It was along this stretch that he had become disorientated and confused by a human on a jet ski machine and then he had been ensnared in a great loop of steel cord attached to a discarded buoy. The thought of it made him wince. He had learned since about how to deal with the jarring noise of jet skis and had encountered them several times since without problems, though the sound did still give him a terrible headache. He was glad when he had swum out of sight of that spot.

'Can you see her yet?' asked Dancer. Spirit took a low leap over the waves to look.

'I think so' he replied uncertainly. He could see a figure sitting on a rock by the water's edge, knees tucked up under her chin, looking out to sea. They got closer. 'Yes, it is her!'

As they approached Lucy spotted them and stood up on the rock and waved in their direction. She called out making noises that they could not understand.

'That's her alright!' exclaimed Dancer. She was pleased to see Lucy too. Dancer had only seen her once since Lucy had returned to the coast. It may be that Spirit had a special connection with Lucy but Dancer was very fond of her too.

When they were a metre or two from the rock where Lucy was standing, she jumped into the sea next to him. Spirit could tell that for a human she was a good swimmer, but she was vulnerable in the sea with its strong currents and undertows and he had to take care of her.

Lucy stretched out her hand and touched Spirits flank. Again he felt a current of energy pass between the two of them and a sense of understanding beyond anything that could be said in words. She said something and looked him in the eye. He could feel that she was happy to be with him, just as he was happy to be with her. Her eyes glowed warmly. They were both set in the front of her face whilst he had an eye on either side. This meant that he was much more aware of what was going on all around him. Humans couldn't click like dolphins could and so he realised that she was unable to echo-locate in the water. This wasn't surprising though; after all humans didn't spend much time in the water at all.

Dancer came up and greeted Lucy too, shyly at first until Lucy touched her gently with her hand. Then Spirit let Lucy pull herself up onto his back using his dorsal fin and they swam off through the low waves together, with Dancer swimming close along side. Spirit went as fast as he could and they started playing chase with Dancer, turning swiftly to try and outrun her. Soon Lucy fell off and rolled in the water, laughing as she did so.

Then it was Dancer's turn and she hoisted herself onto the older dolphin's back and sped off, this time with Spirit in pursuit.

After they'd played that game for twenty five minutes or so, Spirit could hear that Lucy was panting with exertion and he knew that she probably needed a rest. They floated in the water and she lay right down on his back and sort of hugged him, with her arms wrapped as far round his body as they could go.

Eventually they came back close to the shore and Lucy slid off Spirit's back again and sat on a half submerged rock. Spirit nuzzled into her and she gazed into his eyes. Dancer, not to be outdone, came back with a piece of seaweed and they played pass-the-seaweed for a few minutes, with Lucy smiling and laughing as they did so. It was a simple silly game that the dolphins had played together when they were much younger, but it was easy and fun to do and they all enjoyed it.

It felt so natural and easy for Spirit to be close to Lucy, that he wished it could go on forever. Although she was a human, with strange gangly arms and legs and long soft fur on the top of her head, it felt almost as though she were part of him. Spirit knew that it may be a strange thought, but he couldn't get it out of his head. He wished that she could swim back with them to the pod and stay with them forever, but that of course was impossible. He looked at her and saw that she was beginning to shiver, which he knew meant that she was cold. It was time for Spirit and Dancer to go.

Lucy, sensing that their time was at an end, gave them both a big hug and then waded back to the lip of the beach. Spirit and Dancer dared not go too close in to the shoreline. The tide had

31

turned and they could easily become grounded if they were not careful. The two dolphins hung in the water and Lucy turned back to look at them. She called out something and then gave a big wave of her arm. Spirit and Dancer reared up so that their head and top half of their body was out of the water and clicked their goodbyes, before turning towards the open sea. A short way out, Spirit turned and looked briefly back towards the cove where they had left Lucy. Spirit thought he could see another small human at the top of the cliff looking down on her, but he could not be quite sure. It was early and the light might have played tricks on him.

'That was fun' said Dancer contentedly, as they swum lazily back towards the pod. 'It reminds me of the time that we used to play with Star-Gazer when we were both much younger calves.'

Spirit thought back to those days and the way his mother had played with them both, a look daring and fun in her dark eyes. Spirit realised with a jolt that he had never felt so close to another living being since his mother had disappeared, as he now felt about Lucy. He glanced at Dancer. Dolphins do not cry and Spirit said nothing, but Dancer could tell that he was feeling emotional and gave him a companionable nudge with her nose as they swam slowly along.

'If only she hadn't disappeared' he said eventually in a quiet voice. 'I just wish I knew what happened to her.'

Chapter Three:

Before Lucy could ask the boy any more, they heard voices echoing up the walls of the gulley they'd just come up. The boy frowned.

'I'm off' he said. He turned and ran up the grassy bank behind them and then disappeared through a gap in the broken fence. The two older kids who'd been chasing him suddenly appeared below Lucy. They were both much bigger than the boy they'd been chasing, and were wearing their Heavy Metal t-shirts and had thick unkempt hair and spotty complexions. Lucy didn't like the look of them.

'Where is he?' the taller of the two asked Lucy with a menacing edge to his voice.

'I don't know who you mean' replied Lucy with feigned nonchalance. The boy eyed Lucy suspiciously.

'You're not from round here are you?' he said.

'Nope.'

'And you didn't see a scrawny kid with curly hair come through here?'

'Nope' said Lucy again.

'You say anything else other than nope?'

'Nope'.

The boy turned to his friend.

'That figures. He got away again' he said to his companion. They turned to go back. 'We'll get him next time.' Lucy's curiosity got the better of her.

'What did he do to you anyway? Do you always pick on kids smaller than yourself?' she called out to them. The boy turned briefly to reply.

'He's always making up stories' the taller boy replied. 'Thinks he's something special when he's not. He needs to be taught a lesson.' They clattered off back down the path of the stream, slipping on the slime-covered stones as they went.

Lucy looked around her. The hill reared up behind. There was a grassy slope with what looked like a couple of apple trees, some nettles, then a fence and behind that some houses. Looking in the other direction, Lucy could see the roof tops and then the harbour and sea not so far away. The walled gulley where the stream trickled was like a secret street for kids. 'Cool' she thought to herself. There was nothing like this were she lived. It was all signposts and safety railings there. She half expected the boy with curly hair to reappear from behind the fence, but he didn't. He must have been long gone.

Lucy wondered how to get back down to the harbour. She glanced at her watch and realised that she was late for her rendezvous with Bethany. She guessed that there must be a road or a path or something, but the most direct route was back down the stream she'd just come up. She didn't want to come across

34

those older kids again, but the noise of them had receded and she hoped she would miss them. She made her way cautiously back down the walled gulley, holding on to the sides of the stone wall on either side to steady herself and then carefully stepping from one dry stone to the next when she was back on the main stream bed. She carefully picked her way along the stream, walked under the main road again and soon found herself back where the trickle of water came out onto the pebble beach. The children had gone, but the tide had come in during the short time she'd been away and there was almost no beach left under the harbour walls. It was that easy to get cut off by the tide.

She found the cast-iron ladder again and climbed up over the wall onto street level. Bethany was there waiting for her, looking distractedly at her watch.

'Whoa!' Where did you pop up from?' she asked.

'Oh' I've just been exploring' replied Lucy.

'Well another ten minutes and you'd have been swimming' Bethany went on, peering down at the rising tide.

'Find anything interesting?'

'I was nosing around up that walled stream that runs from the beach under the High Street.'

'Oh that? That's a storm drain really. A town like this built on a hill is like a funnel in a storm and could easily flash-flood if they didn't have that kind of thing. I hope you didn't come across any rats or anything down there.' They turned to walk back to the Land Rover.

'Bethany, what are the local kids around here like?' asked Lucy shyly. Bethany grinned. So that was why Lucy had been off exploring.

'You tell me.'

'I'm not sure they're that nice' replied Lucy.

'Well there's good and bad anywhere you go Kiddo' said Bethany, placing a companionable arm around Lucy's shoulder as they walked. 'But I'm sure you'll find some good ones. I'm sorry I've not been able to fix you up with any play dates' she continued, 'but I just don't know the kids your age round here. And I'm sorry that your friend Amy couldn't come down to join us. Are you getting bored stuck down here with your old aunt?'

'No way' said Lucy resolutely. 'I like it here.'

'And I like having you here' Bethany laughed, turning the key in the lock of the car. They got in. 'Maybe we can ask Thelma tomorrow at tea' she went on. 'She seems to know everything about everything around here.'

When Lucy had turned up in Merwater a fews months ago unannounced and without Bethany's address, it was Thelma who'd helped Lucy get to Bethany's studio. What's more, if it wasn't for Thelma and her husband Nate and his fishing boat the Lady Thelma, Lucy might never have been able to save Spirit that time. Lucy already felt as though Thelma was like another aunt to her. Thelma's own children had already grown up and left home. Lucy wondered if Thelma would really know much about what the local kids were up to. Still, it was always nice to see her and she just loved having tea there.

They drove back home to the studio. It was about lunchtime and they grabbed a quick sandwich and drink of squash. Lucy wondered what Spirit was doing. In fact her thoughts turned to what Spirit was up to several times a day. She'd reach out to him with her mind later on and see what he was up to.

Bethany had to work on her painting that afternoon and told Lucy that she also had an important visitor. If all went well it might lead to another commission. She told Lucy that she was welcome to stay when the visitor showed up, but that she needed to be on her best behaviour.

Lucy mooched out into the farmyard and wondered if she could hang out with Mary, but she could see that Mary was in her cramped office with the phone clamped firmly to the side of her head, so she guessed not.

Lucy strolled over into one of the fields next to the farm. There was no livestock there at the moment and Lucy sat down on the grass and chewed a long stalk. The sun was warm and she lay back with her hands behind her head. She could hear the drone of insects in the distance and watched absent mindedly as a bumble bee made its erratic way from one buttercup to the next. Lucy thought she'd rest her eyes for a moment. After all she'd got up very early that morning.

Lucy soon dozed off and dreamt of Spirit and the pod cruising lazily along through the waters off the coast. What seemed like freezing cold sea to her was warm to the dolphins and especially with the sun on their backs they were enjoying the summer temperatures too. They'd eaten earlier and were contented enough to play and talk without overly exerting themselves. Lucy had dreamt of dolphins for as long as she could remember but it was only earlier this year that she'd realised that they were more than simple dreams and that she was able to actually stretch out with her mind and communicate with the dolphins and Spirit in particular.

Lucy woke up again forty minutes later with a stiff neck but a happy feeling in her heart. Dreaming about dolphins almost always made her feel contented inside. The sun had passed behind the hedge and it was that which had saved her from getting sunburnt. The air was cooler out of the sunshine. The insects still buzzed in the grass and she heard the plaintiff baa of a sheep in a field nearby.

She rolled over onto her tummy and stared at the tuft of grass in front of her. A small beetle with a brilliant iridescent green wing casing was crawling laboriously through the stems of grass. She wondered if it realised that a giant was watching its every movement, just centimetres away. What if people in turn were being observed by aliens from a far-away galaxy, as oblivious to the fact as the beetle was? The thought made her mind reel.

She plucked a blade of grass from the tussock and held it out so that the beetle crawled up it and then down onto her hand. The beetle paused, sensing a change in the air, opened its wing casing and flew away on the breeze.

Lucy got up and stretched, before ambling slowly back to the farmyard. A car had pulled up outside Bethany's studio and she guessed that it must be the special visitor that Bethany had talked about. Lucy decided against barging in on their conversation and opted to stay outside instead. Just then she noticed Mary's husband Darren sitting on the stone steps at the front door of the farmhouse drinking a mug of coffee in the sunshine. She walked over to him. He'd taken off his jacket and had loosened his tie.

'You're back home early' she commented. Darren patted the stone slab next to him for her to sit down too.

'I escaped from a meeting. There wasn't time to go back to the office so I thought I'd just come on home. How are you Lucy? Having fun?'

'Yeah, it's great here. I wish I could stay forever.'

'Oh it's not quite so lovely when you're milking cows at six o'clock on a cold winter's morning. I do my fair share of that too you know.' They sat in companionable silence for a minute or two, both lost in their own thoughts.

'Darren,' Lucy asked eventually 'are there folk stories about dolphins round here?'

'Oh yes, there are plenty of them. Haven't you been to the Merwater town museum yet? There's a whole display about them. Dolphins are famous round these parts. They've been part of the town for centuries. Before engines and radar came along,

39

dolphins used to lead our fisherman out to find shoals of herring, or so they say. Doesn't happen now of course, we're all too modern and have forgotten the old ways. Look at me, I spend all day tapping at a computer.' He chuckled and took another sip of coffee.

'Darren, what's a Dolphin-Child? Lucy asked. Darren sucked in his breath.

'Oh those poor souls' he said. 'Sometimes a youngster would become enchanted by dolphins and have some sort of special thing with them you know? They'd slip away at night to be with them and then never come back. Or so I've heard tell. Not that it's happened for a very long time as far as I know. There was some story or other about one when I was a kid I think. I forget what happened as a matter of fact. Nothing too dramatic I don't suppose or I'd remember.' He glanced at Lucy. 'Where did you hear about Dolphin-Children anyway?'

'Oh, you know, from some kid in town' replied Lucy warily.

'Don't you go believing everything that the kids in town tell you now will you. Sometimes they like to tell tall tales to gullible tourists. There's generally a simple explanation for most things that happen. I like a good folk tale myself, but they're best taken with a pinch of salt, you know?

Just then Bethany's visitor got in his car and rattled over the cattle grid and up the lane. Darren looked at the bottom of his empty coffee mug.

'I think I might get my overalls on and go and help Mary for a bit' he said. 'I expect she's got some job or other for me to do if I ask.'

'See you then Darren' said Lucy, getting up. She walked back over to the studio. Inside Bethany was in an expansive mood.

'Hey Kiddo!' she exclaimed when Lucy walked in. 'What do you say to going out for some celebratory fish and chips tonight? I've just got myself another commission!' She seized Lucy's hands spontaneously and danced her round the room.

'Sound's good' replied Lucy. 'I'd better phone Dad before we go though.'

Lucy missed Dad, but was glad to have a bit of freedom from all his rules during the summer holidays. Things seemed less heavy when he wasn't there. She realised that it had been pretty difficult for him too when they'd lost Mum, but sometimes he was hard to be around. He was coming down for a week in a few days and they were going to do some day trips to see the local sites and go walking on the coastal paths. When he came she wasn't sure how much she'd be able to see Spirit and so she was determined to see him as much as possible before Dad came down to join them.

Lucy went over to the farmhouse to use the phone there. Bethany didn't have a landline and the mobile phone reception was very erratic. Bethany had an understanding with Mary that Lucy could use their phone to call Dad whenever she wanted. She called his mobile number, but after a few rings, it went straight through to voicemail, so Lucy left a message instead.

'Hey Dad' she said after the beep, 'Just phoning to say hello. We went into town today and I met some local kids. Bethany's got a new commission to paint a portrait so we're going out to celebrate with fish and chips tonight. We might not be around if you call later. Missing you!' Lucy hung up the phone. She always felt awkward leaving a message. Dad was probably in a meeting or something when she called.

When Lucy walked back over to the studio, she sat down at the kitchen table whilst Bethany had a quick shower before they went out. She took the chance to reach out with her mind to Spirit, swimming not so far away in the cold waters of the sea. She had to focus her thoughts and then relax them, so that somewhere between consciousness and sleep, she could find the hidden gateway that led through to Spirit's watery world. It was still hard to do, but she was getting better at it and after one or two attempts, she suddenly felt herself falling and the next thing she knew, she was gliding along effortlessly through the cold salty water at Spirit's side.

'Hello Spirit' she said.

'Hello Lucy' replied Spirit. 'It was great to be with you this morning. We had so much fun, especially Dancer. She's been talking to everyone about it all afternoon.'

'Me too' replied Lucy. I want to see you everyday if I can, before my Dad drives down here.' Spirit wondered what driving was, but didn't ask. Lucy could tell from the way that he moved and spoke that Spirit wasn't quite his normal self.

'What's the matter Spirit?' she asked.

'Oh something Dancer said reminded me of my mother before she disappeared' Spirit answered.

'I know what you mean' replied Lucy sympathetically.

Lucy chatted away to Spirit for a few more minutes and then she felt her strength fading. Before she knew it, she found herself back sitting at the kitchen table in Bethany's studio. Bethany came down the steps from the sleeping and living area.

'You ready?' she asked.

The next morning was stormy and wet. Huge foaming white waves crashed in against the shore at the foot of the cliffs and the rain beat down rhythmically on the roof above them. Lucy got up at dawn with the idea of setting out to see Spirit again, but even she realised that it just was not possible on a stormy day such as this. Spirit, Dancer and the rest of the pod would be riding the waves out at sea, away from the danger of submerged rocks and cliff faces. Lucy sat disconsolately and watched the rain drumming against the windows of the studio. It was disappointing but there was nothing she could do about it, so she decided to make breakfast for Bethany instead.

That morning Lucy mooched around the studio whilst Bethany worked on her commission. She was too restless to read her book but paced the floor before idly working on a drawing of her own while she waited for it to stop raining. She was looking forward to going round to Thelma's house that afternoon, not only to get out of the studio but because it felt really comfortable and cosy in Thelma's kitchen. What's more, Thelma was really good at baking things. Bethany wasn't bad, but certainly wasn't in the same league.

Eventually it was time to set off. The rain had eased, but it was still wet and they ran to the Land Rover quickly and clambered in. Bethany started the engine but no sooner had they set off up the lane towards the main road, than the windscreen fogged over and Bethany had to pull over to wipe it clear again.

Thelma and Nate Merryweather lived on the edge of town in a relatively modern semi-detached house. Nate had been born in a fisherman's cottage, but they were too expensive for the local people to live in now and the one that Nate had been brought up in was now owned by some out of towner from London who only came down three or four times a year.

Nate and his first mate Bob went out in their trawler, 'the Lady Thelma' each morning to check their lobster pots and then Bob would take any that they caught round to the local restaurants to sell them. In the afternoon they both worked on one of the boats that took tourists round the harbour and out along the coast to try and spot seals and maybe if they were lucky even a dolphin or a basking shark. As Nate was still at work, it would be just them and Thelma. Her children had long since grown up and left home.

Bethany pulled up off the road and parked the car. Thelma came out to welcome them.

'Hello there Bethany. Hello there young Lucy. Get yourselves inside and out of the rain why don't you?' Lucy gladly ran up the drive with her coat over her head and in through the side door into the kitchen. When Lucy had read the Famous Five books when she was younger, this was how she imagined tea in a country kitchen to be. A big home-made cake was positioned in the middle of the kitchen table and a couple of plates of sandwiches sat alongside it. Thelma brewed up the tea in an old brown teapot kept warm with a tea cosy. Lucy was hungry and couldn't wait to tuck into all the food that Thelma had made.

They sat down, chatting away as Thelma got even more food out. They talked about Lucy's holiday down in Cornwall, Thelma's work in the surgery and Bethany's latest commission. Lucy could tell that Thelma was curious to know more about her mother. Every so often she would slip a question into the conversation to elicit more information about her.

Bethany would tell her what she could about her sister Megan, but Lucy got the feeling that Thelma wanted to know more about what Mum had taught Lucy when she was younger. Lucy was very fond of Thelma, but wasn't ready to open up to her about Mum. What memories she had were very precious to her and she didn't want to cheapen them by telling them to everyone, or even someone like Thelma. She was already worried that she could not remember exactly what Mum's voice sounded like and details about what Mum did and said and laughed at were not as clear as they used to be. She felt that the more she talked about Mum, the less personal her memories would become.

Lucy wondered what Mum would say if she was there drinking tea and eating cake with them. She often liked to imagine Mum there next to her, doing or saying something familiar as she used to before she died. She pictured Mum now, sitting on the fourth chair of Thelma's table, leaning forward on her elbows and smiling as they chatted. Lucy took another bite of cake and then glanced back, but the vision had gone. It was just an empty chair.

Eventually the conversation came round to the children that Lucy had encountered in town the previous day. Bethany mentioned that she'd been slightly alarmed when she found out that Lucy had disappeared up the walled stream and hoped that there were no rats about down there.

'Oh the children love running up and down those gullies' said Thelma. 'My own lot were always mucking around down there when they were growing up. How did you get on with our local kids then?'

'I don't really know' replied Lucy. 'The other children seemed to be picking on this one boy and then two of the older kids chased him up the stream. I went after them to make sure he was okay. I got to speak to him a little bit, but then he disappeared.'

'And who was that then dear?' asked Thelma.

'He was a couple of years younger than me, a bit small, but with lots of curly hair. Do you know him?' asked Lucy. She really hoped that Bethany might. Bethany seemed to know everyone in town and Lucy was not disappointed.

'Yes I know him, or I'm pretty sure I do' replied Thelma. That would be Mrs Treddinick's son. Paul his name is. Paul Treddinick. You're right Lucy. He's a couple of years younger than you, about ten I'd say, but very thin.'

'How do you know him?' asked Lucy.

'You know I work in reception at the doctor's surgery?' replied Thelma, 'Well his mum Rachael Treddinick comes in to the surgery all the time. She's a troubled lady.' Thelma seemed to suddenly realise that she'd said a little more than she should do and stopped.

'You mean she's receiving treatment for depression or something like that?' asked Bethany.

'Something like that' replied Thelma. 'She's alone with two kids, got no job and can't pay the bills. It's enough to get anyone down.'

'Where do they live?' asked Lucy curiously. She wanted to speak to that Paul Treddinick again and find out why he said she was a Dolphin-Child. Bethany, Thelma and her husband Nate knew that Lucy had a special relationship with dolphins, but she hadn't realised that there might be other children out there with the same gift. What Darren at the farm had said worried her a little, but she thought that the boy might tell her something that the grown-ups wouldn't.

'Oh they don't live far from here' replied Thelma. 'You know the recreation ground on the Truro Road, they live in the end-of-terrace house there. Can't miss it. Needs a lick of paint mind, that house and the front garden is a mass of weeds'.

Bethany and Thelma started talking about country doctors and Lucy began to lose interest in the conversation. She'd eaten and drunk as much as she wanted and had nothing in particular to keep her at the table. It had stopped raining now and Lucy thought that she could do with some fresh air. When Thelma poured another cup of tea, she took her opportunity.

'Can I go up to the swings for a while? I'll be back in half an hour.' Bethany agreed and five minutes later Lucy was walking up the Truro Road to the recreation ground. She wouldn't be brave enough to knock on the door of Mrs Treddinick's house, but she thought that she might just bump into Paul if she went past where he lived.

Lucy got to the recreation ground and walked in. The grass was sodden and rain still clung to the swings and the slide. Because it had been raining so much, it seemed like everyone was indoors. Lucy could see the Treddinick's house at the end of the terrace. It did look a bit run down she thought. It didn't look very inviting.

Lucy glanced around her. A hedge ran round three sides of the recreation ground and five or six chestnut trees grew up out of the hedge. Glancing up, she suddenly realised that there was someone sitting in one of the trees, on a low branch not far from the ground. Lucy walked over. She recognised the curly hair. It was Paul Treddinick. As Lucy approached she could see that he seemed to be whittling a stick with a penknife and was quite absorbed in what he was doing.

Someone had hammered some six inch nails into the tree to act as steps and Lucy was halfway up before Paul realised that someone was joining him. This time he couldn't just run away.

'Hi' said Lucy, as she sat down on the branch next to him.

'Oh it's you' said Paul gruffly. Lucy got the feeling that he was trying to be tough, but wasn't really. 'What do you want?' He stopped whittling and looked across at her. If he thought she was a Dolphin-Child, then he must be curious about her too.

'Are you a liar like those big kids said you were?' Lucy asked, hoping to throw him off guard.

'I am NOT!' he replied defiantly.

'When I saw you yesterday you told me that you dream about dolphins. What do you dream about when you do?'

'I dream about what I saw' Paul answered.

'And what's that?' asked Lucy simply.

'Who wants to know?

'I'm Lucy, Lucy Parr. I'm twelve years old and staying with my aunt over the holidays. You said you thought I was a Dolphin-Child, but I don't even really know what that means. Tell me what you dream about dolphins.' Paul thought. He didn't seem to know whether to tell her or not. Then, as if he could not keep a secret, he went on.

'I often go out cycling on my bike out of town. I like to get out of the house and away from Baz, Mike and the rest of their gang. I hate them. I like to go all over the place on my own and often I'm out all afternoon. There's this inlet off the estuary where the river comes out at the sea. It's part of the grounds of this big house and you have to shinny over this old wall to get to it. Then you have to creep through the wood and watch out for the guards. The last bit is a rhododendron thicket, then you come out at the inlet, which is a bit like a lagoon coz there's a fence across the end blocking it off from the estuary. In this lagoon there's this dolphin. I think they keep it as a prisoner there, but it should be free. That's what I dream about. In my dream I remember that dolphin looking out of the water at me all sad-like'.

Chapter Four:

As the light crept over the horizon the next morning, Spirit swam alone towards the mainland a couple of miles away. He felt more confident to swim out on his own now and happily looked forward to seeing Lucy again. The seas had been rough the day before and he'd not been able to see her. Every day that they could meet felt precious and he knew that these days of being together in real life may not last long. Her father would be coming soon and then he would take her back far from the sea again. It was a pleasure to swim together though while they could.

As he neared the cove, Spirit could see the silhouette of Lucy standing on the shore line in her black wet-suit, up to her shins in the sea. Humans had very thin skin and even in the summer they could get very cold very quickly in the sea. Lucy waved as he got near and then waded into the water and started to swim. She swam up close to him and stretched out her hand, holding it lightly to his flank and looking into his eyes. As she did so, Spirit could feel the tingling energy passing through her hand into his skin. After a while Lucy pulled herself up onto his back, using his dorsal fin to hold on with and he swam off with powerful strokes away from the shore.

Spirit would have loved to have been able to dive with her now and show her the landscape at the bottom of the sea, but he knew that she couldn't breathe down there and wasn't able to hold her breath very long either. Anyway, he could still show her the depths when she stretched out to him with her mind. He wished that he could do the same and visit her world above water, but he just did not know how to. It was frustrating having to wait for her to come to him every time.

He knew that like him, Lucy loved to swim along the coast line and see the rocky inlets and caves that they passed as they swam along. Spirit wanted to show Lucy a particular formation of rock along the coast that looked like a dolphin. It made him smile to see it and he thought Lucy would enjoy it too. It wasn't too far to get to and when Lucy saw it, he felt her laugh in recognition.

Laughter was a strange thing that humans did when they enjoyed themselves. Their chests convulsed and the noise that came out of their mouths did not mean anything. Spirit thought that Lucy's laughter sounded like music. They explored the coast together for an hour or so, but eventually he had to bring her back to the cove they had met at. He was supposed the join the others to fish together and knew that Lucy would get tired and could not hang on to his dorsal fin forever. Humans seemed so weak and vulnerable, he wondered how they managed to survive at all.

Spirit got as close in to the shore as he dared, before Lucy slid off his back. Standing with her feet on the pebbles, but still up to her shoulders in the water, she turned and looked deep into his eyes again, before saying something he could not understand and then turned to wade out of the sea again.

He left Lucy as he had found her that morning, standing on the shoreline, waving to him. Spirit swam off back to the rest of the pod. He was hungry and wanted to hunt for fish.

Breeze led Chaser, Storm, Moonlight and Dancer in a wild hunt for squid which they all loved to eat. Spirit hung back. He hated squid and could not understand how any dolphin could eat them; they were so rubbery and flavourless. Summer swam alongside him with her calf. No-Name was not ready to join in the chase and the others would bring her a squid or two which she could then eat while she looked after him.

'I see you still haven't developed a taste for squid!' joked Summer gently. Spirit looked at her calf.

'It looks like your little one hasn't either' he replied with a smile. The calf had chewed a spare tentacle cautiously, but then spat it out in disgust. Milk was evidently much better.

Spirit hoped that the pod would move on and find a shoal of fish that he might actually like to eat, but they didn't. He was hungry but he didn't mind. He thought he might go off again later when they were resting in the afternoon and find something by himself. It didn't seem fair to drag Dancer out with him. She liked squid after all.

He hung peacefully in the water whilst the others hunted. Dancer peeled away from the rest of the pod and swam up to him.

'Let's go out again later and find you a tasty bite' she said playfully.

'That sounds good' he replied. He knew he could rely on Dancer. It would be much more fun to go out with her than to go alone.

It often surprised Spirit where the day went. After the hunt, Chaser had recited one or two of the old stories as they relaxed and before Spirit knew it, midday had passed and the sun had started its slow descent back to the horizon. By this time though Spirit was even hungrier than he had been when he left Lucy that morning.

'Come on then', he whispered to Dancer as the others started to doze off. 'Let's go.' They made their excuses again and swam off together companionably.

'Let's head for the coast.'

Soon they were swimming within a short distance of the shore. It was a hot sunny day and as they passed by a beach, they could hear the sound of humans nearby, splashing and shouting as they played in the water. The two dolphins were too far out to be spotted and it was funny for them to think that even though they were so close, the humans were oblivious to them.

'Those humans couldn't see a squid if it squirted them in the eye' joked Dancer as they swam along.

Though Dancer wanted to swim on, Spirit was curious about the humans on the beach and they lingered at the edges, just out of sight. Spirit was intrigued by the noises that they were making.

'What do you think makes them come to the water?' he asked.

'I don't know. Do you think they're looking for fish?' replied Dancer.

'But all that noise would frighten any fish away.'

'Maybe they just swim in the sea for fun?' continued Dancer.

'There's just so many of them' said Spirit, glancing over the surface of the water towards the beach. 'Why would they want to cram themselves up so close to one another like that?'

'Well I suppose they just live in one big heap all the time. They don't need open space around them like we do' replied Dancer.

Spirit thought that even though he was so close to Lucy, he would never understand the ways of humans. They were such strange creatures and much of what they did seemed completely nonsensical. When they went somewhere, they didn't just want to visit it, they wanted to change it out of all recognition or destroy it altogether. They were almost never alone and always seemed to want to be in a big group. Humans could barely keep themselves afloat in the water and yet they seemed to be irresistibly drawn to it.

Spirit might have dismissed them altogether, like Storm had, if it weren't for Lucy. He knew that there was more to them than met the eye. He wanted to learn as much as he could about humans and the world above the sea that Lucy inhabited.

As Spirit and Dancer listened to the humans splashing and playing in the water, something large and plastic floated past them. It was clear and not easy to spot until it got close. The two dolphins hung underneath the surface of the water and looked up at it.

'What do you suppose that is?' Dancer asked.

'I expect it's just some more rubbish that they've thrown away' said Spirit. There seemed to be something on top of the floating plastic, but he couldn't make out what. They were well used to seeing plastic floating along in the water, though not generally a piece of plastic this big. When he was still a young calf, Spirit had taken a bite out of something white that drifted past him in the water and almost choked on a plastic bag as a result. They let the thing float on past them. It got caught by a gust of wind and was blown on to the rocks just out of sight of the beach with all the people on it. The clear floating plastic thing seemed to snag on something sharp and then crumpled as the air leaked out of it.

Suddenly there was screaming sound from the direction of the floating thing and Spirit and Dancer glanced back to look at it.

'What was that?' asked Dancer in alarm.

'I don't know' replied Spirit turning back towards the plastic thing in the water. The airbed sagged and as they looked they realised that a child had started scrabbling around on top of it.

'Is that a human?' asked Dancer.

'It looks like a child' replied Spirit. The human was much smaller than Lucy and Spirit guessed that the child was about half her age.

In fact the girl on the airbed was about six years old and had fallen asleep as her brothers had played catch with a ball next to her. Another boy had stolen the ball and her brothers had chased him down the beach to get it back. Unattended, the airbed had floated away from the safety of the shallows, seemingly without any one noticing. Her parents thought she was with her brothers and her brothers thought she was with her parents. No one knew that she was out here at all.

The girl started to shout something and although the two dolphins could not understand what she was saying, they could imagine.

'She must be shouting for help' guessed Spirit, overwhelmed with concern for the young girl. Her face was red with tears and hot with fear. However the sound of her screams and cries would not carry far and no one on the beach could hear her over the gentle slosh of waves around them and the noise of the crowds.

The airbed had got caught on a shelf of rock a few metres out from the main shoreline, which rose up out of the sea like a small island. The sea was still coming in though and when high tide came, the rocks would be fully submerged. They were slimy with seaweed. The airbed was rapidly losing its air and soon became unable to support the girl's weight. She clambered off it onto the rocky islet. In doing so the airbed got pushed free of the rocks again and floated away again out of her reach.

'Look!' exclaimed Spirit. 'The girl's trapped on those rocks.' The rocks were so slippery that the girl could not stand upright on them, but instead clung onto them, tears streaming down her face. The two dolphins swam over to where she was and put their heads over the surface of the water in an attempt to whistle encouragement to her.

'Do you think that she will get on your back like Lucy does?' asked Dancer. Instead of being encouraged though, when the girl saw the two dolphins, she shrank back in fear. She'd never seen dolphins before and was too scared and too upset to appreciate that they were friendly and wanted to help her. He realised that even if the girl had wanted to, she wouldn't have the strength to pull herself up onto his back.

'I don't think there's any chance of that' replied Spirit. Just as he spoke, a slightly larger wave came in and washed over the legs and feet of the young girl. It wouldn't be long before the tide rose higher and larger waves started to batter her. They had to do something.

'Well what can we do then?' asked Dancer anxiously, looking at the scared child a couple of metres away from them on the rock. Spirit shook his head. If only he could reach out to Lucy like she could reach out to him. He could tell Lucy what had happened and she could fetch help. He had no idea how to do that though.

'I'd better swim to the beach and find someone who can come back and get the girl' said Spirit. 'You stay here and keep an eye on her.'

Spirit swam quickly back towards the beach. It was the kind of beach that shelved away fairly rapidly and so it was possible for him to get reasonably near to land without fear of grounding himself. As Spirit swam in close to the beach, his dorsal fin showed above the surface. Although a dolphins dorsal fin is completely different to that of a shark and despite the fact that pretty much only harmless basking sharks patrol the coast round Britain, someone shouted 'shark!' loudly in alarm. Suddenly there was a clamour of cries and stampede of children as they all tried to get out of the water as quickly as possible.

Spirit put his face above the surface of the water and reared up as much as he could to try to click and whistle that a girl was in danger and needed their help. As soon as people saw the friendly face of a dolphin, realising that there was no shark in the water, people turned and stormed back towards him.

'Look Mummy a dolphin!' yelled a hundred children, as they all rushed towards him, eager to pet him and stroke his side. 'Isn't he adorable!' replied their parents as they converged on him.

Spirit was alarmed at all of the humans coming towards him, each with their hands outstretched to pat and caress him. The noise and the clamour made him nervous and he retreated to slightly deeper waters. He put his head up again above the surface and tried to click and whistle his warning about the girl stuck on the rocks just out of sight, but none of the humans on the beach knew what he was trying to say, or cared. The adult humans started to hold little black boxes up their face, which made clicking sounds. The youngsters on the beach strained to touch Spirit, but he was worried that they'd cover his blow-hole and kept just out of their reach.

Spirit swam a short distance along the edge of the beach, in the direction of the rocks where the girl lay caught and then turned again, in the hope that they would follow him. Spirit realised though that it was no good. He may as well try to communicate with a shoal of mackerel. He simply could not think of how to tell them that a girl was in trouble and needed help. He swam back to where Dancer was waiting in the hope that at least one or two humans would come off up the beach and round the headland to try to find him again, but it seemed that none of them did. All he could hear was shouting and splashing behind him.

'It's not good' warned Dancer as he approached her again. 'The tide's coming in fast now and that girl is going to get swept off the rock soon. She's scared of us. We can't carry her to safety and I'm worried that if she falls off that rock, she'll drown. What can we do?' called Dancer in increasing agitation.

'Lucy!' thought Spirit in desperation. 'Lucy, Lucy, LUCY!!'

Lucy suddenly sat up with a jolt. She'd been lying in the grass of the field just behind the studio, looking at a brilliant green beetle climbing a grass stem and listening to the buzz of grasshoppers and insects around her. She suddenly felt a sense of great urgency, but she didn't understand from where. Then she thought, 'Spirit'. There was something to do with Spirit that was not right.

She realised that she needed to reach out and contact him straight away.

Lucy composed herself and then focused her mind to concentrate before relaxing, letting her thoughts wander to the corners of her conscious mind. It was still hard to do and she was never sure when it would work, but she was in luck and suddenly she found herself floating in the salty waters next to the two dolphins.

'Spirit, what's the matter?' she asked.

'Lucy!' he replied. 'You came! I called out for you and you came!' Lucy looked around her, surprised to hear the sounds emanating from the beach nearby.

'But what's the matter?' she asked again and then she saw the scared frightened little girl clinging to the rock, as another wave rolled in and almost knocked her off.

'We can't get the humans to come and save her. She's scared of us and no one seems to know she's missing' said Spirit. 'In another few minutes she's going to fall off that rock altogether'. Lucy nodded. She wanted to emerge from the water to comfort the little girl, but she knew that when she came to Spirit in this way, she had left her physical self behind in the field where she'd been lying just a couple of minutes before. She'd look like a ghost to the little girl and scare her even more. The shock might make her fall of the rock by itself. Lucy looked around her.

'Where are we?'

A minute later Lucy burst through the door into the farm office where Mary sat working on a spreadsheet on her computer. Mary looked up in alarm.

'Whatever is the matter Lucy?' she asked.

'We've got to call the Coastguard, NOW!'

Lucy had disappeared almost as quickly as she'd come and Dancer and Spirit were left wondering what good she could do. But barely five minutes later two lifeguards had come running across the rocks and plunged into the water before swimming to the spot where the little girl lay clinging to the rocks, half submerged in the waters of the encroaching tide. Spirit and Dancer watched with satisfaction as the life guards carried the little girl off to safety.

The two dolphins turned away, relieved that the crisis had been averted and that they could swim away again. They wondered by what magic Lucy had been able to communicate with the humans on the beach, but it seemed to Spirit that she must be able to reach out with her mind to other humans in the same way that she was able to do so with him. The ways of humans were very strange and he would never be able to conceive what a telephone was.

What amazed Spirit though was that for the first time, he'd been able to send her a message. Normally, he would never know when Lucy might appear and when she wouldn't. He could never contact her and had to rely on her coming to him. Yet when he really needed her, Lucy had the strong feeling that she had to reach out to him. Together, they had saved a little girl. It was a good feeling.

'But how did you do it?' asked Dancer, as they swam along quietly a safe distance from the shore.

'I don't know' he replied. 'I just really needed her and somehow, she knew.' Suddenly Spirit felt light and happy. They chased each other round and round and leapt into the air for the sheer pleasure of it.

An hour or so later they arrived back where the rest of the pod was basking with the warm afternoon sunshine on their backs. Dancer soon regaled them with the story of the little girl in trouble and how Spirit had been able to contact Lucy and get her to help the little girl. The pod gathered round.

'That's a very useful gift you've got there Spirit' commented Breeze, eyeing him speculatively. 'A very useful gift for the pod.'

'What do you mean?' asked Dancer.

'Oh, you know' replied Breeze. 'What you've got to ask yourself is 'how can I help the pod?''

'But I do help the pod' answered Spirit. 'All the time.'

'It's true' said Summer coming to his defence, 'Spirit does help the pod all the time.'

'Yes but think what more Spirit could do for us with his gift' continued Breeze.

'Like what?' asked Dancer.

'Well you can help when we're in danger and you can work with the humans to help them and then they can bring us more fish.'

Spirit glanced over at where Storm hung in the water. He regarded them all seriously, but didn't say anything. Spirit wondered why.

'Well that's just silly' replied Dancer. 'Why would the humans bring fish to us?'

'More fish to eat sounds good to me' chipped in Chaser, 'but we don't need handouts from the humans. We can hunt for our own fish.'

'Do you remember seven winters ago when Spirit was still very young. There were no fish in these waters and we nearly starved. You'd have been glad of a handout then' replied Breeze.

'That's true enough' said Moonlight, who'd been following the conversation with interest. 'We've got a little one in the pod now' she continued, looking at Summer's calf.

'I, I don't know what my gift is for' said Spirit hesitantly. 'I just know I have something special. I….' he trailed away, as Summer's calf swam up to him and gave him a friendly nuzzle. Of course he'd do anything he could to help the pod, wouldn't he? There was a pause.

'I think that humans are dangerous and not to be trusted' said Storm. 'I've seen more bad come from involvement with humans than good. We're better off without them'. He paused. 'But I've met Lucy and though I could not speak to her in the way that Spirit

64

and Dancer can, I've looked into her eyes. There is something dolphin-like about her. I believe her to be a good human.'

'Great' said Breeze. 'All the better for us! Just think, Spirit could send her instructions and she could get the humans to bring us fish any time we need it.' Spirit and Dancer looked back at Storm. He was quiet for a moment, lost in thought.

'A long time ago we all gave Star-Gazer a promise, before Spirit was named. We all vowed that we would look after Spirit, come what may.'

'And now we have another youngster in the group and Spirit will join us to pledge to look after Summer's new calf' replied Breeze.

'You forget the stories of old' Storm replied, 'and what it means to be a Child-Seer.'

'Who cares about the old stories?' asked Breeze defensively. 'We've all got to pull together to help each other. What use is Spirit's gift unless it puts fish in our stomachs?'

'I agreed with Storm' said Summer, her calf nuzzling into her flank. 'We must think about the old stories.'

'That's right' said Dancer, 'And Lucy has already saved Spirit.'

'I say that it is still too early. I trust Lucy but I do not trust other humans. We cannot use Spirit's gift when we do not yet know what it is' said Storm.

There was a murmur of assent around the group. Breeze was silent. The conversation passed on to other things. Moonlight wanted Spirit to tell the story of how they saved the little girl all over again and Dancer was happy to oblige. Spirit felt shy and let himself drift off a short distance from the pod. Chaser was debating with Storm the best way to tell when a shoal of sprat might be approaching. Summer, noticing that Spirit seemed withdrawn, swam over to him with her calf by her side.

'One thing I know' she said, 'is that Star-Gazer would be proud of you'. Spirit looked back at her, worried and unhappy.

'Do you really think so Summer?' he asked.

'I do' she answered decisively. 'She was my good friend. I wish she was here to see the dolphin you have grown up to be.'

'I wish she was here now too' replied Spirit. 'I still wonder what became of her.'

'So do I Spirit' she replied. 'It must be twelve full moons ago that Storm and I swam out with Star-Gazer. You know the story. We were separated when a squall blew up. A ship crossed our path and the terrible noise of its engines confused all three of us. After the ship had gone, I found Storm easily enough and then we both wondered where Star-Gazer was. She'd disappeared. Storm thought there were traces of her blood in the water, but I wasn't so sure. I wish I knew where she was now.'

'Do you think maybe she's alive now?' asked Spirit anxiously. Summer shook her head.

'I really don't know Spirit' replied Summer. 'I wish I did. It would be great if she was, but then why hasn't she come back to us? I don't want to build your hopes up. You know she's probably joined the stars up in the night sky that she so loved to look at. If she's looking down on us from up there, she'll be smiling at you.'

At that moment Summer's calf No-Name started to wander off and with an apologetic look, she went after him.

It had been a long day and Spirit needed to rest. That evening, the sky was especially clear and bright with what looked like a million stars. Whilst the others dozed off into their waking sleep, Spirit stared up at the stars spread above him in the night sky as his mother had done so many times.

Chapter Five:

For some reason that she could not quite understand, the form that swam through Lucy's dream upset her. She could not see well, as the water in her vision was murky and all she could really make out was a vague silhouette in the shallow brackish water. It seemed to be restless and turned fretfully this way and that, not as though it were looking for a means of escape, but more like a creature that needed to do something, anything, rather than just hang there in the water. Lucy could barely make out the shape of the animal, but she knew it was a dolphin. There was nothing else around it, just the muddy water and there were no other dolphins to keep it company. Lucy could sense a deep, painful loneliness in the dolphin, but was powerless in her dream to do anything about it.

When Lucy awoke, she could not tell if it was a vision of an actual living dolphin, or merely an imaginary scene conjured up out of the depths of her subconscious. She lay there in the camp bed on the platform in Bethany's studio, staring up at the rafters, feeling anxious and unsettled. 'It must just have been a nightmare' Lucy said to herself. 'I'm sure that's all it was'. Yet despite her attempts to convince herself otherwise, Lucy just couldn't be sure.

Sometimes when Lucy had a bad dream, it would hang over her like an oppressive cloud even though she had already woken up. She worried that she would fall back to sleep again and slip back into the nightmare she had just escaped from. Lucy forced her eyes wide open and blinking, looked around her. The morning light was streaming through the studio windows below them, but Bethany was still fast asleep.

Lucy looked at her watch. It was a little before seven o'clock. There was still time to cycle up the hill to old Man's Cove with the hope of swimming with Spirit. She hurriedly pulled on her clothes and slipped out while Bethany was still sleeping. Lucy felt intensely private about swimming with Spirit and didn't want anyone to see her when she did. If she left too late there would be too many people around.

In any case she could not put the image of the solitary dolphin out of her head. She thought about what might have caused it. It must have been brought on by her conversation with that strange boy Paul Treddinick the previous day, she thought to herself.

An hour and a half later when Lucy got back, she went straight to the kitchen area and made herself some warm chocolate milk. Bethany was not there and she guessed that she'd popped over to the farm office for a chat with Mary. Lucy sat down at the kitchen table to drink it. Even though she'd been out swimming with Spirit, it was the first morning of her holiday down here in Cornwall that she didn't feel all that happy.

Lucy's encounter with Paul's mother the day before had really upset her. She recalled how she'd found Paul in the recreation ground when he told her about the dolphin trapped in the lagoon. Lucy had been sitting there on the low bough of the tree next to the recreation ground, conscious that the wetness of the branch was seeping through her jeans and making her bottom uncomfortably damp. Paul had been whittling a piece of wood with his penknife, but now that she had suddenly appeared next to him, he put his penknife down on the branch next to him. Lucy noticed enviously that Paul was sitting on a plastic carrier bag. His bottom was still dry. Lucy could understand why the other kids called him scrawny; he really was very thin and his mass of curly hair merely accentuated the slightness of the rest of his body.

Lucy wondered whether Paul might be a liar like those big kids had claimed, yet when he described the grounds of the house where he said a dolphin was kept in a saltwater lake, she wasn't so sure. He seemed to tell her with utter sincerity and a kind of shyness that made her realise he wasn't just saying it to show off.

'Where is this place?' asked Lucy curiously. 'Can you take me there?'

'I go cycling on my own' replied Paul. 'I don't take no one with me.'

'Oh go on, you could take me' Lucy urged him. 'You told me all about it the other day.'

'No' said Paul defiantly. Now he wished he hadn't said what he told her the other day, even if she was supposed to be a Dolphin

Child. With a fluid and practised twist of his hips, he half jumped and half slid from the low branch that they were both sitting on, landing on the wet grass of the recreation field with a thud.

'Hey, come back!' Lucy called, too nervous to jump down herself and looking around for the nails driven into the tree trunk which she had used to climb up in the first place. Paul started walking away from her towards the swings. Lucy hastily clambered back down the tree, ripping the sleeve of her t-shirt on one of the nails in her anxiety to get down and go after him. She jumped the last bit and ran to catch up with him.

'What's with you then?' she asked.

'You've got your dolphins in the sea' he said, turning to look at her. 'You get to swim around with them. You're a Dolphin-Child. You come from a big town and your aunt's a well-known artist. Everything's easy for you.' Lucy wanted to say that things certainly weren't easy for her, but she knew her words would sound hollow and insincere if she said so.

'I just thought I could….help' Lucy replied simply.

'Well I don't need your help' he answered sharply. 'I shouldn't have told you what I did. I can sort things out on my own. My Mum said…., well...' He trailed off and then turned to walk towards the gate to Truro Road. Lucy remembered that Thelma said he lived just next to the park in the end-of-terrace house with peeling paint and weeds in the garden. Lucy followed Paul. She wanted to say something more to him, but she wasn't sure what.

'I don't even know what a Dolphin-Child is' she said eventually as he neared the road. 'Why can't you help me?'

'Go look in the museum' he replied, without looking back at her. Lucy just could not understand why he should suddenly switch like this. Just then Mrs Treddinick emerged from the house. She wore a shapeless cardigan and looked tired beyond her years.

'Paul, who is that?' she shouted across the road at her son.

'It's, well.....'

'It's not that girl you told me about is it?' Paul didn't deny it. 'Come over here this instant' she called to Paul, anger catching in her voice. Lucy stopped where she was, while Paul crossed the road over to where his mother stood at their front gate.

'You stay away from my boy, you hear!' Mrs Treddinick shouted back across at Lucy. 'You and your kind are dangerous. You stop following him around. You'll be the death of all of us!' She marched her son into the house and banged her door shut behind her.

Lucy stood there, shocked and disbelieving, unable to comprehend what had prompted the outburst from Paul's mother. She had no friends of her own here in Merwater and even Paul, who was picked on by other kids, had turned his back on her. Now his mother was shouting at her and she didn't understand why. Lucy burst out into bitter tears. She turned to walk back down the road to Thelma's house where she and Bethany were still chatting over the tea things.

'Lucy, whatever is the matter?' exclaimed Bethany as she walked back into Thelma's kitchen. Lucy's eyes were puffy and red. It was obvious she'd been crying. Lucy hesitantly recounted the story of her encounter with Paul and what his mother had said to her.

'That Rachael Treddinick' said Thelma angrily. 'I'll be having a word with her when I next see her, you mark my words.'

'But what did she mean?' asked Lucy miserably.

'Oh I shouldn't worry about her' said Bethany, her arm around her niece's shoulders. 'She's not a happy woman. Some people say thoughtless things when they're miserable themselves.'

'That's right young Lucy' added Thelma. 'She doesn't know what she's saying. Take no notice now.'

Bethany had been ready to leave when Lucy got back and so after a few more minutes they thanked Thelma and made for the door.

'My Nate was wondering if you'd like to go out in the tourist boat with him and Bob tomorrow afternoon' said Thelma as they stood by the door. 'They'll be going out seal watching. He reckons you've got a good pair of eyes for that kind of thing. Now what do you say?'

'How about it Kiddo?' asked Bethany. 'It'll get you out of the studio sure enough.'

'Yes I'd love to' smiled Lucy wanly, still feeling tearful.

'Good. I'll let Nate know to expect you' replied Thelma. They waved and walked back to Bethany's Land Rover. As they drove through the town on their way back to the studio, Lucy stared out of the window, half expecting to see Paul Treddinick on the street again, but she saw no one she knew and they were soon rattling down the lane that led to the farm.

Later on, after her daily phone call to Dad and Bethany had announced it was time to get ready for bed, Lucy's thoughts turned back to Paul Treddinick and his mother.

'That boy said I was a Dolphin-Child' she told Bethany, but I don't know what that means, not really.'

'Well I suppose it means that you've got a special gift' replied Bethany cautiously.

'Like Mum did?' asked Lucy.

'Yes, yes I suppose so.'

'Did people call her a Dolphin-Child?' Bethany paused before replying.

'Not that I know of Kiddo' she said eventually. 'Now come on, let's get you off to bed.'

'And then Paul's mum said my kind were dangerous. Do you know what she meant by that?'

'One thing I'm certain about Kiddo' said Bethany with passion in her voice, 'is that there's absolutely nothing wrong, bad or dangerous about you and your gift. Don't listen to that woman. She's just silly and confused.'

Despite the assurances of Bethany and Thelma, Lucy had laid awake for a long time, staring up into the rafters and wondering about what Mrs Treddinick had said. When eventually she had drifted off to sleep, it had been into fitful and restless dreams. Then just before waking up, she had had the unsettling dream of the lone dolphin in the murky saltwater lagoon.

Later today she'd be going out on the tourist boat with Nate and Bob to look for seals. She had some time to kill before that though and wondered what she might do. A lazy morning reading her book in the field behind the studio would be just the thing she decided.

It was like an electric shock when Spirit had broken through to her, telling her quickly about the little girl trapped on the rocks at the beach. It jolted her upright and although she was pleased and amazed that Spirit had been able to reach out to her instead of the other way round, it had been an almost painful sensation when he did.

When Spirit had told her of the danger that the little girl was in, she realised that she had to do something that instant. She'd burst into the farm office to get Mary to call the coastguard, but could hardly believe that Mary or anyone else would listen to her. Yet Mary had unquestioningly picked up the receiver and called the coastguard straight away, telling them that there was a little girl in trouble on the rocks at the side of Black Gull Sands. When Mary put down the receiver, she looked up at Lucy, who was standing anxiously in the doorway of the small office.

'I just hope you're right' she said, 'or I'm going to have some serious explaining to do.' Lucy was relieved that she was right too, though then she realised that she might still have trouble explaining how a twelve year old lying in a field chewing a stalk of grass might know that a little girl was in trouble at a beach two miles up the coast.

Mary had to drive into town later in the van for an appointment and offered to give Lucy a lift into town. Bethany would pick her up again at the end of the afternoon.

Mary dropped her off at the side of the harbour in Merwater.

'See you later then Lucy' called Mary. The van door clunked shut behind her and with a wave Mary drove off. Lucy glanced up at the sky. It was bright and sunny, but there were clouds on the horizon and she wondered if it might rain later. The ever-present gulls swooped and soared above the town, looking out for a discarded fish head or a half eaten sandwich on which to feast. In nesting season gulls could swoop down aggressively on anyone who happened to be walking up the street. Fortunately at the moment they were more interested in looking out for their next meal. There were many unsuspecting tourists in town for them to prey on.

Lucy crossed over the road to the harbour wall. In the mornings Nate and Bob went out in their fishing boat the Lady Thelma to check their lobster pots. In the afternoons, especially in tourist season, they took out visitors in the tourist boat 'The Merry Widow' round the coast to look for seals or even if they were lucky enough, a glimpse of a dolphin or a whale. 'It's easier to haul in a few tourists than a few lobster' Nate would say. Making a living from fishing had never been easy and now it was just getting harder.

Lucy walked up to where the Merry Widow was moored. Nate was sitting on one of the plastic chairs bolted to the foredeck drinking tea from a chipped mug. He was a comfortably built, middle-aged man with thinning grey hair above his friendly red face.

'Ahoy there young Lucy' he greeted her. 'You're a full fifty minutes early. Still though, you're welcome to come on board now and wait. The tourists will start arriving soon I expect.

'Do you think there'll be good sailing today Nate?' she asked. 'Do you think we might see some dolphins?'

'Well Lucy, with you on the lookout who knows, maybe we will' Nate laughed.

'I hope so.'

'My friend Steve from the coastguard station tells me that there was a strange call from a farm recently. Turns out a little girl was stranded on some rocks at the edge of Black Gull Sands. The woman on the farm told them exactly where to find the little girl, but how could she have known, he asked me. You wouldn't happen to know anything about that now would you young Lucy?' Nate turned to look at her with a half knowing, amused expression on his face.

Lucy shifted from one foot to the other. If she didn't know him any better, she'd have thought that he was putting her on the spot.

Instead she realised that he was only half serious in asking the question.

'I might' she replied with a smile on her face. Nate grinned back at her.

'Strange things have been going on down here since you turned up my gal' he joked. 'You best keep your eyes peeled for them dolphins this afternoon. Make some tourists happy and keep yourself out of trouble!' He gave a chesty laugh. 'Anyhow, you're a tad early for the boat ride, so if you don't want to wait here, you feel free to wander into town for half an hour or so.'

'I might just do that' replied Lucy. She strolled back towards the town again, past the booth selling tickets for the boat trip, wondering how she might spend the time.

Just then Lucy saw a sign; 'Merwater Museum'. In fact she'd passed the museum half a dozen times at least. It was a small building, run by the local council and situated just close to the harbour. It was one of those places that Lucy thought she might go to on a rainy day, but she'd always had some excuse or other not to go and so she had never actually ventured inside. Now, as she passed, she remembered what Paul Treddinick said to her the day before when she'd asked what a Dolphin-Child actually was.'Go look in the museum' he'd said in answer to her question. The museum was free and Lucy thought she may as well take a look around inside.

There were only three rooms to the museum which Lucy quickly realised, really was very small indeed. Half a dozen tourists were quietly looking around. A display with an old wooden fishing boat and a fisherman's net dominated the main room. Lucy read the sign of the exhibit explaining how fishing nets were made and maintained. She turned to look at the sequence of glass cases running around the edge of the other side of the room. There were various old photos, clay pipes and tinder boxes on display. Lucy ambled around haphazardly, looking at the exhibits out of order.

One exhibit seized Lucy's interest in particular. It was a diorama; a sort of model of the town of Merwater in perspective, showing how it might have looked two hundred and fifty or more years ago, with a crowd of model people gathered at the harbours edge. There were some figures who appeared to be drowning in the water and some men in rowing boats struggling out through the high waves towards them.

There was a telephone handset next to the exhibit with a recorded voice to tell people what it was all about. Lucy picked it up and sat down on the bench next to the exhibit to listen.

'The town of Merwater was mentioned in the Doomsday book almost a thousand years ago and as recently as two hundred and fifty years ago was still famous for its fish and the tin that was mined nearby. The scene in the exhibit in front of you shows a famous story from the town's past, which most people think is a myth.

The town is called "Mer" Water because legend has it that Mer people once lived here. Sometimes known as mermaids, Mer People were as comfortable in the sea as on dry land. However they were not the half-fish, half-woman that pictures and pirate stories portray. So the stories go, the Mer people all had a special connection with dolphins and so are sometimes known as Children of the Dolphins, or Mer children. At one time, it is said that almost a quarter of the population of Merwater were Children of the Dolphins. Stories recount how the locals would swim out to be with the dolphins and would work with them to bring fish to their nets.

Since that time legend has it that there are only one or two Children of the Dolphins born in every generation. About two hundred and fifty years ago, a young girl aged ten or eleven called Susan Penhaligon told everyone in the town that she was a Mer Child too. She claimed that she could teach the other children how to become Mer children as well. Two or three-score children became her followers. The town people started to become concerned about what Susan Penhaligon was telling their children and forbade them from associating with her. Some people believed she was under the power of dark forces and called for her to be tried as a witch. Susan Penhaligon went into hiding, but her followers remained faithful to her and would steal away at first light to see her and to be with the dolphins, who they thought were a type of angel.

On Easter Sunday in 1756 it is said that Susan Penhaligon's followers left their homes and swam out to sea at sunrise, to perform a mystical ceremony that she had devised and which she told them would enable them to all become Mer Children like her.

However that very morning a storm hit the coast. Of the thirty or so children that followed Susan Penhaligon out into the waves, only one boy survived. Ten or so children were drowned and washed up on the coast. Susan Penhaligon and the other children were never heard of again. They too were lost, presumed drowned at sea, but legend has it that they turned into dolphins and lived on amongst the waves.

Some local families still believe the old stories of Mer Children and dolphins. To this day those families whose children were never found are always kind to dolphins, believing that the descendents of their lost children still swim with them. The families of the children that were washed up drowned on the beach are mistrustful of dolphins and anything to do with them.

The diorama you see in front of you shows the townsfolk of Merwater at the harbours edge vainly trying to save the children from the storm.

Although this story was recounted in locally printed pamphlets from about 1850 and has been passed down from mother to child for generations, there are no contemporaneous records to corroborate that these events ever actually occurred. The story of Susan Penhaligon and the Mer Children is a legend that continues to fascinate generations of visitors.'

The recording ended and Lucy put down the handset back on its rest. Lucy felt shaky and had to sit down briefly on a bench to steady herself. She felt a strange swirl of emotions. She was pleased to learn that she was not alone and that other people might have had similar experiences to her own in the past. The story of Susan Penhaligon and the children she took to their death in the seas disturbed her though. How could associating with something so wonderful as a dolphin lead to death like that?

Lucy thought back to Paul's mother Mrs Treddinick and what she had said only yesterday. 'You and your kind are dangerous' she'd said. 'You'll be the death of all of us!' Those words cut into Lucy like a knife. She wondered whether Mrs Treddinick believed the old stories and what she'd said to her son Paul about Lucy.

Lucy glanced at her watch. She'd have to get back to Nate and Bob in a few minutes. She wandered around the museum a little more. There in another display case was one of the original pamphlets telling the story of Susan Penhaligon and there was even an old oil painting of what an artist imagined her to look like. It was a dark picture, with a girl in the foreground and the sea and leaping dolphins in the background. The girl's eyes were too close together, Lucy thought and the dolphins in the picture all looked strange. The next room told the story of tin mining in Cornwall, but Lucy didn't have time to look at that properly and left the small museum, still feeling disturbed by what she had just heard and seen.

There were quite a few tourists already onboard the Merry Widow and Nate greeted her again in a friendly tone.

'Hop on board young Lucy, we're leaving in five minutes.' Nate looked at her more closely. 'You okay?'

'You know. I've just been in the museum' she replied quietly. A look of understanding passed across Nate's face. He could imagine which displays she'd been looking at and what it meant to her.

'Oh I see' Nate replied simply. He had to busy himself with preparations to cast off and leave the harbour. Lucy went and stood at the stern of the Merry Widow. The weather had cleared up and a light breeze was coming off the sea. There were twenty or so tourists on board, cameras at the ready, eager for the glimpse of seals basking on the rocks, a great plankton-feeding basking shark perhaps, or even a dolphin.

Lucy contented herself with standing at the bow of the boat and looking down at the low waves beneath her. She imagined Susan Penhaligon and her followers swimming out to sea and their mysterious fate. What was going through their minds when they did so? Lucy looked back at the town. Merwater was disappearing in the distance as they went round the headland. The sheer rock of the cliffs steeped up to their left.

Nate gave the tourists a commentary over a loud speaker as they sailed along. They were heading towards a rocky outcrop a quarter of a mile from the shore. Lucy had never seen a seal in the wild and was keen to see them up close. Before long Bob cut off the engine and the Merry Widow sat quietly in the water near the seals basking on their rocks. It wasn't possible to get up too close, but they had a good view and the tourists on the boat snapped away happily with their cameras. There were some young seals amongst the group and oohs and aahs emanated from the tourists on deck. It made Lucy think about Summer's calf. She had only seen No-Name in her visions and had never been able to meet the tiny dolphin in real life. She longed to do so.

On their way back Lucy scanned the sea for any sign of dolphins. At one point she saw what looked like a dorsal fin briefly breaking the surface of the water, but then it disappeared again and she could not tell whether her eyes were deceiving her and it was really only a wave. Nate beckoned her to join him and Bob in the cabin and he gave her a turn steering the vessel, as he did with all of the other children who came out on the boat and who were old enough to have a go.

The two hours quickly passed and before she knew it, they were back at the harbour, ready to disembark and go home. Bethany would be waiting for her in the Land Rover at five o'clock. Lucy chatted to Nate and Bob for a while and then glanced at her watch. She thought she'd better go and find her aunt. She thanked both the two of them again for the trip on the boat and then headed off.

As she started on her way back to the car park where Bethany would be waiting, there sitting on the harbour wall was Paul Treddinick. His distinctive curly hair was easy to spot. He was looking out at the waves rolling in to shore and seemed to be frowning unhappily.

Chapter Six:

Spirit stirred from his waking sleep. Half of his brain was alert to the changes in the waves and the current in order to stay close enough to the surface to breathe through his blow hole. On the other half of his brain he dreamt troubling dreams.

At first he dreamt about the girl on the rock that he and Dancer had helped. Just before he awoke though, he dreamt that there was a dolphin some distance ahead of him in the water. He couldn't see the dolphin, as in his dream the water wasn't clear. He clicked rapidly and using his echo location was able to ascertain the shape of a dolphin in the water. The dolphin didn't answer though and although Spirit swam and swam towards the shape, he simply could not reach it.

For some reason he felt that the silhouette of the dolphin ahead of him was familiar but he couldn't say why. He desperately wanted to get to it, but the more he tried, the further away he seemed to be. Eventually the dolphin just appeared to dissolve into the water.

Spirit woke up with a start. Dancer was already awake.

'What's the matter?' she asked.

'Oh I just, you know, had sort of a nightmare.'

'Was it of a herring as long as a ship?' joked Dancer. 'That's what I dream about. And that herring's really, really hungry and chasing me!' Spirit smiled. Already the memory of his own dream seemed less immediate, disturbing though it was.

'Are you hungry?' asked Dancer.

'Actually I'm famished' Spirit replied. They slipped away from the main pod and hunted around on the shallow seabed for flounder, but without success. As they did so, Spirit felt a tingle of anticipation run down his spine and then Lucy suddenly came into focus in the sea just in front of them, appearing as though an apparition, not quite there because her physical self was still miles away on dry land.

Spirit had learned now that when a human pulls up the corners of its mouth, that is mostly a sign of friendliness, although not always. Lucy smiled broadly at them both. Human expressions were very hard to read. They seemed to mostly just use their faces to show how they felt, while dolphins expressed themselves in a myriad of ways; the way they swam, jumped or flicked a fin, or clicked and whistled. Even though he knew he would never fully understand the strange ways of humans, he was sure that Lucy really cared for him. He felt the same way about her. Though they were so different from each other in so many ways, he felt that somehow at a fundamental level they were quite alike.

'Hi Spirit, hello Dancer' she said. When she came to them as a vision, they were able to communicate with each other without human words or dolphin clicks and whistles. Spirit had spent many hours trying to figure out how it worked, but he just couldn't. Somehow thoughts seemed to pass straight from her mind to his. All three of them started to glide along through the water companionably.

'Did you dream of us last night?' Spirit asked. He often asked. He'd had been enchanted to discover that Lucy had dreamt of him and the rest of the pod almost every night since she was a little girl and he was still a very young calf.

'Actually, I didn't' admitted Lucy 'I sort of dreamt of dolphins, but not any one in particular, I don't think'. Spirit quickly told Lucy about his own dream. He thought that she might make a joke about it like Dancer did, but instead she seemed surprised and startled. Spirit wondered whether she was going to say something, but she seemed to hold back. Instead she changed the subject.

'How did you feel about helping the little girl?' she asked the two dolphins.

'Oh, you know, when we saw her in trouble, we knew that we simply couldn't leave her until she was safe' said Dancer. 'But she was scared of us, otherwise we might have been able to carry her to safety. That's when Spirit reached out to you with his mind.'

'I'd never done that before' said Spirit, wondering why Lucy had changed the subject away from dreams and what it was that she wasn't telling them. 'I didn't think I knew how to do it. I had to use all my mental energy to reach out to you. I was glad that I could though. I don't know how we'd have helped the little girl if I hadn't got through to you. I tried to swim up to the people splashing in the water at the edge of the beach, but they didn't seem to understand.'

'It was amazing when you contacted me' replied Lucy. 'It was as though an electric shock ran through my body. Every nerve stood to attention.'

'Well I'm glad' said Spirit modestly.

'You were a sensation at the beach' continued Lucy. 'Everyone's talking about the dolphins appearing there and hordes of people are going there now to try to catch sight of you again. It's even been on the local TV.'

'Oh I'm not going there again' laughed Spirit hurriedly. 'It was scary having all those arms and legs in the water around us, trying to touch and grab at me. I'm not going to put myself through that again unless I really have to.'

'Why do humans go in the water like that anyway Lucy?' asked Dancer. After all, humans are not sea creatures are they?'

It's difficult to explain really' Lucy said. 'The sun makes us feel healthy and happy and so does the sea. But we only like the sea when it's sunny, otherwise we get too cold.'

'You humans need a layer of fat round you to keep you warm' joked Dancer.

'But it's strange isn't it' said Spirit thoughtfully. 'You humans can't really swim properly at all, well not like us anyway. You should be afraid of the sea shouldn't you, instead of being attracted to it.'

'I know' said Lucy turning slowly in the water, 'maybe we'd all secretly like to return to the sea again. You know scientists say that all the animals on dry land evolved from sea creatures millions of years ago. They say that whales and dolphins were land-living mammals once which evolved to return back to the sea again.'

'I don't really understand that' said Spirit. 'Dolphins have been the same since time itself began. That is what the elders teach us. You couldn't just grow flippers and a blow hole could you?' Lucy laughed and then paused for a few moments. Spirit felt that she was deciding whether to ask him something.

'Spirit' she said eventually. 'I know its silly, but have you ever heard of humans turning into dolphins?'

'No, never' replied Spirit. 'Not in any of the old stories that I've been told. Why?'

'Oh, well…' Lucy hesitated again and Spirit could tell that she was uncertain about how to continue. 'Amongst people, there are stories about humans turning into dolphins and I just wondered….' She trailed off.

'I can ask if you like' said Spirit, his imagination aroused. 'I can ask Storm or some of the other older dolphins.

'That would be good' she replied. It was Spirit's turn to become thoughtful. Her question reminded him of what Moonlight had said the day before.

'Why do you think that we are linked together in this way; I mean you as a human and me as a dolphin. Is there a purpose to it?'

'I don't know, I….' Spirit could see that Lucy's energy was giving out and that she was fading away into the water as she and Dancer looked at her.

'Goodbye Lucy' he called to her. Then she was gone.

'You really shouldn't worry about what Moonlight said to you' Dancer reassured him once Lucy's image faded away into the salt water. 'He's never going to understand that there's more to life than eating fish.'

'But he's right though in a way, isn't he Dancer' replied Spirit, his voice tinged with doubt. 'There must be some reason for the link between me and Lucy.'

'Sometimes we cannot understand the reasons for things' said Dancer after a few moments thought, 'but we just have to accept them. Maybe we will never discover the reason for the connection between you and Lucy, but my guess is that your life is better knowing her than not.' Spirit looked at Dancer's face. There was wisdom behind those normally playful eyes.

'Why do you think that Lucy asked about humans turning into dolphins?' asked Spirit.

'I don't know' replied Dancer. 'Storm believes that humans are foolish creatures. He says that they're more like children than fully grown adults and that they just pollute the seas and destroy everything around them. Maybe they actually do believe stories like that. I don't imagine that any dolphins would though.'

With these curious thoughts still fresh in their minds, they swam back to join the rest of their pod, still hungry. It would be better to hunt all together. When they got nearer, Summer's young calf No-Name saw them and swam enthusiastically towards them. The little calf became separated from his mother's side doing so and before anyone quite realised, No-Name was some tens of metres away from both Summer and Dancer and Spirit.

Vulnerable and alone, he could fall easy prey to any larger predators that might be prowling the waters. As if to confirm their worst fears, suddenly the white and black bulk of a killer whale appeared off to one side of the calf, swimming rapidly in No-Name's direction, appearing as if from nowhere.

Spirit himself had been the subject of an attack by orcas only a few months before and knew just how dangerous they could be. He had learned a lot since then and gained greatly in confidence, but orcas still scared him.

'Orcas!' he cried as loud as he could. He could tell that the same thought passed through Dancer's mind as his. The orcas would try to attack No-Name. It was always easier for them to attack the young, weak and inexperienced dolphins in the pod. A calf makes an easy meal for a pack of hungry killer whales.

Dancer darted forward through the water to try and protect Summer's calf, with Spirit just behind. The orca closed in on No-Name rapidly and it looked like they would not be fast enough to save the lone calf. Dancer gave a last burst of speed and slammed into the side of the killer whale just in time, forcing it off to one side, just before it was able to close its jaws on Summer's calf.

Spirit got there a moment later and used his body to shield the calf against any further attacks. Summer swam up anxiously moments later and in no time at all the whole pod had come to No-Name's rescue, circling around him defensively.

The orca, recognising the overwhelming force of numbers on the part of the dolphins, gave up and disappeared back into the vastness of the ocean.

'Thank goodness you got to him in time!' Summer said to Dancer, relief in her voice.

'Yes, that brute nearly got him. You did well Dancer. No special powers needed there' added Moonlight pointedly. Dancer had been winded badly when she slammed into the side of the hefty Orca and took a while to calm down and recover her breath.

'It was Spirit who saw the orca coming' Dancer said eventually, suspicious that Moonlight's compliment might be at Spirit's expense.

'We work better as a whole than as individuals' intoned Storm, his voice calm and serious. 'It is vital that we all look to the security and wellbeing of each other. We had better take extra care if there are orcas in these waters at the moment.'

The dolphins swam on, scouting for shoals of fish. The sun made its way across the sky. The pod was extra vigilant for any signs of orcas and No-Name stayed close to his mother. Spirit, still thinking about his conversation with Lucy that morning, swam up and joined Storm by his side.

'Storm' he said eventually, 'have you ever heard about humans turning into dolphins?' Storm almost jumped in surprise.

'Where have you heard of such a thing?' he asked.

'Lucy came to me and Dancer this morning' Spirit replied, nervous at Storm's reaction. 'She said that she thought it was silly, but that some humans told stories of other humans turning into dolphins. I don't think that could happen, but humans know about a lot of things that we don't. Storm snorted contemptuously, but then he stopped and turned to look Spirit in the eye.

'We do not tell such stories in this pod because we do not believe them' he said seriously. 'But you should know that there are some dolphins that do believe it to be true and tell stories of humans becoming dolphins. There are some dolphins who actually believe that they are descended from the humans that swam out into the sea. It's nonsense of course and we don't abide with such old superstitions.'

'But how do you know its nonsense?' asked Spirit. 'After all, I myself have connections to humans that we do not understand.'

'That is true' replied Storm. 'Humans may be able to do many things that we cannot, but we remain the wiser, older and more superior creature. They cannot be capable of transforming themselves into us.'

'I do not think of Lucy as any lesser an animal than I am' replied Spirit. I think of ourselves as equal.' Storm smiled.

'Perhaps you are right Spirit. Maybe I can be too harsh about humans. But always remember that they are dangerous, more so than orcas, or sharks or any other predator in the sea.'

'Who are the dolphins that believe they are descended from humans?' asked Spirit.

'I knew that you would ask me that' said Storm resignedly. 'They live many days swimming from here and though I know of them, I have never met them myself. They live too far away from us to come together in the great dolphin council.'

'So there is no easy way of contacting them then?' asked Spirit, immediately disappointed. Storm sighed.

'Not quite' he replied. 'In fact I believe you have already met one. It is Blue's mother, Sunlight'. Immediately Spirit thought back to his recent mission. Blue had run away from one pod and joined another. He had not met Blue's mother then, but had probably done so at an earlier council of the dolphins.

'Is she one of them then?' he asked in surprise.

'She believes she is' replied Storm. 'She came from that same pod far away.'

'So she ran away from her own pod and now her son Blue has run away from his?'

'I am not sure what led Sunlight to leave her own pod' replied Storm cautiously. 'but she is born of those dolphins who believe themselves descended from humans.'

'Can I speak to her about it?' asked Spirit eagerly. Storm sighed once again.

'I think that you must' he said. 'Until you do you will never rest. Her pod is not so far away, just to the east of the islands. A couple of hours swimming will bring you there.'

'Then can I go?'

'I'd be happier if you took Dancer with you. That orca will still be in these waters and besides, they're a strange pod.'

Spirit hastened away to tell Dancer the news. Soon they were skimming the surface of the sea together as they swam along towards the waters to the east of the islands. Small waves picked up on the surface of the sea. Clouds blotted out the sun and looked heavy with rain. The weather was changing. Dolphins have a sense for the weather. They are so in tune with the currents and the temperature of the water, that it is almost as though they can smell it. Spirit felt reassured. There might be rain, but there would be no storm.

'So what are you going to say to Sunlight when you meet her?' asked Dancer quizzically as they swam along.

'Well, I just want to ask her what her kin told her about being descended from humans' Spirit replied.

'It's not going to be easy you know. You were sent out on a mission to speak to her son Blue. Now you come to her and want to talk about some far-fetched old tales. She'll just want you to tell her about her son.'

'Well that's no problem' Spirit replied, I can do that too.'

'And do you want to find out just to answer Lucy's question this morning?' she asked. Spirit thought for a moment, as they swum on towards the islands.

'It's not just that I want to answer Lucy's question. It's more than that. There's something between humans and dolphins, something between Lucy and me that I don't understand. I want to know the answer to Moonlight's question; what's the point of my gift at all?' Spirit felt the unanswered questions boiling up inside him. 'If there's anything at all to these stories about humans turning into dolphins, then it must help me, mustn't it?'

At that moment the image from his dream of the night before returned to him; the dolphin that he could just make out through the murk of the water, but who, try as he might, he could not get close to.

Presently they could make out the calls of dolphins echoing outwards from the seas just east of the islands and they honed in on their target. They found the pod at rest, after having just eaten. The eldest and most senior dolphin in their pod of twelve or so was called Speed, because in her day she had been the fastest dolphin in all of the seas hereabouts. She was old now and bad tempered. Spirit and Dancer offered the traditional greeting and said that they wanted to speak to Sunlight.

As her name implied, Sunlight was a positive, warm and open dolphin, but she had been hurt and upset when Blue had left them to join another pod. She was eager for news of him and Spirit was happy to oblige. While Dancer chatted to the other members of the pod, Spirit filled Sunlight in on his recent visit to Blue.

'Do you think he will come back to us?' she asked anxiously.

'I cannot say for certain' said Spirit cautiously, 'but I think that he is less angry than he was and that must surely be a good thing. It is my belief that before long he will visit you again.' They talked on for a while about Blue, while Spirit wondered how he could bring the conversation round to what he really wanted to speak about.

Later, when Spirit felt that he had said all that he was able to tell Sunlight about Blue, he thought that it was safe to change the subject.

'Sunlight. I am trying to learn as much as I can about all of the stories of the dolphins. I have heard that you originated from a pod far away from here'. Immediately Sunlight's face clouded with worry and she glanced down.

'I don't like to talk of those times' she replied. Spirit started to worry that he would not be able to get Sunlight to tell him anything at all. He tried again.

'You see it is important for me. I am what the others call a Child-Seer, that is I am able to communicate with a human child

98

that comes to me in visions. I have met her in real life too. I have heard that in the pod of your birth, it is believed that you were all descended from humans. Is that true?'

Sunlight looked at Spirit with anxiety in her eyes.

'I thought I had left all that behind me.' She glanced away into the depths of the ocean, memories swimming before her eyes and then looked back at Spirit.

'My real name is not Sunlight' she said in a quiet voice. 'That is the name I took after joining this pod. In the pod in which I grew up, we are given names at birth. My birth name is Susan. It is a human name for a girl and it has been passed down the generations.'

Spirit looked at Sunlight. The name Susan meant nothing to him. The only human name he knew was Lucy and which she had told him meant light. Sunlight was evidently troubled by what she was telling him, but he was intensely curious and did not want her to stop.

'There were twelve dolphins in my pod and there had always been the same number as long as any dolphin there could remember. The eldest were Edgar, John and Mirabel. Then there were Florence, Jethro, Jane, Agnes and Michael. The youngest were Anne, Simeon, Arthur and myself. These are all human names you see, the same names as the humans carried when it is said they changed from their human form many years ago.' Sunlight and Spirit turned and swam along slowly just under the surface of the water.

'When I grew up, the older dolphins would tell us young ones stories of what it was like to live on land, of the dark cold boxes that humans lived in and green hills and tall things called trees that were like rigid kelp. It was said though that our human ancestors were not free, and had do what other humans told them and work many hours of the day. They could not roam the land like we roam the seas. Sometimes the males would be sent to dig in deep dark holes in the ground, in what were called mines. Many of them died there, or became ill and died while still young. It was a hard desolate life, full of toil and sadness.'

This all seemed strange to Spirit. He thought that humans were as free as dolphins. He knew that they lived in tiny boxes and that Lucy had to go to a place called a school to learn things, but she was mostly happy to be there he thought. He had not heard about humans dying young as Sunlight described.

'Why did they leave the land?' he asked.

'It is said that there was a young girl that could visit a particular dolphin in visions and communicate with him. His name was Midnight and he was a Child-Seer like you. The girl was terribly unhappy. She could see the freedom and the beauty of the seas when she visited, but hated her life on the land. She persuaded other children that life was better out here on the seas and that if they wanted to, they could join her out here and live forever in freedom and happiness.'

'What happened then?' Spirit asked. Sunlight sighed. 'It is told that a number of human children swam out from the land, but were engulfed in a storm and that their shattered bodies scattered back to the shore like so many broken twigs. But it is also told that the spirits of a few of the children became dolphins and that their descendents form the pod into which I was born.'

Spirit gasped. He was shocked at the death of the children. He was all too aware of how frail and vulnerable any human was in the sea. Even Lucy, who was a good swimmer, easily tired and he could see that she was no match for the currents and tides that swelled and surged along the coast.

'You keep saying it is told', he said to Sunlight. 'Do you believe in the stories yourself?' She gave a small shake of her head and looked away again for a moment before replying.

'I was brought up on those stories. Something must have happened to inspire them, I know that. Now my pod lives a long way away from the waters around the human town of Merwater, from where the human children are said to have swum. As a young calf growing to maturity, I could not accept or believe that our ancestors could be born of such a sad and terrible story. I left my pod to travel back here to try and discover what really happened. None of the dolphins that live in these parts now believe the story I just told you. Neither do I anymore. I could not go back to my pod to live a lie so I stayed here and have sought out happiness and peace where I can.'

'Why do you think the stories are told then, if they did not really happen?' asked Spirit.

'I think perhaps that Midnight, the Child-Seer, was so overcome by grief that he invented the story to comfort himself. It is the only explanation that makes sense to me.'

'And the human girl, that told the others to swim out to sea. What was her name?' asked Spirit.

'It was Susan. Yes', Sunlight smiled sadly. 'The name I was given by my pod at birth.'

Chapter Seven:

At first Lucy thought that she would just walk past Paul, sitting there on the harbour wall, and pretend that she had not seen him. It didn't look as though he was aware of her presence and it seemed to be a coincidence that he happened to be there as she came off the Merry Widow after her trip with Nate and Bob and the tourists to go seal watching. But Lucy had become used to confronting difficult situations and knew that she could not walk on by without saying at least something to him. She went up to him.

'Hey' she said.

'Hey' he replied quietly. Paul did not turn to look at her, but instead continued to stare determinedly out to sea, as if by returning her gaze he would reveal some weakness. She realised that he was trying not to cry. Something must have happened to upset him.

'What's up?' she asked. Paul gave a slight shake of his head, as if to say he would not tell her, while still looking away from her. Lucy glanced around her, as if by doing so she could see the cause of his distress. There was no one in sight other than a few tourists and visitors to the town.

'Was it those kids again?' she asked, guessing at the truth.
Paul gave the slightest of nods, but still would not return her look.

'Will I see you around?' she asked. He gave a shrug.

'I'm not supposed to talk to you' he mumbled eventually.

'Well suit yourself.' Lucy walked away feeling rejected. She
saw that Bethany had pulled up in the car park behind the
harbour. She hooted the horn and waved out of the open window
when she saw Lucy coming in her direction.

'Hey Kiddo, hop in!'

Lucy was glad to climb into Bethany's old Land Rover and sit
down. It had been a surprisingly tiring afternoon. Just as she got
to the car she cast a last look back in Paul's direction. He was
staring down at his feet.

Later on, after a dinner of salad and freshly caught plaice that
Bob had wrapped up for Lucy to take home, it was time for Lucy to
call Dad. Bethany and Lucy sat outside after they'd washed up,
enjoying the late afternoon sunshine. Swifts skimmed along the
hedgerows and over the meadow like miniature fighter pilots,
catching insects on the wing.

'I can't believe those tiny little birds fly all the way up from North
Africa to spend each summer here' said Bethany admiringly,
gazing up at them in the sky.

'It's time to call your Dad' she added after a while. 'Bet you've
got lots to tell him.'

'Well yes and no' said Lucy noncommittally. Although Dad knew that Lucy was what Paul called a Dolphin-Child, she was keenly aware that he did not like it and did not approve. He was so adamantly opposed to it, that she felt she could not tell him anything about Spirit and the other dolphins at all. It seemed better just to keep quiet and avoid trouble. Yet the strange thing was that not so long ago he'd objected to her even doing swimming practice at lunchtimes. Now he'd agreed to her coming down to Cornwall to stay with Bethany alone and without his supervision. It didn't make any sense.

'He'll be coming down in a few days, you looking forward to it?' Lucy pulled a face. 'Hey, he's your Dad you know and he loves you. He's stuck in that office working while you're down here enjoying the summer. You'll have a great time when he comes down I'm sure.'

'But will I be able to see Spirit though when he comes?'

'I thought that might be worrying you Kiddo' replied Bethany. 'I guess it won't be quite as easy, but we'll have a word with him and make sure you still can. Don't forget, it's been tough on both of you after your Mum died, but he's had to look after you, carry on working in a difficult job he doesn't like very much and keep the house and home together. Maybe he's starting to relax a bit now. A holiday will be good for him. It'll be good for both of you.'

'I guess so' said Lucy. She wasn't so sure, but didn't like to say. It would be their first holiday together since Mum died. It didn't seem right to be away with Dad unless Mum was there too.

She'd just about got used to living at home with only Dad, but a holiday with him would bring all the memories back to her and that great aching sense of loss.

Lucy dutifully went over to the farmhouse to call Dad. Mobile phone reception was still bad at the farm. Darren opened the door then Mary came out from the living room.

'Hello there Lucy' she said amiably. 'Just before you call your Dad, I thought I'd tell you that I had a bit of a surprise visit from the Coast Guard this afternoon. They wanted me to tell them how I knew there was a little girl stranded on the rocks off Black Gull Beach.'

'What did you tell them?' asked Lucy nervously.

'Well I didn't know what to tell them. I didn't think they'd understand if I told them what really happened and I thought you might not be so keen on getting an earful of their questions. So I'm afraid I told them a bit of a fib' she confessed awkwardly. Lucy was grateful and relieved that she hadn't been put on the spot and wondered what on earth Mary could have said.

'So I told them that a friend of mine was walking down the coastal path to the beach and saw the girl and that she called me on her mobile so that I could ring the Coast Guard' Mary continued. 'Not sure if they completely believed me, but it kept them quiet though and off they went again.'

'Trouble is' said Darren coming through, 'that my Mary always blushes scarlet red when she tells a lie. Known for it in these parts she is. So I'm guessing they didn't believe her at all' he laughed. Lucy smiled awkwardly.

'I'm sorry you had to fib' she said to Mary, 'but thanks anyway.'

Lucy went to the phone in the hall and called Dad. She told him all about the boat trip with Nate and Bob earlier and the strange boy she'd encountered in the town. She didn't tell him what Paul's mother had said about her, or helping to rescue the little girl, or her swims with Spirit. In fact she didn't tell him any of the really interesting stuff at all. Towards the end of the call he cleared his throat and then asked the question that she knew he really wanted to ask all along.

'So, err, how are things with your, err, dolphin friends?'

'Oh, you know, fine' she answered as uninformatively as possible, hoping that he wouldn't ask anything else.

'And are you swimming with them?' he asked. Lucy knew he hated the idea of her doing so and could not bring himself to use Spirit or Dancer's names. It was Lucy's turn to fib now.

'Oh you know, Bethany and I have gone down to the cove a couple of times and I, well, said hello to them.' At least on the phone he couldn't see her blush.

'Good girl' replied Dad. 'At least you know better than to try and go down there on your own. Those coastal waters are incredibly dangerous. The undertow can pull you out a quarter of a mile before you know it, even a strong swimmer like you. At the end of the day Luce those dolphins are just animals. They may look smiley and nice but you can't trust them to save you if you get into

107

trouble. At least I'll be down in a few days and then I can look after you properly.'

'Yes Dad' said Lucy obediently, her heart sinking.

Lucy slept badly that night. At first she'd slept well enough and dreamt of Spirit, Dancer, Storm and the others, which made her feel happy and calm. Then towards the morning the image of the lone dolphin came into her mind once again, floating suspended in the murky waters a few metres away from her. She tried to swim towards the vague silhouette of the dolphin, but the more she strove to get closer to it, the further away it seemed to be.

Then suddenly the calm waters turned choppy and she could see children above her on the surface, their arms flailing, gasping for air as the waves crashed over them and then floating down, still and lifeless into the inky depths.

Lucy woke up with a start, anxious and sweaty. Though she had slept for nine hours, she felt as though she had barely slept for two. She felt drained and exhausted. Although she wanted to, she didn't feel able to cycle up to Old Man's Cove at first light in the hope of seeing Spirit and Dancer. Besides, she wasn't sure if they'd be there that morning anyway.

Lucy stretched out instead to Spirit with her mind. She had to focus her thoughts and then relax, so that she could find that elusive door between her conscious and unconscious that would allow her to slip through and tumble down into their world of water.

108

She already felt tired from her disturbed night's sleep, so the effort to maintain the vision was more difficult than usual.

Lucy's thoughts kept returning to Susan Penhaligon and her ill-fated attempt to take to the sea with a crowd of other children. Could humans really turn into dolphins? It seemed unlikely, but then her own ability to communicate with Spirit and Dancer defied understanding. She asked Spirit, but he hadn't heard anything of the story. Of course it happened over two hundred years ago and maybe it was unlikely that such a tale would pass down through so many generations of dolphins. Spirit said that he would ask the others about it, but she doubted he would be able to find anything out.

She didn't like to tell Spirit about her dream of the lone dolphin in those murky waters, perpetually just out of reach. She thought it might disturb him. Eventually her energy gave out and she found herself sitting on a kitchen chair in Bethany's studio, feeling tired and hungry.

Bethany had also got up and had crept down the stairs from the sleeping platform so quietly that Lucy had not noticed. Now that Lucy had emerged from her reverie, she dared to make a noise.

'Hey Kiddo, how about some chocolate milk?' she said.

Sunlight flooded in through the windows and after three slices of toast and a bowl full of cereal, she was beginning to feel more herself again. Sometimes she wondered what it would be like to live exclusively on a diet of fish and squid like Spirit had to and was quite glad she didn't have to try.

'So what do you fancy doing today?' asked Bethany as she cleared away the breakfast things. 'I've got stuff to do this morning but we could hang out together this afternoon. Maybe we could book ourselves a lesson with your friend Dan at the surf school? One day I'm determined that I'll be able to stand up on that surf board without immediately falling off it again.'

'That sounds good' replied Lucy. 'I'd like that.'

'It's a deal then. I'll call Dan this morning and fix up a lesson for this afternoon. I'm pretty sure the tide will be coming then, so the waves should be a bit bigger.' Four months ago Lucy had given Dan the fright of his life when she'd swum away from shore by the surf school to save Spirit.

Lucy had the morning to herself and she decided to ask Mary if she could borrow her bicycle. She wanted to cycle into Merwater and buy a postcard to send to her friend Amy back home. Amy had demanded that Lucy send her regular updates over the summer. Lucy wondered whether she would see those kids when she went into town, or that boy Paul. She didn't want to go up to the recreation ground as she was still worried about encountering his mother Mrs Treddinick again.

She left the house, bumped over the cattle grid on Mary's bike and started cycling up the lane. The verges were overgrown with weeds and flowers now and the hedges behind them were tall and unkempt. The occasional butterfly fluttered past and Lucy could hear the distant hum of bees as they flew from flower to flower. The first bit was uphill and Lucy soon broke out into a sweat in the warm sunshine. The lane levelled out where it joined the main road that followed the coast. It was busy with tourist traffic and Lucy cycled on the grassy verge to keep out of the way of cars. After a quarter of a mile or so another lane branched off again and Lucy knew that she could get into Merwater on this quieter road.

Within another ten minutes she was free-wheeling down the steep hill towards the harbour and the High Street. Lucy chained her bike up to a railing and began to amble along, casually looking into the shop windows as she went. She had the whole morning to herself after all. She bought a postcard and a stamp in one of the gift shops and then sat on a wall in the sunshine to write it before dropping it into the post box outside the 'Clotted Cream' Tea Room.

As Lucy walked along the road, she got to the point where the walled stream passed under the road and continued for a short distance before it came out at the sea wall and the muddy strip of beach beyond. She stopped and looked down to see how much water was in the stream. It was sluggish and green with algae and there seemed to be less in it than when Lucy had followed Paul up it only a couple of days before.

Just as she was about to turn away, Lucy suddenly heard thudding noises echoing down the walled stream from up the hill and then she caught the sound of children's voices yelling angrily. Lucy's heart started to thud as Paul Treddinick came round the bend, running as fast as he could along the bed of the stream. He stumbled on the algae covered rocks and almost fell as he did so, righting himself just in time. The two bigger kids that had chased him the other day were almost on top of him, barely an arms length behind him and seemed intent on catching Paul and pulling him down. As quickly as they came into view, they disappeared out of sight under the road.

Lucy felt a clutch of anxiety. She couldn't just stand there. She had to do something. There was a pedestrian crossing across the road only twenty metres away and immediately beyond it a narrow side road that led to sea wall. Lucy walked briskly up to the crossing and then once she was on the other side, ran as fast as she could till she got to the wall. Looking down, she could see that the tide was out to its fullest extent and beyond the thin pebble beach there was thick sludge. The two older kids had caught up with Paul and it looked like one was holding him while the other had scooped up a handful of sea mud and was trying to stuff it down the back of the neck of Paul's tee-shirt.

'Hey, leave him alone!' Lucy called angrily. The two boys either didn't hear her or didn't take any notice. Quickly she found the rusted iron ladder fixed to the side of the wall and climbed down onto the beach. She ran across to them.

'I said leave him alone!' she yelled, this time trying to pull one of the boys away, so that Paul could run away. The thick sludge squelched up over her sandals and onto her feet. It felt horrible. One of the boys turned to face Lucy.

112

'Ooooh' he taunted, 'Paulie's got a girlfriend!' The other boy sniggered. Lucy's heart was thudding in her chest now. She scooped up a handful of foul-smelling sludge herself now and made as if to fling it at them.

'You want it too then?' Lucy said, referring to the sludge. The boy leered at her, but started backing off.

'Come on' he said to the other boy, 'let's leave Paulie to his girlie. They're mud for each other.' They laughed again at their weak joke and swaggered off. Lucy dropped the sludge and looked at Paul. They'd managed to splatter sludge down the back of his tee-shirt, in his hair and over his face.

'You look terrible' Lucy told Paul as he straightened up. 'Come on, let's clean ourselves up. Paul didn't say anything as they walked back to where the pebbles edged directly onto the sea. Lucy had muddy feet and one muddy hand. They could soon be washed clean in the sea though. For Paul it wasn't so easy. He resolved the problem by dunking himself in the clean salt water so that the sludge washed off him.

Lucy looked at him. He was wearing shorts and a tee-shirt and so although his clothes were now soaked in salt water and his hair was dripping wet, at least the worst of the stinking wet mud had washed off him. It was sunny and warm, thought Lucy. He'd dry out. Paul avoided her gaze though and seemed embarrassed and upset. She wanted to know why they'd picked on him, but in her heart she knew there was probably no reason at all. They didn't need an excuse to make his life miserable. He was probably too easy and convenient a victim.

Instead of approaching the subject directly, Lucy thought she'd find out if there was anyone who would stick up for Paul.

'You got any brothers or sisters then?' she asked.

'I got a sister, but she's only five' he replied. So there was no older brother or sister to help him she thought.

'What's your dad like?'

'Can't remember. Haven't seen him for a long time' Paul replied.

'Who's your best friend?' she asked.

'He moved to Bristol at Easter.'

'Who else then?'

'No one. You know, they all have a go at me' he said. If he was at school the teachers should stop the bullying Lucy thought. But it was the summer holidays now and maybe there was no one he could turn to. No wonder Paul preferred to go off on his bike into the countryside alone.

'How come they've all got it in for you?' asked Lucy. Paul shrugged.

'Dunno' he said.

'Who are those kids anyway?' she asked instead.

'They're Baz and Mike' he replied. 'They live round the corner from me. Think they own the place. They don't know nothing though.'

There was a big rock just under the sea wall. Lucy gestured towards it.

'Let's go sit over there till you dry out a bit' she said. Paul was hardly chatty, but neither was he keen to get away from her. He followed her over to the rock and sat down. They perched there for a while in silence, looking out at the sea. A couple of gulls strutted stiff-legged across the rocks a few metres away. A bit further along a small wader bird was probing the sludge with its long slender beak.

'You always lived here?' she asked.

'Yeah. Us Treddinicks have lived round these parts for just about forever' he replied with a hint of pride.

'What does your mum do?' Lucy asked as much for something to say as anything else.

'She says it's too hard to get a job, what with one thing and another. She's not worked for a year or two. She gets down. That doesn't help.'

'What's your mum got against me then?' Lucy was afraid of the answer, but still needed to know. Paul shrugged.

'She doesn't like you coz you're a Dolphin-Child. You know, like you've got a special thing with them. I told her about seeing you at Old Man's Cove. She says that from way back the Treddinick's don't hold with dolphins and all that. She says we've been hurt once already and that it's bad and dangerous. She says never again.' Lucy could not understand how anyone could think that a dolphin could be dangerous, but then she remembered the story of Susan Penhaligon.

'What do you think then?' asked Lucy shyly. Paul paused.

'I don't know. You seem okay to me' he replied eventually. He looked her in the eye. Like, I don't think you're bad. And…' Paul broke off again. He seemed to want to say something more, but appeared to be battling with conflicting feelings which he could not put into words.

'Yes?'

'Well. Like I said. I've seen one in that lake, all trapped and sad looking. It saw me. I… Well, I can't get its eyes out of my head. No one believes me, but it's true.'

'I believe you' replied Lucy. 'You can take me there' she exclaimed, the thought suddenly striking her. 'We can do something together.' Paul seemed to half shake his head and shrink back into himself.

'I don't know. You've got dolphins. You've got everything. Why do you want my one too?'

'So we can help her of course!' Lucy didn't have any idea how they might help, or even why she thought the dolphin was a she. It just came out before she thought about it. Paul stared at the ground.

'My Mum says we Treddinicks don't hold with anything to do with dolphins and all that. Never have. But since I saw that dolphin, well I…' Paul trailed off again. Lucy felt she knew what he meant though. He couldn't turn his back on the dolphin, not now that he'd seen her.

'Let me help you help that dolphin' she urged him, trying to press home her point. Paul just gave another half shake of his head though. It seemed as though he wanted to confide in her, but was mistrustful at the same time.

'You'll take her away from me' he replied. 'You'll go away and I'll be on my own again with nothing.' Lucy didn't know what to say. She couldn't say that she wouldn't. If they could save that dolphin, it might swim off and away from Paul forever.

'But you don't want to leave that dolphin trapped in that lagoon do you?' He shook his head more firmly now.

'No, no I don't' he said. He looked out across the mud towards the sea, as though he was expecting to see a dolphin appear in front of him there and then. The tide was coming in now and the mud was quickly disappearing under the incoming sea. Paul's clothes were still heavy with the salty water and he smelt slightly as the sun slowly dried him.

'What if I did?' he asked after a moment. Lucy didn't quite understand.

'What if you did what?'

'What if I showed you the lake with the dolphin in it?' She still didn't follow what he meant. 'Well, could I meet your dolphin, like?' Finally Lucy realised what he was getting at.

'Oh, I see!' she exclaimed. 'You want to meet Spirit. Well, yes sure. Why not?' she said hesitantly.

'Let me see him first' Paul said quietly. It was half a demand and half a plea. 'Let me meet your dolphin first and then I'll take you to the lagoon.'

Chapter Eight:

Spirit was troubled by what Sunlight had told him about her pod and the human children that had died in the sea so many years ago. What he still needed to know was; what was the point of his gift at all? He thought that maybe he had discovered the answer when he'd been able to reach out to Lucy and help the little girl that was stranded on the rock. Now he wasn't so sure. Susan Penhaligon had led those other children out to their deaths. Her Child-Seer Midnight had not been able to save their lives.

He wondered whether children really could turn into dolphins. A whole pod believed that it actually had happened. The dolphins of his pod and others in the area though did not. Spirit himself would ordinarily be equally sceptical. However it was already inexplicable and magical that he could communicate with Lucy, a human that lived far away on the land. How could that be? And if that was possible, why couldn't children turn into dolphins? Spirit didn't know what to believe.

It had been fun to visit the pod near the islands. Dancer in particular had played with two other young dolphins there called Twister and Singer. When they left Twister said that he hoped that he would see Dancer again soon and Spirit had been amused to see how she was both pleased and embarrassed by the attention he gave her. He was happy for his friend and she chatted excitedly as they swam back to their own pod. Spirit only half paid attention to what Dancer was saying though and was lost in his own thoughts.

What should he say to Lucy? She had asked him if he knew about any stories of human children turning into dolphins. Now he knew that there were indeed such stories, but would it disturb Lucy as it had done him if he told her? Then again, if he kept secrets from her, it would weaken the bond between them. He tried to imagine Lucy now, in a little box somewhere, looking out of one of those small translucent squares they called windows onto the greenness beyond. Or maybe all she could see were those grey little boxes? He thought about Susan Penhaligon again, leading those children out into the stormy sea. When he did so, Lucy's face came irresistibly into his mind. Was that girl Susan all those years ago like Lucy? Yet he could not believe that Lucy would ever do such a thing. What was it that Storm sometimes said? 'If we do not learn from the past, we never learn at all.' It was far better that he share what Sunlight had told him so that they might both learn from it.

As they swam back Dancer and Spirit occasionally broke the surface of the water, taking in the view of the world above the waves as they did so. The sun seemed particularly large today and was tinged with orange and red as it made its slow descent towards the horizon. Sunlight sparkled off the gentle lapping waves, dazzling them as they made their steady progress back to their home pod. When he was younger, Star-Gazer had told him that she thought that the sun was like a big ball of fire in the sky and that it was their world that went around the sun, and not the sun that went around them.

Moonlight had said that it was a ridiculous idea. He said that it was a disc of fire that the dolphins at the edge of the world in the East set aflame every morning and then flung up into the sky. He said that when it came down again it would fizzle out in the sea and the world would turn dark again for another night.

Star-Gazer told Spirit that there was no edge to the world and that if you swam far enough in any particular direction, then providing there was no land in the way, you would eventually come back to the same spot. She asked how dolphins could set anything aflame, as they lived in water and did not have the power of fire. Moonlight tried to stick up for his theory, saying that perhaps it was humans or some other creature that set the disc alight every morning, but that that was definitely what happened.

Another time when Spirit was young, Chaser tried telling him that the world is contained in a huge shell and that every night the lid of the shell simply closes. The stars you can see are nothing more than pricks of light that penetrate through the ancient shell where it has worn thin. Then Star-Gazer asked why you could not see the edge of the shell as it came down. She said that the world went dark when the Sun disappeared over the horizon and that if

121

Chaser's theory was right, the Sun would always stay in the same place in the sky.

It was Star-Gazer that pointed out to him that when the Moon is at it's fullest, the tides are at their highest. She spent many hours trying to understand the power that the Moon exerted over the waters of the seas, but she never could make sense of it. 'It's as if the Moon was pulling the sea' she would say, 'but how can that be?' Even Moonlight, despite his name, was unable to offer an answer to that question.

There was much that dolphins did not understand. Spirit had asked once whether humans knew more than they did. Storm said that humans might know more about certain things than dolphins, but that they understood much less. He said that it was their lack of understanding of the harmony of all living things that made them so dangerous. Occasionally he wondered whether it was humans that had caused his mother Star-Gazer to be taken from him. Perhaps he would never know for certain.

Spirit and Dancer reached their own pod just as the Sun descended into the west, glad to play awhile before resting.

'Paul, have you tidied up your room yet?' Mrs Treddinick called upstairs.

'Not yet Mum!' he shouted back at her. It was true. His room was a mess. He just couldn't see the point of tidying it up, because a day after doing so it would just be as bad as it was before. When his Mum really insisted, he just shovelled everything loose under the bed. It was done in five minutes and if Mum did put her head around his door, she would be satisfied. She never did take too close a look. Paul knew that just as quickly as she would get worked up about the chaos in his room she would forget it again, no matter how bad it was.

She was like that. One day she'd be full of enthusiasm for something, then she'd forget all about it again. When she felt really low, she'd just sit there, staring out of the dirty window, smoking cigarette after cigarette, a plate in front of her full of cigarette butts and ash. Paul hated the smoke and hated it when his Mum fell into one of those low moods. He'd have to look after his younger sister Hayley as best as he could when she did. He'd cook cheese on toast for tea and walk Hayley to school all by himself. Dirty plates would pile up in the sink and she'd forget to put the bin bags out. Fortunately Mum had been okay for the last couple of months and she'd really been trying hard to get a job, but you never knew when she might change again. It was like waiting for a reed to snap in the wind.

Paul looked out of the window. The paint was peeling off the wood and in places he'd picked at the putty holding the glass in place with his penknife. In the depths of winter icy crystals would trace their way along the inside of the glass, but at the moment it was hot and sunny and he stared out of the window towards the recreation ground. The trees seemed bleached of colour and the listless wind shovelled a couple of frail clouds along high in the sky.

Paul was always delighted when the school holidays began, but after a fortnight or so of freedom, they began to drag. They couldn't afford to go away on holiday and each day merged into the next. When his best friend Richard still lived in Merwater, they would spend hours and hours together, but now that Richard's family had left and moved to Bristol, Paul had no one to spend time with. Even Hayley could go round to her friend's house two doors down the road. Paul didn't really have anyone else now that Richard had gone.

When he could, Paul would take his bike and cycle off for whole afternoons down the country lanes to explore the fields and woods beyond the town, or up along the coastal paths at the top of the cliffs. He'd let his imagination fly free and pass the time as he cycled with fantastical make-believe stories, in which he was always the hero, saving someone's life or fighting off smugglers.

For the last few days his bike had had a puncture. Mum said she'd buy a bicycle puncture repair kit, but first she forgot and then she said she didn't have enough change. She always had enough money to buy cigarettes though, thought Paul ruefully. It was for this reason that he'd been stuck round town for the past few days, waiting for the kit to repair his bike so he could go off exploring again.

Paul wondered what to do. He hated staying indoors, but going out was fraught with risks as well. Just recently Baz and Mike had started picking on him. Now the other kids had turned against him as well. The more he tried to stick up for himself, the more they just ridiculed him.

Paul looked around his room again. He made a vague attempt at tidying up and then trudged downstairs. He'd agreed to see Lucy the next morning at first light, but he had the sneaking feeling that she wouldn't turn up, or that she'd join in with the other kids and start laughing at him. He didn't dare let himself look forward to it. If he couldn't repair his bike before the next day, he might not get there anyway.

'Your sister's playing next door. Why don't you get out into the sunshine instead of hanging round here all day' said Mrs Treddinick, fingering an unlit cigarette.

'Yes Mum' replied Paul obediently.

'And you tell me if that girl approaches you again. You keep away from that one you hear me? She's no good.'

'Yes Mum' Paul replied again, his head down. He didn't want to get drawn into another argument. He didn't understand what Mum had against her. He wished he'd never said anything about her in the first place.

'Don't forget my puncture repair kit', he added. His Mum fished in her purse, pulling out a fistful of loose coins.

'Here's some money. You go to the bike shop and buy yourself one. I want my change back now mind.'

'Thanks Mum!' Paul said, seizing up the coins and thrusting them into his pocket. e He made He made for the door. At least he had somewhere to go now. He cut across the recreation ground to get to the parade where the bike shop was. He'd almost got to the exit on the other side when Baz and Mike walked into the park from the other direction. They hung around the gate waiting to confront him. Paul would have gone the other way if he could, but he had to pass them.

'Well look who it is' said Baz loudly. 'If it isn't that little liar Paulie Treddinick.' He thought for a moment that they were going to block his way, but he could tell that they weren't going to cause him too much trouble today. Even so, his heart thudded in his chest and his tongue went dry.

'Found any ditched space-ships? Saved any dolphins this week then have you?' sneered Mike.

'Yeah, like we so believe you' snorted Baz. Paul put his head down and kept walking. He'd been out by the Brenham farm last week and seen burn marks in the cornfield there, which he was sure were from where a spaceship had landed. He'd blurted it out, trying to impress the other kids in the recreation ground, but instead everyone had just laughed at him. Now he couldn't go anywhere without someone throwing it back in his face, even the little kids that his sister Hayley played with.

'I'll get you next time!' called Baz threateningly behind him as he walked on towards the bike shop. 'You'll get more than just mud down your neck then!'

At the bike shop, Paul had just enough change to buy the puncture repair kit and then headed back home to fix his bike. He hoped that Baz and Mike would have disappeared by then, but instead they were still hanging around in the recreation ground, messing around on the swings just next to the path.

'Where's your girlfriend then Paulie?' Mike jeered.

'Is she blind?' added Baz, laughing.

Paul wanted so much to fit in and for Mike and Baz and all the others to stop sneering at him. He was dying to tell them that Lucy was actually a Dolphin-Child and that the next day she was going to let him meet her dolphin. He thought how jealous they would be when they knew and how much they'd be in awe of him. They'd stop jeering at him then he thought. It was so tempting just to tell them. It would be so easy. This time they'd listen to him for sure.

Paul stopped and started to open his mouth. Before he could say anything though, a piece of dry mud whizzed across and caught him square on the face. Baz and Mike burst out laughing and Baz made to throw another lump in his direction. Paul turned and ran up the path towards his house.

'So you want to bring another human child with you, a boy?' asked Spirit. He was a little surprised by Lucy. She'd never mentioned this other human child before and he couldn't understand why she wanted one to come now. He felt that it was special when they could meet in real life. She'd be able to gently stroke his flank, or they would play together in the water. It was obvious though that Lucy wanted to say something more, but wasn't sure whether to or not.

'Yes, he … err asked me and I, err, said I thought it would be okay'. She sounded edgy and uncertain.

'I'm not sure' he replied. 'It doesn't seem, well, right.' In her heart of hearts, Lucy felt the same thing. But still she needed Spirit to agree to meet with Paul.

'Please Spirit!' implored Lucy. 'There is a reason, but I'm not sure if I can tell you yet. Not till I know more anyway'.

The apparition of Lucy floated in front of Spirit in the water, her hair floating around her head like a cloud. The late afternoon sun dappled the water above them. They were in the shallows, three or four metres up from the sandy seabed. The other dolphins were swimming off in the distance. He knew of course that she wasn't physically there and that if he nudged her with his beak, he would pass straight through her. Yet when she came to him like this, she seemed so real that he could hardly imagine otherwise. He wished that he could visit her world in the same way that Lucy visited his. Right now that dream seemed a long way off.

'But I tell you everything' he replied, feeling left out. He had decided to tell her all about what Sunlight had told him the day before, though he had not yet had a chance to.

'Yes I know' said Lucy with a frown on her face. 'I want to tell you, but I need to find out more first. If I said something now and I was wrong, it would just upset you needlessly.'

'Alright then' decided Spirit eventually. 'But you tell me as soon as you've found out. I'll meet this boy, I suppose' he added grudgingly.

He told Lucy briefly what he had found out from Sunlight. He said that there were some dolphins that believed that humans had turned into dolphins, but that even though Sunlight was from that pod, she wasn't sure. What's more, he said, none of the local pods believed it either.

'What do you think?' asked Lucy.

'I just can't say for certain. If I can communicate with you, then maybe humans did once turn into dolphins. It doesn't seem so extraordinary to me. In Sunlight's pod, they were all given human names. Her name was Susan and the others were....'

'Did you say Susan?' Lucy asked incredulously, thinking of her visit to the museum and the story of Susan Penhaligon.

'Yes, that's right' replied Spirit. The others were Edgar, Simeon, Mirabel, Florence, Jethro and…oh I can't remember the others. Human names are harder to remember for dolphins.

'That's amazing!' exclaimed Lucy. She told him what she had found out in the museum in Merwater. 'Whatever actually did happen to those kids, it's more than just a story. Something must have happened to make both dolphins and humans remember it all these years later.'

'Storm says that humans have weak and gullible minds' said Spirit. 'He says that it is too easy to believe in a dream and promises of escape from ordinary life. He thinks that's why those human children swam out with Susan Penhaligon. Life was so horrible for them on land and seemed easier and better in the sea with the dolphins. He says that that type of dream never comes true. But then I look at you and you're almost like a dream in front of me now. I don't know what to believe.'

'My science teacher says that if something seems too good to be true, it probably isn't true' replied Lucy thoughtfully. 'She says never accept what people tell you at face value. She says we should always question what their motivation is for telling you something and test what they say. According to her a lot of people out there are willing to con you and won't tell the truth, or don't even know what the truth is themselves.'

Spirit didn't know what science was or what conning was either, but still, he got the idea of what Lucy meant.

'Sunlight says that she thinks that Midnight, the Child-Seer of that girl Susan, was so overcome with grief after those children swam out to sea and died that he gave other dolphins in his pod human names to make himself feel better' said Spirit.

'That makes sense' replied Lucy. 'My science teacher says that if there are two explanations for something, you should generally choose the one that is the most likely. I guess it's more probable that he gave the dolphins human names, than that humans turned into dolphins don't you think?'

Spirit started to tell her more about what Sunlight had told him the day before, but when he glanced back at Lucy, he realised that her image had faded away into the water. Her energy must have run out again. There was just the faintest outline of her shape still hanging there and then it was washed away in the current.

'Till next time Lucy' he said to himself quietly.

Paul woke up at first light. He didn't need his alarm clock, though he had set it just in case. Despite himself, he felt tense, nervous and excited about the prospect of meeting Lucy's dolphin. He'd hardly been able to sleep at all and when he did eventually drop off, he kept waking up every half hour or so, as though the morning might take him by surprise if he didn't.

Paul glanced at his watch. It was five thirty. He'd agreed to meet Lucy at Old Man's Cove where he'd seen her with the dolphin a few days before. It wasn't unusual for him to leave the house early and his Mum wasn't particularly bothered if he did. She let him run wild, his aunt had said, adding that they'd better not let Social Services find out. He'd never crept out this early before though and he was wary in case she put two and two together and realised that he was meeting Lucy. Anyone would think Lucy had committed mass murder the way Mum went on about her.

Paul climbed out of bed. The floor boards in the house had an unfortunate habit of creaking and it sounded all the louder so early in the morning when the rest of the house was quiet. Mum was a restless sleeper too and more than once he'd almost jumped out of his skin when he'd gone downstairs early and found her silently smoking a cigarette on her own in the front room. He slipped on his jeans and tee-shirt, and then put on his trainers. They were his prized possession, but had seen better days. There was a big hole where his toe protruded through the fabric. His trainers were another thing that Baz and Mike made fun of.

He contemplated climbing out of his bedroom window and shinnying down the drainpipe. That's what kids did in movies, but by the looks of the drainpipe on his house, it'd just collapse if he tried that. The safer option was to go downstairs, as quietly as he possibly could, taking particular care over the third and fourth steps, which were especially creaky. Luckily, neither Mum nor Hayley seemed to hear him and he was soon out in the backyard where he kept his bike.

He was dead lucky, he thought, that Mum had given him the money for the puncture repair kit the previous afternoon. He didn't know how he'd get to Old Man's Cove otherwise. He wheeled his bike out, making sure that the gate didn't bang behind him. The street outside his house was perfectly still and the early morning light filtered weakly through the trees of the recreation ground. The only sound was of the birds singing in the trees. It was as though he was the only person up. It felt quite eerie. He couldn't even detect the sound of the milk float doing its rounds.

Paul glanced at his watch again briefly before he pedalled off. He should be able to get there in plenty of time, but he didn't want to be late. He still didn't know if he could trust Lucy, even though he had to admit that she'd been really nice to him, and he couldn't leave anything to chance.

Even though it was summer, the early morning air was sharp and chilly. His body soon warmed up as he pedalled along, but his hands still felt cold on the handle bars.

The last bit of the journey was a tough climb on his bike up the hill towards Old Mans Cove. There were a few cars on the main road, but nothing compared with usual. He was glad to be able to get off his bike and give his legs a rest. He heaved his bike over the stile and climbed over after it. Lucy was waiting for him on the other side, sitting cross legged on the grass.

'Hi' she said.

'Morning' he replied coolly. They stood awkwardly for a moment.

'I didn't think you'd come' Lucy said.

'Well I guess I did' he answered defensively. He hadn't been sure whether she'd come, or else he thought she might have some nasty trick up her sleeve for him, like the kids in town. He'd trusted kids before and then they turned on him. Lucy might be just like them.

'You know what we agreed though' Lucy continued. 'I'll let you meet my dolphin, but then you've got to take me to the dolphin that you told me about. The one in the brackish lake I mean.'

'Course I will' replied Paul, trying to sound more certain that he actually felt.

'All right then' said Lucy cautiously. 'I guess we'd better get going. I don't suppose you've got a wet suit?' Paul shook his head. 'Well I'm a fair bit taller than you, but you'd better wear mine. I've already got my swimming costume on under my sweatshirt.' He could see she'd stuffed her wetsuit into her backpack along with a towel. He realised that he'd completely forgotten a towel for himself.

'You swim okay don't you?' Lucy asked him as they walked up the path. 'The currents are really dangerous here and you've got to be dead careful.' In fact Paul hated swimming and at lessons at school he was always stuck in the learner's pool when most of the other kids were splashing around noisily in the deep end.

'Course I do' he lied. 'I can swim like a fish.' He hoped he wouldn't be put to the test. They walked up the footpath to the edge of the cliff and the steep path that led down to the cove and the small beach. The sea sparkled in the early morning light. He'd seldom seen it look so beautiful or inviting. He felt excitement and fear in equal measure. There below them, a short distance from the edge of the beach, he could see the dorsal fin of a dolphin swimming languorously in the lapping water.

Chapter Nine:

Lucy glanced at Paul's face as they looked down from the top of the cliff into the cove where Spirit was waiting for them. A look of wonder and surprise stole across Paul's features as he stared down. Lucy was pleased at his reaction, but she still had a nagging doubt in the back of her mind. This wasn't supposed to be the first dolphin he'd seen. When they'd sat together on the wet bough of the tree in the recreation ground, he told her he'd seen a dolphin in that salt water lake. Would he really be so surprised and delighted to see a dolphin now if he'd seen one before? Perhaps it was different today though, seeing a dolphin that he was actually going to meet free in the sea. She just could not be absolutely sure that he was telling her the truth. They started making their way down the steep path.

An hour before Lucy had still been asleep in her bed in Bethany's studio. She'd dreamt the same, comfortable and familiar dream that she so often had of the dolphins all swimming together, relaxed, peaceful and happy. Then as she had dreamt on, the water had turned murky and dark and she'd almost expected to see the silhouette of the dolphin that Paul had told her about and which now haunted her. Instead she couldn't make out anything in the watery gloom. She wondered why. Was that dolphin in trouble?

Lucy woke up as the early morning light streamed in, with an uneasy feeling in the pit of her stomach. As soon as she awoke, a vivid image came in to Lucy's mind. It was a memory of Mum before she'd died when Lucy herself had still been very little. The two of them had been walking in the woods near their house. Lucy ran on ahead of Mum, her short fat legs kicking the leaves as she went. She felt so happy and secure, but then she suddenly realised with a shock that she didn't know where Mum was. She found herself standing in a shallow depression between tall birch trees and she had the impression of being in a natural bowl. All directions looked the same and Lucy couldn't remember which way she'd come from. She called out again. She could hear Mum reply, but still had no idea where she was. Mum's voice sounded muffled and distant. It felt as though Mum was a million miles away and that she was completely alone. Suddenly she became scared and started to cry.

A second or two later Mum had appeared and Lucy was soon engulfed in the warm comfort of her embrace. Yet Lucy felt shaken by just how easy it was to lose all that was familiar to her. Lucy couldn't remember quite how old she had been when it happened, but she must have been very young at the time.

She kept Mum very close to her for a while after that and years later Mum had told her not long before she died that as a toddler she'd gone through a very clingy phase, following her about everywhere. Lucy was much older when she'd lost Mum forever and more able to rationalise and understand what had happened. It didn't make losing her any bit easier though. In fact it was indescribably worse. Somehow that memory of losing Mum in the woods and dream of the shadowy dolphin seemed to belong together, but she couldn't quite say why.

Lucy got up and quickly put her swim suit on and then her jeans and sweatshirt over the top. She didn't have to creep around now like she used to. Lucy knew that Bethany was willing to give her the freedom to go and see Spirit unaccompanied. Sometimes she wondered why Bethany was so relaxed at letting her venture out like this. Just then Bethany put up her bleary and tousled head, her curly blond hair half obscuring her face.

'I just don't understand how you manage to get up so horribly early every day' she sighed, before slumping back into the bedclothes. 'I guess you're off to swim with Spirit? I must be mad letting you go like this.'

'You are!' joked Lucy. 'Don't worry. Spirit will take good care of me.' Lucy decided not to mention that Paul was going to be there with them too. Bethany would have woken up pretty quickly if she had.

'You betcha he will' Bethany mumbled sleepily, 'or he'll have me to answer to. Like I always say Kiddo, don't do anything silly.'

'I'll be okay' Lucy reassured her, pulling on her trainers and then padding down the steps from the living platform to the kitchen area. She quickly spooned some cereals down her and then called out goodbye before clicking the studio door closed behind her. Mary was walking across the farmyard in her wellington boots towards the tractor shed.

'Hello there Lucy' she called. 'You off out early again?'

'That's right' Lucy called back.

'You know you should be a farmer when you grow up' Mary joked. You're a natural for getting up at an unearthly hour of the morning.' Lucy smiled.

'See you later.' Lucy gave Mary a little wave and then climbed astride the bicycle before pedalling off over the cattle grid out of the farmyard and up the lane.

She loved this time of morning. It was before anyone was around that she would see rabbits nibbling at the edge of the road, or even a deer grazing shyly in the field next to the copse. The bird song seemed more vivid and bright when the sun had just risen and on a morning like this she always experienced a surge of optimism. It felt like all the problems of the world could be solved before the sun had burned away the dew on the grass. Lucy glanced at her watch. She wanted to get to the cove in good time before Paul got there.

As they walked down the steep path to the cove, Paul was torn between the sensation of excitement that he would soon be swimming in the sea with a real wild dolphin and the feeling that something was bound to go wrong, that it would all be snatched away from him before anything good could happen. Lucy seemed so confident and assured. It was as though she had been living here all her life, not him. He felt gauche and awkward walking down the sheer path behind her. Sometimes Paul felt like everyone one else had been invited to a party except him and that all he could do was to look in from the outside. Even now he felt as though he wasn't really on the invitation list at all.

'What's his name then?' he asked, trying to crowd out his thoughts.

'His name's Spirit' Lucy replied.

'And you can speak to him can you?' Paul continued.

'Not when I'm with him like this. It's, well…it's difficult to explain.' Paul nodded. He was used to people not bothering to explain things to him. It didn't surprise him that Lucy didn't want to explain either.

They got to the bottom of the path and crunched onto the pebbles of the beach. They could see Spirit more clearly now, swimming just off the shore, as close to land as he dared to come. He looked in their direction and Lucy gave him a little wave. Paul stood transfixed.

'Well, let's get changed then' said Lucy, struggling to pull the wetsuit out of her backpack. It was awkward to roll up and carry like that. Eventually she got the wetsuit out. Paul was a good head shorter than Lucy and it was evidently going to be too big for him. Once he got into it though, the suit fitted well enough and he immediately felt warmer with it on.

'You don't need arm bands or anything like that do you Paul?' she asked with a worried expression on her face.

'Don't be daft!' he replied. He just hoped with all his heart that he'd be able to swim all right when it came to it.

He could see Lucy shivering as she stood there in her swimming costume. It might be summer, but the sun was barely up and there was a cool breeze coming in from the sea.

'Come on then' she said. 'We can't stand round here all day.' Paul paused.

'Do you think…do you think he'll like me being here?' he asked, suddenly uncertain again. Lucy turned and looked back at him. She smiled reassuringly.

'You'll be okay' she said. 'He knows you're coming. You just stick close to me and do everything I say. Remember, you can absolutely trust Spirit with your life and he'll keep you safe even if you're pulled out by the current or something. Just hang onto him if you need to. Don't try anything clever and you'll be all right.'

Paul had expected Lucy to just plunge into the sea from the shallow crescent of beach and swim out. Instead she picked her way over the rocks at the edge of the beach. Paul followed just behind her. It was low tide and the rock shelf was more fully exposed as a result. Barnacles and limpets encrusted the rock and it was uncomfortable to walk over in their bare feet. Lucy came to a boulder at the edge of the water and sat down with her lower legs and feet submerged in the salty water. Paul did likewise. It felt icy cold.

The water was deeper here and Spirit was able to swim right up close to the rocky outcrop. Spirit put his head out of the water a looked up at them with a calm, intelligent gaze. Paul felt as though the rest of the world melted away and focused all his senses on the dolphin in front of him, trying to drink in every aspect of the experience; the fascinating and intelligent creature in front of him, the gentle lapping of the waves, the salty tang of the exposed seaweed in his nostrils. He smiled.

Spirit regarded the two figures on the rock in front of him. Despite the fact that he had only encountered a few humans, he had an instant feel for the nature and character of each human that he had met. He could see that Paul was still just a young inexperienced calf and his nervous jerky movements told Spirit that he was very unsure of himself. Spirit had been the youngest in the pod himself, but at least all the other pod members cared for him, even if they did also poke fun at him occasionally. Spirit had the feeling that Paul was not so lucky. He got the impression that Paul had been picked upon once too often and that even with his attempts to show otherwise, all he was really doing was waiting for the next kick. 'I'm glad I'm a dolphin and not a human' he thought to himself as he looked at them both. The life of humans seemed so complicated and unfriendly.

Lucy slipped into the water and Paul followed suit. By dolphin standards Lucy could barely swim. In comparison to Paul though,

Lucy was a natural in the water. Lucy could see that Paul seemed extremely nervous as he lowered himself into the sea and as he did so he tensed up as if he expected to receive an electric shock. She wondered whether he'd be able to swim in the sea at all. The current was unusually weak though and there were barely any waves. As the water enveloped him Lucy could see that Paul kept looking at Spirit with a kind of happiness and light in his eyes. Lucy was immensely relieved. She'd been worried about how another child would react to being so close to Spirit. Now she could see that that was one thing at least that she didn't have to concern herself with.

Paul trod water and Spirit moved slowly towards the boy in front of him. Very gently, Spirit brought his head closer to Pauls face, all the while regarding Paul with calm eyes. Paul put out a hand and placed it lightly on the side of Spirit's head. A smile broke out across Paul's face again and he closed his eyes for a moment as though touching the dolphin was like the sun warming his face. Lucy could see that Paul was relaxing.

Spirit turned slightly and offered Paul a fin to take hold of. He swam slowly in a loose circle with Paul clinging to his left fin. Lucy trod water and watched them together. Paul might have been the human, but Spirit was definitely in charge. Lucy was struck by the level of care and sympathy with which he treated the young boy. It was as if he realised that Paul needed to be looked after very carefully and gently. Lucy had her own reservations about Paul, but now she began to see him in a new light. All the cares and worries of life above water seemed to drop away from him as he revelled in the excitement of swimming with a real live dolphin.

They swam back to where Lucy was treading water and Spirit cast her a long, understanding look. It was difficult to not speak to Spirit when they met together in this way, but words did not always convey everything that there was to be said.

Lucy swam up to Spirit and took his other flipper, so that the dolphin could gently propel them both further out before returning to the edge of the rocks. Then they let go of his flippers and he regarded Paul again calmly, before nuzzling him briefly with his beak. Then he approached Lucy and did the same with her before turning slowly to swim out to sea again.

Lucy and Paul climbed out again onto the shelf of rock. Lucy glanced at Paul and realised that now was perhaps not the right time to speak. He was smiling and his eyes were full of light, but silent tears were streaming down from them at the same time as he sat there. Lucy put her arm around his shoulders briefly and gave a little squeeze.

Dolphins had been in her mind and in her dreams for as long as she could remember. When she first swam with dolphins for real, it had been to try and save Spirit when he had been trapped and so even though the experience was incredible, it was in a very different circumstance to Paul meeting Spirit now. She could see that he was overwhelmed by everything that had just happened and that he needed to be left to his own thoughts for a few moments.

As she knew he would, Spirit made two great leaps in salute from the water before turning and swimming back out to sea. Lucy and Paul waved back. They sat silently for a few minutes, but Lucy was not in her wetsuit and she began to shiver sitting there in just her swimming costume.

'Come on, I'm freezing' she said to Paul. They got up and walked back over the rocks to where they had left their clothes and towels on the beach.

'How was that then?' she asked Paul, as she quickly towelled herself down.

'That was, well…that was just…amazing' he said eventually, a smile spread out across his face. He sniffed and quickly wiped away his tears with the back of his hand. Lucy nodded.

'I know' she replied.

Paul felt as though he was still in a dream as they quickly changed back into their dry clothes, carefully looking away from each other as they did so. Once they were dry and fully clothed, they sat down again at the edge of the beach, staring out to sea whilst they recouped their energy. Now that they were dry, the sun soon warmed them. Lucy handed Paul a chocolate bar she'd taken from Bethany's kitchen. She had one too and they sat in silence while they ate.

'I wish I was a dolphin' said Paul eventually.

'Yeah, I know what you mean' replied Lucy.

'Don't you think they've got a better life than ours?' he continued. 'They don't get told what to do, they don't get picked on and life is so easy and straightforward for them. They just play, eat fish and sleep don't they?' Lucy thought about what she knew about Spirit, Dancer and the pod. It was hard for her to put it all into words.

'It's not really as simple as that' she said. 'Spirit nearly got killed. Dolphins get dragged up in fishing nets and poisoned by waste in the sea. Killer whales have a go at them too.'

'I just know that I should be a Dolphin-Child like you' he replied, ignoring what Lucy had said a moment before. Lucy gave an embarrassed smile. It still felt strange to be called a Dolphin-Child. 'I mean', he continued, 'you can swim with dolphins in real life and you can speak to them whenever you want to' he continued. 'It felt so amazing to touch Spirit. Why can't I do what you can do?'

'I don't know.' Lucy hesitated. 'It's weird. I've had dreams about dolphins for as long as I can remember. Then I realised I could stretch out with my mind and communicate with Spirit. It just sort of happened one day. I don't know how. It's just a gift I suppose.'

'Do you think I can learn how to do it?' Paul asked. Lucy shrugged.

'I'm not sure if its one of those things that you can just learn' she answered cautiously. 'Maybe its just something that you are born with.'

'I bet there's some trick or other to it' Paul replied, unconvinced.

'No, no gimmicks. No tricks' said Lucy. 'I really wish I knew how it happened as well, but I just don't. Paul paused a few moments in thought and Lucy could see he was reliving the experience in his minds eye.

'When I touched Spirit, it was like there was electricity passing between us' he said. 'Then I felt so calm and peaceful. It was like I wasn't scared at all then.'

'Were you scared before?' asked Lucy.

'Well, a bit' admitted Paul. 'Just wait till I tell…' he started, before trailing off. He thought of Baz and Mike and the other local kids and how he could impress them with stories of swimming with dolphins. 'No…' he said after a moment. Suddenly the idea of showing off to the other kids didn't seem such a great idea after all.

'Maybe best not to go round telling everyone about this' said Lucy. 'Anyway, your Mum's already a bit weird about me. Who knows what she'd say if she found out.'

'You're right' Paul replied decisively.

'Anyway, you've got to keep your side of the deal' Lucy went on. 'I've let you meet Spirit. Now you've got to take me to meet the dolphin in the lake.' Paul shifted uncomfortably on the rock where he was sitting.

'Oh, yeah, sure' he said. 'We can bike out there tomorrow afternoon if you like' he said uneasily.

'I really look forward to it' replied Lucy. The truth was that her dreams about the shadowy dolphin in the murky water exerted such a fascination upon her, that she just had to find out whether it was Paul's dolphin that she had been dreaming about. She still had the suspicion that Paul wasn't entirely telling the truth, but for the time being she simply had to take what he said on trust.

After a while they got their things together. Lucy tried to cram the wetsuit back into her rucksack, but she just couldn't manage it, so she slung it over her shoulder instead as they started to make their way up the path. A man in shorts and with binoculars round his neck started to make his way down the path as they went up it. He cheerily said 'Good morning' to them and they politely replied 'Hello'.

'Good thing he wasn't here half an hour earlier' Lucy muttered to Paul after they passed him. At the top, slightly out of breath, they turned and looked back down at the stretch of sea below them.

'Do you think… Do you think that Spirit is like, well, like a person, I mean a person like us?' Paul asked Lucy. 'Do you think he's smart like we are?' She hadn't thought about it before, but now Paul asked, the answer came to her instantaneously.

'Yes, I'm sure he is' she answered. 'He's just as much a person as you or I are.'

'That's what I thought' said Paul. 'I just had this….sort of idea that he must be. He looked so smart and understanding when I looked into his eyes.' Paul seemed so positive about Spirit and the other dolphins, but she knew his Mum thought differently and hoped that Mrs Treddinick would not find out.

'What about your Mum, what does she think?' she asked. Paul shook his head, a frown passing across his face.

'I don't know' he replied. 'She says some strange things sometimes. I don't think she understands what it's like to meet a dolphin. If she did....' Paul looked at his watch. It was later than he thought. 'I suppose I'd better get back' he said, changing the subject. 'I'll get my bike.'

They walked across the field and hoisted their bikes over the stile onto the side of the road.

'Where shall we meet tomorrow then?' asked Lucy. Paul thought for a moment.

'You know the church at the end of Bussey Lane?' he asked. Lucy wasn't sure, but she could find out from Bethany or Mary anyhow. 'Meet me there at twelve. Then we'll cycle down together.' They parted, with Paul pedalling along the main road back into town and Lucy heading off down the lane back to the farm.

Lucy felt happy as she free-wheeled along. Things seemed to be working out. By tomorrow she'd find out whether Paul was telling the truth about the dolphin in the lake and then maybe the strange dreams that she'd been having recently would make more sense to her. Maybe after tomorrow she'd have something to tell Spirit. She didn't like not telling him everything. If she was right.... No. It was best to find out first.

The verges of the lane seemed to buzz with insect life as she approached the farm. Swifts wheeled overhead, catching flies and midges on the wing. She saw a pile of earth shift slightly, as the mole below it pushed up the soil as he extended his tunnel. She could hardly imagine the dark subterranean world that the mole inhabited, deprived of sunshine and light. Lucy clattered over the cattle grid into the farm yard still full of all sorts of thoughts and then braked suddenly, overcome with surprise. There was their familiar car parked next to the studio and there was Dad standing next to the open boot, pulling out a suitcase.

'Dad!' she exclaimed in surprise. He looked up.

'Hey Lucy!' She jumped off her bike, let it drop and ran over to Dad and hugged him.

'What are you doing here?' she asked. 'You said you wouldn't be coming down for another few days.'

'My project finished early so I thought I'd drive down straight away. I managed to get the cottage a couple of days earlier. We can have a good old bucket and spade holiday together now Luce. You and me.'

Chapter Ten:

Spirit swam back to join Dancer and the rest of the pod.

'Hey, it's a good thing you're back' Dancer told him. 'Chaser's just been out and he's told us about a shoal of squid in the deeper ocean west of here. We're all going after them together.'

'I hate squid' said Spirit. 'But I am starving.'

'And did you have a nice time with Lucy?' asked Dancer, almost shyly.

'She came with a short male human' replied Spirit, eager to tell his friend what had just happened. 'He's smaller than Lucy, which I suppose means he's younger. You know the fur stuff on human's heads called hair? Lucy has long straight hair, but his was all curly and in a big blob on his head. He seemed very uncertain of himself and almost vulnerable.' Spirit hesitated.

'How do you mean?'

'You know how some fish can puff up to make you think they're bigger than they really are? Or other fish shake their tale at you like they're really fierce when you know that they aren't?' Dancer nodded. 'Well I just had this strange feeling that boy was like that. I felt as though he'd just crumble if you touched him. Yet there was…. There was fear and wonder in his eyes and it made me feel very strange.'

'Why was that?'

'I don't know really' said Spirit quietly. 'I just think there's something not quite right about him, like when you look at white clouds on the horizon but somehow know that a storm is just behind. You just know without understanding how.'

'So did this little human swim with you too?'

'Yes he did. When he got in the water I thought he was going to sink like a rotten lump of wood, he was so bad at swimming. I had to let him hold onto one of my fins and pull him through the water so I could be sure he'd be okay. I thought he'd want to get back out of the sea as soon as possible, but instead it seemed as though he wanted to stay there with me forever. I felt this strange kind of energy come off him. Lucy gives off energy too when she touches me in real life.

'Yes I know' replied Dancer, thinking back to the time that she had carried Lucy on her back, with the girl clinging on to her dorsal fin as they swam.

'But Lucy's energy is more calm and constant' Spirit continued, 'while this boy's energy reminded me of one of those insects you see flying just above the surface of the water; all full of jerks and starts and sudden turns.'

'So why did Lucy bring this boy to you then?' asked Dancer curiously.

'I don't know. She says she wants to tell me and that there's some reason or other why she can't just yet. I wish she would though.'

'Hey you two!' called Breeze. 'Are you ready to hunt for squid or not?' Spirit glanced around. Even Summer's tiny calf seemed to be ready for the foray, though he still only drank his mother's milk.

'We certainly are' Dancer called back. They set off, moving along as fast as they could without Summer's calf falling behind. He'd quickly gained strength though and despite his size was much better able to keep up with the pod than he had been even just two weeks before.

It was always exciting to be on the verge of a hunt and even though Spirit was not so keen on squid, his heart quickened as they approached the shoal and his stomach reminded him that it was hungry and needed feeding. They fell upon the squid and snatched hungrily at their white rubbery bodies and their tentacles. As was their way, they did not seek to eat all the squid that were there. Storm always said that it was better to take a few and leave the rest to live on. That way the dolphins could live and so could the squid and the delicate balance of life would be maintained. Storm said that that was a lesson that humans, with their big clanking ships and rapacious nets had yet to learn.

Just then, the call of other creatures echoed across the seas.

'What's that?' asked Dancer. All the dolphins listened intently for a few moments.

'They're pilot whales' replied Summer. 'It seems to me like there's a lot of them'. Spirit had never encountered pilot whales before. He gulped down the squid he had in his mouth. Summer's calf instinctively sought the safety of his mother's flank as while they watched, the pilot whales quietly appeared all around them, sighing languorously as they broke the surface for air.

Spirit had imagined that they'd be as least as big as orcas, but instead they were little larger than the dolphins themselves. Their great bulbous foreheads glistened as they broke the surface of the water. Their eyes and mouth seemed dwarfed by their foreheads, which were their most prominent feature. They were such a dark bluey-black colour that it was hard to see them amongst the shadows of the waves and if it weren't for his echo-location, Spirit would have had trouble at guessing how many there were around him. As it was, he could tell that there must be forty of them at least.

'Do they talk?' Spirit whispered to Dancer.

'We talk' replied a pilot whale surprisingly close to him in a slow lazy accent, before sighing again dreamily and rolling heavily onto one side. If the Pilot whales too had been intending to hunt, the squid had by now dispersed and the pilot's seemed in no hurry to pursue them. Instead they appeared happy to rest and Spirit felt many sets of eyes trained on him and the others, calm and unhurried under their huge foreheads. Spirit heard Storm speak up.

'Cousin Pilots, it is good to see you in these waters. What brings you here?'

'We go' said one of the pilots and then paused for a long moment before continuing, 'We go towards the North islands. There is good fishing there'. 'Yes, good fishing' murmured others behind him. It was a wonder to Spirit that they had energy enough to do any fishing at all, they seemed so slow and lethargic.

'And which waters have you come from?' continued Storm in an effort to draw them into conversation.

'We come from everywhere and nowhere, we are of all of the seas and none of them. We are at one with the tides' replied another pilot enigmatically, but uninformatively. 'We have come from the deep ocean where the days are long and the sea is wide.'

One of the pilots brushed against Spirit's side as it passed and Spirit jolted nervously in surprise.

'Don't worry little dolphin' the Pilot said slowly, turning to fix Spirit with calm eyes. 'We mean you no harm. You are safe with us.' Spirit half expected the pilot to fall asleep in mid-sentence, it was so calm and somnolent. He was glad that they were benign though. Spirit glanced at Summer's calf. He thought with a shudder of his own experience not so many months ago when orcas had tried to attack him as he and Storm swam alone. He was immensely glad that the pilots were so different from the great black and white orcas and that the pilots were no threat to

Summer's calf or any of the others in the pod. He was reminded almost of a great cloud of jellyfish, floating along where the current took them, blind to the seas around them.

'And have you news?' another pilot asked, as they drifted around the few dolphins. Breeze answered.

'We have a Child See-er amongst us, though the reason for his gift is not yet apparent to us.' A murmur of surprise rippled through the congregated pilots.

'Who is this Child See-er' asked the pilot which had just brushed against Spirit. Breeze nodded with his head in Spirit's direction.

'It's this one' he said, indicating towards Spirit. All of the eyes in the great pod of pilots now seemed to be focused on Spirit. He found their steady gaze unnerving.

'You speak with…humans?' asked the pilot.

'Only one human' mumbled Spirit shyly.

'We do not like humans' sighed another pilot. 'In the past humans have herded us onto the rocks to kill us. They do not do so anymore, but still we do not trust them. They are dangerous. They still cause death. Another pilot added his voice.

'This human. The one that you talk to. Has it pledged to safeguard the life of all living things in the ocean?' Spirit was surprised by the question.

'Err, I'm not sure' replied Spirit uncertainly. 'I know she would never do anything to harm us. I…' The pilot whale seemed dissatisfied with Spirit's answer.

155

'Look at these calves' he said, indicating with his great bulbous head toward a group of five pilot juveniles swimming in a group just to his left. 'None of them now have mothers and for three of them, humans caused their mother's deaths.'

'But how?' asked Spirit. The pilot whale continued to regard him seriously.

'One was killed by a propeller, one was poisoned by rubbish and one was captured and taken alive by the humans. They lifted her out and took her away.'

'I don't understand why humans would do that' said Dancer.

'Neither do we' replied the pilot, 'they are a mystery to us too.'

The dolphins looked at the orphaned pilot calves. They seemed so young and vulnerable. Spirit looked at Summer's calf, nuzzling into her flank. Spirit knew that Lucy was absolutely committed to help all the dolphins in the pod. After all, she had risked her own life to help save Spirit himself. But what about the small human that he had met with Lucy only that morning? Who knew what he may do to threaten their safety.

In the same way that they came, the pilot whales sighed again dreamily and turned to swim on.

'Farewell dolphins, farewell!' Slowly they eased away. The group melted into the background of the ocean and then they were gone. The dolphins had been overwhelmed by the pilots and now they had swum on, they felt a very small group in comparison.

'What did you make of that then?' exclaimed Chaser. 'They're a strange bunch. They all seem the same as the next one.'

'Only to us' said Storm. 'Pilot whales have very strong bonds within the pod, stronger even than us. They will not leave a fellow pilot hurt or in danger, even if that means that they may die themselves. They value each member of the pod equally, large though it is.'

'What do you think they meant about humans herding them to their death?' asked Dancer.

'It is true' replied Summer. 'Humans have hunted and killed whales and dolphins in years gone by. Once my own mother told me that she saw a great blue whale swimming in the ocean with not one but two harpoons stuck in its side.

'And what about that calf's mother being captured and taken away by the humans. Why would they do that?' continued Dancer incredulously.

'Who knows?' said Breeze in reply. 'Maybe you can ask the human child' he said to Spirit. Spirit had been equally affected by the story.

'I will' he murmured, 'I will. Do you think…?' he began to ask, before tailing off again, lost in thought.

'What?' asked Dancer.

'Oh nothing' replied Spirit awkwardly, turning and swimming off a short distance. His mind began to swirl with uncomfortable thoughts, but he did not want to share them with the others, not yet at least.

157

The dolphins rested lazily amongst the gently lapping waves. Summer and her calf floated off a short distance from the others. Spirit turned to Dancer.

'I need to speak to Summer about something. Come with me' he said.

'What about?' Dancer asked.

'You'll see' he replied. They swam up to her.

'Summer, I need to ask you something' Spirit said.

'Of course, anything' she replied.

'It's about my mother, Star-Gazer. All I know about the day that she disappeared is that you and Storm had swum out with Star-Gazer to feed. A squall blew up and then a ship crossed your path. The noise of the ship's engines disorientated all three of you. After the ship had passed you and Storm found each other, but you could not find Star-Gazer. She had disappeared. Is that right?'

'Yes that's right Spirit' Summer replied with a worried look in her eyes. 'Why do you ask?'

'I don't know, but I can't seem to get it out of my head and what the pilot whales were saying just made it all come back. Surely there must be something more, some detail that I don't know about. Something that would help me make sense of her disappearance?'

'Well you know all the important things' said Summer uncertainly.

158

'Where did it happen for example?' asked Spirit. Summer brightened at the thought that she had something more to tell him.

'Oh, in fact it wasn't far from these waters. We were near the mainland at the time. You know the rock on the cliffs that looks a bit like a dolphin leaping, before you get to the mussels? Yes? Well it was along there.'

'Oh I know where that is!' exclaimed Dancer. 'I was swimming along there just the other day.'

'It wasn't such a big ship' continued Summer, but it gave off such a strange sound. Storm said it was the sound of the engines, but I felt at the time that it was something else. I couldn't be sure though.'

'And a storm blew up?' Spirit continued.

'Well, I'm not sure you could call it a storm, or even a squall really' replied Summer, glancing back at her calf idling peacefully by her side. There were some choppy waves, but nothing that we're not used to. It was mostly the strange noise from the ship that confused us, not the seas.

'Do you think that humans could have seized her, like they did with the pilot whales?' asked Spirit, anxiety snagging his voice.

'I don't know. Maybe, I suppose. I couldn't say.' Summer answered. 'We certainly didn't see the ship taking her. The noise didn't last that long and afterwards Star-Gazer had simply vanished. We called and we called and we looked and we looked, but we couldn't find her.'

'Did you see anything suspicious, or anything unusual that you could not explain?' continued Spirit, with the same edge of anxiety and concern in his voice.

'No, but the sound from the ship had made us feel very unwell. You know when a really terrible headache makes it hard for you to see properly? Well it was a bit like that. My vision was all fuzzy round the sides. Maybe we just weren't well enough to search for anything suspicious. In fact I thought that Star-Gazer had already swum off to rejoin the rest of the pod. I told Storm that we'd find her with the others when we got back. Instead when we did, they said that they had no idea where she was. It was a mystery that we never did find the answer to.'

'The ship. Do you remember what colour it was?' asked Dancer.

'Oh yes' replied Summer. 'It was red with a white stripe up the side. But Spirit…' she continued. 'Whatever happened to her, your mother's lost to us now. We can't bring her back. You've got to let go and accept that what's happened has happened. If you let yourself live in the past and ask 'what if…'. Well, you will never find the answer. It will eat you up.'

Spirit felt a turmoil of emotions inside him, but didn't know how to express them so he didn't say anything at all. He thanked Summer and he and Dancer swam off a short distance again.

'So what's going through your head then?' asked Dancer after they had left Summer.

160

'It's just…. It's just that I've begun to feel so close to Lucy and so I've started to trust other humans as well. But then I still don't know much about them and Storm says not to trust them at all. Then we come across the pilot whales and they say that humans actually capture them, or else herd them onto the rocks to kill them. And then I think…. Well I think that if no one knows what's happened to Star-Gazer, maybe humans did something to her too!' Spirit sighed.

'I know but….like Summer said, you've just got to let go of it. We'll never know what happened to Star-Gazer.'

'But don't you see' replied Spirit with true anguish in his voice, 'I can't. Not when I'm linked in this way to a human like Lucy. I have to find out, I just have to!'

'Well I'll tell you one thing that we can do then' said Dancer. We can go and look at that stretch along the edge of the sea and see what we can find.'

Spirit and Dancer decided to head off towards the coast straight away. The other dolphins in the pod were still dozing lethargically after feeding on the squid and there was plenty of the day left. There was no reason why they should not leave now and still get back to the others before sundown. 'I don't know how those young dolphins find the energy' muttered Moonlight to Chaser as they watched the tails of Spirit and Dancer swim off into the blue.

Spirit was glad that Dancer suggested going to see the place where Star-Gazer had disappeared. At least by doing something he felt that worrying knot of anxiety inside him lessen a little. He had no idea what they could do or find now after all this time. After all, it was at least twelve moons since Star-Gazer had disappeared and even if there might have been something to find at the time, there was unlikely to be anything now.

As they approached, Dancer looked up at the rock which Summer had described as looking like a dolphin leaping.

'Doesn't look much like a dolphin leaping to me' she grumbled. Spirit gave her a playful nudge.

'You've got to look at it from the right angle' he said.

'Which angle is that?'

'With your eyes open!' joked Spirit.

The rock loomed up above them as they swam past and when they went into its shadow, Spirit felt his mood darken. This was the stretch of coast which Star-Gazer had disappeared from. The shore formed a gentle curve, as though it were a very wide bay for about three miles before coming to another rocky outcrop in the distance. Beyond that was the mouth of a narrow estuary where a river fed into the sea. The shoreline itself was a mixture of pebble beach and low cliff. Out there somewhere, the ship had passed and during that stormy squall, while the noise from the ship had disorientated all three dolphins, something had happened.

'Come on, lets start looking' said Spirit.

'But what for?' replied Dancer.

162

'I don't know. Let's just look.' That was the problem. Spirit didn't know what to look for. This stretch of coast was long and even if there was some evidence of Star-Gazer's disappearance, the chance of him and Dancer stumbling upon it was remote.

They swam along, scanning the seabed as they went. The rock didn't drop away sharply here as it did along some parts of the coast, but formed a gentle incline. They searched for evidence of humans having been there. They would frequently see small see-through containers on the seabed that Lucy called bottles, or metal ones that were discoloured or crumpled. They seemed to be everywhere. Occasionally they would see a larger black round thing with a hole in the middle. Spirit could not imagine what they were for. Chaser said he'd bitten one once to see what it tasted like. He said it was tough and chewy, like old squid, but that the taste had been acrid and bitter in his mouth.

Every so often there would be larger lumps of metal in the water that were brown with rust and encrusted with small shell fish. They reminded Spirit of the ship-wreck that he and Dancer had explored off the islands, only these lumps of metal were much smaller and spread out. They came across one which was like one of those small metallic drinking containers, only it was much much bigger. Some black liquid was leaching out of it slowly, polluting the sea around it.

'Let's keep away from that' said Dancer as they swam along. The trouble was that they did not understand what most of these things left by humans actually were. In some parts they

163

completely changed the nature of the seabed and instead of the life that Spirit would expect to see there, it was desolate and dead.

'Shall we go closer to the shore?' Spirit asked Dancer.

'As long as we don't get too close we'll be ok' she replied.

A pipe ran out into the sea and from it came a black-ish brown effluent that drifted in murky clouds in the water until the current dispersed it. Spirit, who was used to the mostly cleaner waters of the open sea, found the taste of it in the water disgusting and over-powering. Some shell fish thrived on it and there was a colony of hundreds of mussels just by the outlet pipe, but to Spirit and Dancer it was dirty and unnatural.

'It's like they just throw into the sea anything that they no longer want on land' said Dancer, the unpleasant taste still lingering in their mouths. 'It really is horrid along here. It's like a wasteland. Maybe we should swim out to sea again.' Spirit agreed and they swam out further from the shoreline.

Spirit half expected to see the ship that Summer had described, making its way across the wide bay, but of course there was nothing. Spirit felt increasingly despondent about swimming here. What was the point? Instead he started to try and imagine what had happened to Star-Gazer. Maybe the ship had a claw that had picked her up. Maybe she'd become ensnared in nets that had been left drifting in the water. Perhaps somehow she'd been pulled into the ship's propellers and been killed. It was so hard to say.

At the far end of the beach around the outcrop of rocks was the entry to the narrow estuary, where fresh waters mingled with salt. Dolphins would never risk going up an estuary like that. It was far too shallow and dangerous, so they turned back.

By this time Spirit had completely given up on the idea of finding something and began to turn to head for home. More than anything right now, he wanted to be able to speak to Lucy and he tried to send her that message in the way that he had once before. It was not so urgent this time, but who knew, maybe she would sense that he wanted to speak to her and would come to him.

After a few minutes, Spirit began to get that feeling that he sometimes had that Lucy was just about to appear in front of him. He was not wrong. As they watched, her shape slowly coalesced in front of them.

'Hello Spirit. Hi Dancer' she said as she floated there in the water in front of them. 'I had a strong feeling that you needed me somehow. You know, like last time. Is there something wrong? Is someone in trouble?' Lucy looked around her, half expecting to see some dolphin or person there that needed saving.

'Yes, that's right. I did want you to come to us' replied Spirit. 'I needed to ask you something.'

'What is it Spirit?' Lucy replied. 'Of course. Ask me anything you like.' Spirit hesitated, trying to summon up this thoughts.

'I need to ask you a question' he answered. 'Do humans really steal dolphins out of the sea?' he asked Lucy. She looked awkwardly away, as though thinking about how best to answer.

'Yes, they do' she replied eventually, an unhappy look upon her face.

Chapter Eleven:

Lucy was so used to seeing Dad in his work clothes everyday, that it seemed strange to see him wearing a pair of baggy shorts and trainers. His knees looked white and pasty, as though they hadn't been exposed to sunlight for a very long time. He appeared rather uncomfortable in his holiday clothes, as though he'd got mixed up over the day of a fancy dress party. It was so surprising to see Dad there in the farmyard, suitcase next to him, that Lucy was quite taken aback. He just looked out of place there somehow.

'Lucy' exclaimed Bethany coming round the corner. 'Your dad and I have just been having a chat. Now that you're both here, why don't we go inside and have a cup of tea?'

Lucy wondered what they could have been having a chat about, but the obvious answer was her and Spirit. Bethany and Dad didn't exactly see eye to eye, but Dad had been persuaded to let Lucy come down here and stay, when before he'd been dead set against it. In fact she still wasn't entirely sure why. She felt as though two different worlds that she would rather have kept apart had just clashed and the thought made her feel rather awkward and gauche. Lucy had always known that Dad would be coming down to Cornwall to join her, but his arrival here a few days early brought it home to her even more forcibly.

They went inside. Lucy could see Dad eyeing Bethany's studio critically. He didn't seem exactly pleased at what he saw. Looking at the studio as if through Dad's eyes, she could see that it was quite messy. Canvasses were stacked up along the wall and the wooden floor was stained where paint had dripped down. There was a smell of turpentine in the air and the metal-framed windows looked tatty and old. The kitchen area was improvised and she could see that dust and fluff had accumulated under the cooker. The living and sleeping area on the raised platform seemed restricted and pokey. Dad took it all in with one sweeping glance and Lucy could imagine his disapproval at such a place for his daughter to be staying in.

Dad said nothing, but smiled as he stirred his tea, as though he was determined to be jolly.

'So what have you been up to this morning Lucy?' he asked conversationally.

'Well me and this boy Paul' Lucy started. 'Well we've been to see, you know. Well my dolphin Spirit actually'. Lucy's enthusiasm drained out of her voice as she wondered what Dad would make of her visit to her dolphin friend. Instead he didn't comment about Spirit.

'A boy?!' he asked with a raised eyebrow.

'Don't be silly, not a boy like that. He's this kid I met in town. He's younger than me and a bit scrawny looking. He… well, we hang out together that's all.' Dad nodded sagely.

'So you've been swimming already this morning? Is that safe?' he continued. Bethany shifted uncomfortably in her chair. She was supposed to be the responsible adult, but had allowed Lucy to go and swim in the sea alone and unsupervised.

'Yes I slipped out before Bethany woke up' Lucy replied quickly, before Bethany got into trouble. 'She doesn't allow me to go down to the sea on my own otherwise' she lied. Dad adopted a sceptical expression but didn't say anything. He'd only just arrived and Lucy guessed that he was trying not to be judgemental.

'More tea John?' Bethany enquired brightly, trying to change the subject and filling his mug up from the teapot on the table. Dad explained that he'd rented a cottage.

'Oh Dad!' Lucy exclaimed anxiously. 'I don't have to leave the farm do I? Not already!' Lucy hated the idea of moving out of the studio and the farm in order to go and stay in some soulless holiday cottage. She knew that Dad couldn't stay in Bethany's studio, but didn't see why she had to leave just because Dad had turned up.

'Where's the cottage then John?' asked Bethany. Dad smiled. Ignoring Lucy, he replied to Bethany.

'As a matter of fact, the cottage is not far from here and I'm renting it from a Mr and Mrs Pengelly.'

'Pengelly?' asked Bethany. 'Why that's….'

'You don't mean Mary and Darren do you?' Lucy butted in.
Dad's smile broadened into a grin.

'I might' he replied with a laugh.

'That means we're staying in the holiday cottages on the farm!'
exclaimed Lucy.

'That's right' replied Dad, 'I believe that they're just a short walk
up the lane, so even though I'll be dragging you away from
Bethany and the studio, we won't be very far away.'

'Oh that's great Dad!' Lucy exclaimed happily. Bethany smiled
too.

'Mr and Mrs Pengelly have been very, ah, accommodating'. He
chuckled at his own joke.

'So what do you think that you two will do down here?' Bethany
asked Dad.

'Well there's plenty to do here of course' replied Dad. 'I'm sure
that we won't get bored. But mostly I shall be happy to just hang
out with my daughter. I feel that I have been neglecting her a little
recently.'

Lucy thought of all the times that she'd wished that Dad
wouldn't be so distant and that he'd spend more time with her like
he did when Mum was alive. Now that he was down here though,
Lucy had mixed feelings. She had things she wanted to do and
wondered how amenable Dad would be to her going off for half a
day at a time on her own. Now wasn't the time to raise it though.
Bethany cut them both a slice of cake.

'I'd like to tell you I baked it myself, but in fact I bought it from the supermarket' she admitted bashfully.

Lucy looked at Bethany with her mass of blond curly hair, wearing an old striped tee-shirt and khaki shorts. Then she looked at Dad, so pallid and out of place. These two people, who were so important to her, seemed completely different from each other. Sometimes she'd wondered what drew Mum to be with Dad in the first place.

In between mouthfuls of cake Dad described his drive down at length, complaining about the state of the roads and the queues of cars and caravans on the motorway. Eventually he turned his attention back to Lucy.

'Come on then Lucy. Let's go and find your Mrs Pengelly and get the keys to the cottage.' They went across the farmyard to find Mary filling out forms in the farm office. Mary and Darren had a row of three cottages just a short distance up the back lane from the farm. They used to be worker's cottages once upon a time, but now they let them out to the tourists during the summer. Lucy had never been in them and was keen to find out what they were like.

In fact the cottage Dad had rented was small, but clean and cosy, with a pocket handkerchief-sized garden at the back with views across the valley beyond.

'This is great Dad!' she exclaimed as she explored the cottage, her concern at moving out of the studio evaporating.

'I'm glad' said Dad smiling. 'I want us to have a nice time together Luce.' He looked at her shyly, as though he was afraid that Lucy would drift away from him altogether. In a way Lucy knew that she was. She was becoming more and more independent and the world of Spirit and the other dolphins seemed far more compelling than anything Dad could offer. Still, he was her father and she loved him. She smiled.

'After you've unpacked, let me take you for a walk round the farm.'

'It's a deal!' he replied.

As they walked across the fields, they chatted about what Lucy had been up to and what the people were like in Merwater. Dad asked about Thelma and Nate, whom he'd met several months before when Lucy had come to the rescue of Spirit and laughed at her description of the enormous tea that Thelma had provided last time they'd visited. Lucy was careful to keep talk about dolphins to a minimum, but told Dad about Paul and the way that the other kids had picked on him.

'I've arranged to go cycling into the countryside with Paul tomorrow in fact' Lucy added, wary of how Dad would react. 'There's this place he's promised to show me.'

'Oh no you're not' Dad replied in a forceful tone while still wanting to keep things light-hearted. 'I've not driven two hundred miles just for you to disappear on some cycle trip. We're supposed to be hanging out together Luce. I've seen precious little of you as it is.'

'But Dad…..' Lucy started plaintively, but she could tell that he was having none of it.

'No! We're spending this holiday together and that's final' he replied with a firm edge to his voice. 'I'm sure you can just call and cancel. If he's just some scrawny ten-year-old like you said, he's hardly going to be good company for you anyway, is he?'

They walked on in silence for a while, both lost in their own thoughts. Lucy couldn't help but think of her dream of the murky silhouette of the dolphin. Why was it so important for her to find out about that dolphin? She couldn't say why, but her gut feeling was that even though she could not believe everything that he told her, Paul could help her find out something important about the dolphin in her dream. By now she'd learned that she should not ignore her dreams. What would Paul think tomorrow if she didn't turn up? Would he ever talk to her again?

They came to the gate at the top edge of Long Field and Dad bet Lucy he could hurdle it. It was a tall farm gate made of galvanized steel. He said he'd been quite the hurdler when he did athletics as a young man. Lucy looked at Dad and then at the gate. She really wasn't sure. Dad took a run at the gate and seemed ready to leap, but just at the last moment he broke off. He looked at her sheepishly.

'Maybe it has been a few years since I last practiced' he admitted as he opted to climb the gate instead.

The shadows were starting to lengthen across the fields as they approached the cottage again. But even despite the lateness of the afternoon, the air was still full of birdsong.

They walked up the short path to the cottage door, glad to be able to get their shoes off and have a rest. A small yellow note had been stuck to the door just by the lock. In neat handwriting it said 'Would you like to join us for supper at seven o'clock tonight? Mary and Darren. PS. Bethany will join us too.' Dad seemed pleased to be invited. He didn't have any food in the cottage and didn't relish the prospect of driving to the nearest shop to pick up provisions. It was nice of Mary and Darren to ask, thought Lucy.

They both went to get ready for dinner. Upstairs in her bedroom at the cottage a sudden insistent feeling came over Lucy that she had to reach out and contact Spirit, in the same way that she had when the little girl was trapped on the rocks. Lucy let her mind slip into the trance that she needed to find the secret door in her mind that led to the world of dolphins and of water. She slipped through and found the water thick with shadows in that last half hour before the long summer evening turned into night.

When Spirit asked her whether humans stole dolphins from the sea, Lucy felt a wave of guilt sweep over her as though it was she that was responsible for all the bad things that people did in the world. She thought of the Sea World adventure park they had visited when Lucy was much younger and the dolphins jumping through hoops in return for fish. It had upset her then, but the

174

though upset her more now. She hardly knew what to say to Spirit at all.

'But why would humans capture dolphins?' asked Spirit. 'I don't understand'. Lucy thought of all the children and parents laughing and admiring the dolphins performing tricks at Sea World.

'People think dolphins are beautiful' she replied, trying to explain. 'They want to see them closer.'

'Dolphins are made for the sea though' continued Spirit. 'We can't live in an over-sized swimming pool. We need to feel the currents, to hear the waves crashing above us, to hunt for fish and squid. We need to be free!' Lucy nodded, her eyes downcast.

'I know' she replied quietly. Lucy thought about the dolphin in the briny lagoon that Paul had described to her and which had become such a recurring image in her nightly dreams. She longed to tell Spirit, but daren't do so, not yet. When she knew more then maybe she would, but not now. She turned back to Spirit.

'It is wrong for humans to keep dolphins in captivity' she said firmly. 'I will do whatever I can to set free any dolphin I find that we have taken from the wild. You have my word.' Spirit gave a nod of his head.

'Thank you Lucy. It's just that I started to think that I knew humans, that I could trust them. I know I can trust you, but then I realised that other humans are strange and dangerous and I don't know what to think anymore.'

Showered and rested, Lucy and Dad strolled down the lane the short distance to the farmhouse. Darren and Mary soon made them feel welcome. Bethany was already there and before long all five of them were chatting and laughing, relaxed and happy. Darren had cooked a dish that he'd found in an Italian-style cookbook and even though it had burned rather badly on the top, nothing could dampen the jollity of the evening. The grown-up's sipped at Darren's home-made Crab Apple wine, which Dad said had a kick like a mule. Lucy could see that Dad was starting to unwind, the cares of work and city life falling from his shoulders like a cloak. It made him look younger, she thought.

They ended the evening by playing charades and by the time Dad and Lucy left to go back to the cottage, it was almost half past eleven.

Back in her room in the cottage, Lucy opened her bedroom window, propped her chin on her hands and stared out at the night sky. There was not a cloud in sight and because there was no moon, the stars seemed particularly bright. Out in the country away from the towns, there was much less light pollution to spoil the view of the stars. They seemed to be scattered across the heavens as though the contents of a bottle of glitter had been spilled on water. Lucy thought that she could make out the Milky Way, but wasn't quite sure. A pipistrelle bat flitted across the garden, hunting for moths. Lucy looked down the valley. It was a shame they didn't have a view of the sea. She imagined Spirit's pod, resting quietly on the surface of the water, their dorsal fins casting dark shadows. What must Spirit think of humans now?

If only she could cycle out with Paul tomorrow and find the dolphin trapped in the murky lagoon. Then she really would have something to tell Spirit. But it was impossible. Unless a miracle happened between now and tomorrow morning, Dad simply wasn't going to let her go off with Paul for the day. She'd have to get a message to him one way or another. But how?

She sighed, as she pulled her curtains closed and climbed into bed. It was nice to be in a proper bed again, after the nights she'd recently spent on Bethany's camp bed. Yet it did not feel the same. It felt so natural to live with Bethany at her studio. Sometimes she liked to imagine that all Bethany's paintings would come alive as she lay there snuggled down under Bethany's spare duvet. She would imagine that the animals and people would emerge from their squares of canvas and talk together quietly as Bethany and Lucy slept. Lucy closed her eyes and drifted off to sleep to dream of dolphins free to roam the wide oceans.

The next morning there was still no food in the cottage, so Lucy persuaded Dad to go over to the studio for breakfast. He said he didn't like to impose, but Lucy could tell that after the previous night he was feeling a bit more positive about Bethany and that he was happy enough to go. Lucy still half hoped that he would relent and let her go for her cycle ride with Paul, but Dad announced resolutely over breakfast at the kitchen table in the studio that they would go into Merwater that morning to buy some groceries and then walk along the cliff tops in the afternoon.

'You can show me the pirate coves and hidden treasure Luce' he joked.

Lucy said that she would tidy away the breakfast things while Dad went back to the cottage to get ready. Once Dad had left, Lucy turned anxiously to Bethany.

'I don't know what to do' she half whispered. I promised that boy Paul that I'd go for a cycle ride with him today. It's just that he… Well, he says that he knows a lake or a lagoon or something where a dolphin is kept prisoner. He was going to show me today. There's no way Dad will let me go, so I've got to get a message to Paul to say I can't come.

'Well you can't blame your Dad for wanting to spend some time with you when he's just arrived Kiddo' replied Bethany sympathetically. I can sort of guess at how important it must be for you to go and find this dolphin' she continued, 'if there really is one. Are you sure he's telling the truth?'

'If it wasn't for these dreams that I've been having, I'm not sure if I'd trust him either' said Lucy. 'But ever since he told me, I've been having the same dream about a dolphin all alone in a murky lagoon. I can barely make out its shape and the dolphin always seems just out of reach. I…' Lucy trailed off.

'It could be just a dream' speculated Bethany.

'But my dreams about Spirit turned out to be real' replied Lucy. I have this feeling that….', but she didn't finish her sentence because she didn't want to put into words what was in the back of her mind. Bethany put the tea towel down on the table to come and give Lucy a hug for a few moments.

'You could ask Thelma to get a message to this boy Paul' she said. 'Thelma knows his Mum so she probably knows where he lives too. Your Dad likes Thelma too. They had long involved conversations about something or other the last time your Dad was down here when you saved Spirit. I reckon that's your best bet.'

'That's a good idea' replied Lucy, but even as she said so, she wondered whether she really wanted Mrs Treddinick to know. 'But I don't know if I'll see Thelma in time. Could you call her for me?'

'Oh I expect so' said Bethany, 'but I can't guarantee I'll be able to get a message to your friend Paul'. Bethany glanced at her wrist watch. 'Off you go now' said Bethany. 'Your father will be waiting for you'. Lucy ran up the lane to where Dad was waiting for her in the car, the engine idling.

'You ready?' he asked brightly. 'Then hop in.'

In Merwater Dad was in no hurry to get to the minimarket and suggested wandering down the main road first and around the small harbour to soak in the sights and smells. Lucy didn't mind. She thought perhaps they'd bump into Thelma or Nate if they did.

It was still early in the day and so the town was still relatively quiet. The tourists would arrive later in the morning. Down at the harbour's edge she looked for Nate's boat the Lady Thelma, but it was not there. Nate and his first mate Bob must have been out tending to their lobster pots. Dad was obviously enjoying wandering around the small, picturesque town and they chatted inconsequentially about this and that as they walked. It was nice to be with Dad she realised. It felt a bit like old times.

They nosed around one or two of the shops full of nick-nacks and curios on sale to the tourists, before coming to the gallery where some of Bethany's work was displayed. There in the window was a large oil-painting by Bethany of a stormy, buffeted sea and in it, a tiny figure of a girl swimming, swimming through the huge waves. Dad studied it silently for a long time. Lucy wondered if it affected him as it had affected her the first time she had seen it. Eventually Dad reached out and gave Lucy's hand a short tight squeeze.

'Come on' he said eventually, 'let's go and get those groceries.' They started walking back up the road and Dad wiped something from his eye. Was it a tear Lucy wondered? She couldn't be quite sure.

In the mini market they both grabbed a hand-basket and wandered round the aisles. Dad said he didn't want to buy more than the bare minimum, but before they knew it, both baskets were nearly full. They rounded the corner, looking for bread-rolls.

'Why Lucy!' exclaimed a voice. Lucy looked up from the shelf she was looking at.

'Mrs Penhaligon! What are you doing here?' It was Lucy's English teacher from school. She'd barely thought about school since they broke up for the holidays and to her surprise here was one of her teachers in front of her in the mini market.

'Well I'm from these parts originally and I've just come down to see my family and enjoy a bit of the sea air.' She smiled at Dad.

'Mr Parr, you have a very pleasant and hardworking daughter. If she keeps it up I've no doubt she'll do very well.' Lucy blushed for a moment, but then a more powerful and compelling thought overcame her.

'Mrs Penhaligon, are you related to Susan Penhaligon?' she asked with a serious tone to her voice. Dad glanced in his daughter's direction, clearly wondering who Susan Penhaligon was. Mrs Penhaligon laughed lightly.

'No Lucy. Penhaligon is a good Cornish name. Lots of people are called Penhaligon round here'.

'But in class you told us the story of the girl on the island and the fisherman and how it is said that they both became dolphins. And it was Susan Penhaligon here in Merwater who persuaded the children to swim out to sea to become dolphins all those years ago.' Her teacher smiled, but her answer was thoughtful and serious.

'Yes you are right, but the name is nothing more than a coincidence. I am a Penhaligon by marriage only. There are stories of people and dolphins which stretch back hundreds of years. I know that you love dolphins, but I only gave that story in class as a piece of interesting folklore. I never imagined I'd be chatting to you in a minimarket in Merwater about local history!'

Dad shifted uneasily. He was obviously surprised by the turn the conversation had suddenly taken.

'But…' stuttered Lucy.

'Luce do stop quizzing poor Mrs Penhaligon. She's on holiday too after all' he said with an apologetic glance towards her teacher. Mrs Penhaligon smiled again.

'It's been nice to see you Lucy. I do hope that you and your father have a lovely holiday here.' She hesitated a moment and then said goodbye and walked off down the aisle.

After they went through the check-out, Dad asked Lucy to wait with two bags of shopping whilst he took the other two to the car. Lucy had felt strangely put out by having seen Mrs Penhaligon. In class she'd felt that her teacher knew more than she cared to say and that they'd had a sort of special connection. She felt that Mrs Penhaligon knew about dolphins. Here in Merwater her teacher's comments had been bland and empty. Lucy adjusted the bags at her feet. It didn't make sense.

'Lucy while your Dad's away for a moment I just wanted to say something.' Mrs Penhaligon suddenly appeared at her side again and spoke in a low urgent tone. 'I think that you have a special gift' she said, looking at Lucy. 'Yes, I can see it there in your eyes. I know more about Susan Penhaligon and local dolphin folklore than I cared to let on back there. I have an idea your father is not as receptive to such talk as you are. But you are not like Susan Penhaligon all those years ago. You can make your own destiny. You just need to believe in yourself'. She touched Lucy lightly on the arm.

'I'm helping out most days at my sister's gift shop just down the road' she said pressing a business card into Lucy's palm. Do drop in and see me if you can' she said. With that she slipped away. Just then Dad came back for the last two shopping bags.

'You ready Luce?' he asked.

Chapter Twelve:

Paul lent his bike against the stone wall surrounding the grave yard of the church at the end of Bussey Lane. He was wearing his favourite tee-shirt shirt and a pair of baggy khaki shorts. The church was small and stumpy with a pitched slate roof and low tower. It squatted at the convergence of two roads, just on the edge of Merwater where the countryside started.

Lichen-covered grave stones stood drunkenly at regular intervals in the graveyard, their lettering so old that it had all but worn away. Flowers and nettles sprouted up in the corners where nature was always poised to take over if it was left unattended for more than a few weeks. This was a good place to search for insects and twice Paul had found a slow-worm, a short legless lizard that looked like a snake, sunning itself on a gravestone.

Paul glanced at his watch. It was a quarter past twelve. He thought Lucy would be here by now. A car droned by, as sleepily as a bumble bee. Paul rubbed his knee. It was cut and grazed. Mum had sent him to the corner shop for a pint of milk that morning. She'd wanted him to buy a pack of cigarettes for her as well, but the man in the shop said it wasn't allowed. He'd cut across the recreation ground on the way back. Baz and Mike had

184

come up behind him and stuck out a leg to trip him up. He'd fallen sprawling on the tarmac path while the milk carton had hit the ground and started leaking milk onto the earth. Paul's knee stung and started to bleed.

'Ooh Paulie, you're so careless' jeered Mike.

'Get off of me' Paul yelled back, 'or I'll...'

'Or you'll what?' sneered Baz as he kicked the milk carton into a shrub. Paul didn't know how to finish his sentence, so he didn't say anything. He wanted to say 'You don't know anything about me, I swum with a dolphin yesterday' but something stopped him just in time. He got up and retrieved the milk carton, which by now was half empty and limped off home. Mum was annoyed both for the split carton and the fact that he'd come back without her cigarettes. At least his bike was working again and he'd be able to escape for the entire afternoon.

Paul looked at his watch again. It was almost half past twelve and there was still no sign of Lucy. She'd been so insistent that he take her to the dolphin lagoon and now she wasn't here. He wondered what had happened to her. Maybe she hadn't been able to find the church, or perhaps she'd just been winding him up. It wouldn't be the first time that someone had played a trick on him like that.

He sighed. There was something in the graveyard he wanted to show her. It was the grave of Susan Penhaligon, tucked away in the undergrowth near the crumbling wall, marked by a lopsided headstone.. That's why he'd suggested meeting here. 'Well, it's

185

her loss' he thought. He'd strapped his school lunch box onto the back of his bike. Now he took it off and got out his sandwiches wrapped in cling film. He munched at a cheese sandwich disconsolately.

He still couldn't get over having swum in the sea with Spirit the day before. It had been more amazing than he had ever imagined. The dolphin had looked at him with such calm, understanding eyes that he felt like Spirit had been reading his soul. It made him feel as though he wanted to laugh and cry at the same time. He'd never felt such a connection with another living creature before, not even the dog they'd had before Dad had left home.

Paul wondered why Lucy was a Dolphin-Child and not him. It wasn't fair, like the way it wasn't fair that some kids were brought up in big comfortable homes with everything they wanted, while other kids felt miserable, neglected and poor. Maybe he could learn how to become a Dolphin-Child too he thought. He wanted to find out more about it from Lucy and then perhaps he'd learn the secret too.

Mum was weird about Lucy and told him to keep away from her, but after he'd swum with Spirit yesterday he knew that he couldn't. He just wouldn't tell Mum. That meant he couldn't tell anyone else either and that was something that was going to be really difficult for him. He was just dying to show off to someone about it, but he knew he had to keep it to himself.

By a quarter past one he decided that Lucy was not going to turn up after all. He felt lonely and let down. He thought he'd just embarked on a special adventure with a new friend, but now it seemed that maybe it had ended before it had even properly begun. Perhaps even now Lucy was laughing about him with the other kids.

He wondered what he should do now. After what had happened with Baz and Mike that morning, he certainly couldn't face going back home and risk encountering them again. He decided to head on out to the lagoon all by himself. He'd show Lucy.

Paul climbed on his bike and pedalled off slowly down the road. It dipped down at first and Paul was able to free-wheel, the wind fresh on his face. Then at the bottom the road narrowed into a lane. A small hump backed bridge carried the lane over a stream and up a wooded hill on the other side. Paul panted as he cycled up the hill, but the trees provided dappled shade as he went. Once he got to the top the lane flattened out and Paul came out into the bright sunlight again as it proceeded through fields. Cows grazed on one side of the hedge and horses ambled in the field on the other side of the road. A farm track peeled off to the left and Paul cycled on, swerving to avoid the occasional pot-hole as he went.

Eventually Paul came to the point where the lane passed through a short narrow tunnel under a raised railway track on an earth embankment. As far as Paul knew, trains hadn't run along here for decades and the slope and verge was like a long green wall linking one hill to the next.

On the other side of the short tunnel Paul got off his bike and turned off on to a path that led up to where the railway tracks had once been. A track ran along the top between saplings and small trees that had established themselves there. He left his bike hidden behind a bush and walked on until he left the railway track and plunged down a slope, past the stinging nettles to a long stone wall. It stood, taller than a full grown man and ran along the edge of the railway for as far as the eye could see before it curved round out of sight. The wall enclosed a private estate and was half overgrown with ivy and had ferns growing out of it periodically along the top. Paul could see that at one time the wall had crumbled and fallen down in a couple of places, but in recent years it had been repaired with fresh concrete and stones.

Along the top of the wall was sprinkled broken glass, set into the render, but the last time he had come he had climbed a tree to where he had access to the top of the wall and then beat the glass flat with a stone he'd found at the base.

It was up the same tree that Paul climbed again. He inched along the branch towards the wall. It bent alarmingly under his weight but he was soon standing on the top of the wall. There was nothing for it but to jump. It felt scarily high at the top but the ground below was thick with pine needles. He imagined there were guards patrolling the grounds that he had to evade.

After a minute or so, he pressed on through the wood, dodging the imaginary guards.

At the edge of the pine wood was a huge tangled wall of rhododendron bushes that had spent the last hundred years or more growing to enormous proportions. Paul dived in amongst the rhododendron branches and started climbing up through them until he was two or three meters above the ground. Paul pulled himself up until he was almost at the top of great sprawling rhododendrons. In the distance to the left he could see the roof of the house at the end of the lake.

The lagoon was as broad as two football pitches and four times as long. To his left it tapered to the point where the house stood, its grey stone walls set off by the redness of the roof tiles above. On the other side of the lagoon were low reed beds where Paul guessed that wading birds probably nested. Beyond that was another wood rising up a hill. To his right though was a sort of close-linked fence that rose to about a meter above the surface of the water. The submerged part of the metal fencing let the tidal waters through but cut it off from the river estuary beyond. In truth the lagoon was simply an inlet from the estuary that had a metal fence stretched across it so that no boat, or indeed any fish longer than a hand could get through.

The estuary itself was sheltered from the winds and the waves of the open sea, but was still subject to the tides that flowed in and out. Hills rose up on the other side and gave it a sheltered aspect. Its water was brackish and muddy.

Paul wondered why there was a fence across the inlet at all. He glanced back at the big house. It was completely quiet.

189

Paul sat on the bank of the inlet and trailed one hand in the water. Barely without him having noticed, clouds had obscured the sun and now light rain played upon the surface of the water and the musty smell of warm raindrops rose up from the ground. It wasn't raining heavily enough to make him wet, but Paul idly started wondering whether dolphins minded the rain even though they were in the water anyway. He scanned the surface of the lagoon for any sign of the dorsal fin of a dolphin, but he could not see any. He patted the surface of the water to attract its attention.

'Come on dolphin!' he called quietly. 'Come here!' No dolphin came. It was a big enough lake for him to have difficulty spotting anything that might have swum there, so it did not surprise him that he could not really see anything. It could easily have been hiding behind some reeds or an overhanging bush.

Sitting there and looking at an empty lake was no comparison to swimming with Spirit the day before. Paul began to imagine what it would be like if the dolphin actually did come up to him now, poking its nose out of the water at him and clicking in greeting. He'd stare long and deep into its eyes and then he'd be able to understand what the dolphin's clicks and whistles meant, he thought. Then he'd be able to communicate with it, just like Lucy could with Spirit. He'd be a Dolphin-Child, the same as that girl Susan Penhaligon so many years before.

Paul visualised his own legs and arms becoming flukes and flippers, until he too was a smooth graceful dolphin slicing through the waves. He pictured the children who swam out into the sea with Susan Penhaligon all becoming dolphins as well before swimming off to a new life of freedom and happiness. Paul wished that he could shed all his anguish and unhappiness like a skin and swim off to adventures under the waves like them.

Still there was no sign of the dolphin. Instead of calling, he tried sending it a message with his mind. He strained his thoughts to transmit the message 'I am your friend. Please come to me', but there was no response whatsoever. In truth he had no idea how you could send a telepathic message to the mind of a dolphin.

The rain shower had stopped now and the surface of the water looked as still and unbroken as before. There was the smell of damp dust in the air. Paul wondered if he could catch a fish to tempt the dolphin to come over to him. He looked down into the water immediately in front of him. Something moved in the murk and he splashed his hand in noisily, hoping to scoop up whatever it was. His hand came up wet but empty. Catching a fish would be an impossible task.

Just then a figure emerged from the big house at the end of the inlet. Paul immediately tensed himself and hunched down so that he was hidden behind a clump of nettles growing at the waters edge. He peered carefully round them to see what the figure was doing.

The figure was thin and moved with slow, deliberate movements. He couldn't see quite well enough to decide whether it was a man or a woman. The figure walked around the side of the house and Paul took the opportunity to move along up the bank towards the house to get a better view, ducking low as he did so. As he did so he tripped over a root and sprawled headlong into another clump of nettles. He protected his face but his fore-arms were badly stung. Fortunately some dock-leaves were growing nearby and he grabbed a couple to rub on his arm as he crept up to get a better view of the house.

The figure came round the side of the house again and Paul crouched down. To his surprise it was a woman. She looked old he decided and she had gray hair. She was carrying a bucket and made her way down to a small landing stage at the water's edge. Unfortunately Paul did not have a clear view of what she was doing as there were some reeds growing at the edge of the landing stage and they obscured her. If anything Paul would have had a better view where he had been before, but it was too late to go back there now. Paul scanned the water again for signs of a dolphin, but could see no sign of one.

Eventually the woman came into view again and walked stiffly back to the house. It looked like the bucket was empty now. He wondered what she'd deposited in the water.

Paul sighed. It was a good thing that Lucy hadn't come he thought. She'd have just said that he was a liar and made it all up. He began to doubt it himself. Maybe he'd just seen a log or something in the water the last time and had been mistaken. He'd read stories about people believing they'd seen the Loch Ness monster, but that they'd probably just seen a branch or something in the waters of the Loch instead. Maybe that was all that he'd seen. He sighed again. Even if he saw Lucy again and even if she were to come with him out here, they'd see nothing and she'd never speak to him again. He'd probably never get to swim with Spirit in the sea again either.

Paul glanced at his watch. It was much later than he'd thought and Mum had told him that he'd better be back home by five o'clock. He wouldn't make it he realised. Reluctantly he turned his back on the lake and made his way back to the spot where he'd left his bike.

Once the small human had turned and left, the dolphin allowed herself to break the surface of the water and swam slowly round the edge of the lake to where he had been. She didn't trust humans, especially not one that lurked around behind bushes. She owed her life to humans, but equally she was held as a prisoner here by one.

The lagoon was muddy and it was hard to see more than a meter or so in front of her under the water. Even with her sonar clicking it wasn't much better. The few fish that got through the links of the fencing that divided the inlet from the rest of the estuary were small and insubstantial. She had no choice but to accept the hand-outs from the old lady when she came down to the water's edge twice a day. The fish were dead though and sometimes they were frozen in the middle. She would look up imploringly into the eyes of the woman on the little wooden landing stage above her, but the woman didn't seem to realise what she was trying to say. She'd attempted to find a way through the fence and to escape, but it had proved impossible. It was too high for her to leap over, though she may have been able to do so before the accident. The dolphin swam on slowly and disconsolately, with nothing to do but to endlessly circle the edge of the lake.

Chapter Thirteen:

It was light beyond the curtains of the little room in the cottage when Lucy awoke. She turned restlessly, half aware of Dad's sonorous snoring from the next room. Lucy glanced at her watch; it was only half past five in the morning. It was still way too early to get up.

Lucy dipped in and out of sleep. When she closed her eyes, in her dreams she was swimming effortlessly alongside Spirit and Dancer, leaping through the waves and chasing fish through clear waters. Then she dreamt of Paul's mother, telling her to keep away and the feeling of anxiety and rejection crept over her. In her dream Paul's Mum turned into a raven and flapped away mournfully, cawing as it went 'Dolphin girl, dolphin girl, stay away from the dolphin girl.' Lucy woke up again at this point, a knot of sheets twisted around her. She tried to keep herself from slipping back into the same dream, but eventually the desire to sleep overcame her once again.

Lucy was immediately transported back to the murky waters of the lagoon that she had so often visited in her sleep these last few days. She could not see the dolphin, but sensed that it was somewhere nearby. In the distance she could just make out the restless beating of the dolphins tail as it swept to and fro, backwards and forth along the shore line of the lake.

Lucy had visited a zoo once and seen a polar bear endlessly pacing backwards and forwards the few steps it took to get from one side of its small enclosure to the other, before turning and pacing back. She had a sense that the dolphin was doing the same thing. As Lucy watched she glimpsed it better occasionally as it came past. The dolphin looked stressed and unhappy. 'This is no way for a dolphin to live' Lucy thought to herself.

She tried to approach the dolphin, as if by doing or saying something she could make the creature feel better. The more she tried to swim forward though, the less she seemed to be moving. Thrashing about with her limbs seemed to do no good at all. Then the dolphin came towards her and blind to her presence, paused a moment just by her. 'I need to be free, I need to be free' the dolphin muttered to herself. 'Why are those humans keeping me here? What have I done to them?'

In her dreaming state, Lucy stretched out her hand towards the unhappy animal, but the dolphin turned again and swum off out of sight into the murky void. Of course the dolphin was unable to see her. Spirit never saw her when she dreamt about him.

The last time she had reached out to him with her mind, Spirit had asked Lucy whether humans took dolphins captive. She hated to tell him the truth that they did and that indeed she had seen dolphins at a dolphinarium, but she had had to. How could she explain it to him? There was no good explanation why humans did so. It may be marginally better than catching dolphins in fishing nets, as she knew happened with some deep sea trawlers, but separating a dolphin from the wide openness of the sea was like cutting out a dolphin's soul. It cut them inside to be so confined and Lucy could see that the dolphin in this muddy lagoon was equally badly affected.

'If I don't do something soon, that dolphin's going to go mad' she said aloud to herself in her dream. Her own words shocked Lucy into consciousness and she sat up suddenly, caught in the tangled mess of sheets, her eyes wide with fear for the creature trapped in some place that she didn't know how to find.

Now that she was awake, Lucy's thoughts turned to Paul. If only she had been able to go out cycling with him the day before. She didn't blame Dad for wanting to spend time with her, she was his daughter after all, but she wished with all her heart that she'd been able to cycle along the country lanes with Paul by her side and find that lake and the dolphin within it. She didn't know what she would do when she did, but she felt strongly that something would happen. Something had to happen.

Lucy didn't know whether Paul had got her message via Bethany and Thelma that she was not coming yesterday. If he didn't, he'd never want to talk to her again, Lucy thought. He'd probably think that she was some arrogant out-of-towner. She'd had her doubts about how much of what Paul told her was true, but he was her only chance of finding that dolphin before it was too late.

197

As Lucy was sitting in bed, she decided to stretch out with her mind to speak to Spirit. That usually made her feel better. Try as she might though, Lucy simply wasn't able to find that door in the corner of her mind that would allow her to plunge into his world of water. Sometimes, when she was feeling anxious about something, she'd had this problem before. Lucy kept trying for almost fifteen minutes, but it was no good. Lucy knew that the best thing to do would be to stop trying and come back to it later. Often things seemed easier if she put it to one side for a while.

Lucy opened the curtains a crack and peeked out. It was going to be another beautiful day. The early morning sky was blue except for a few wispy clouds that almost seemed to glow with rays of sunlight that caught them.

She listened to the dawn chorus of birds and imagined that in field after field after field, all the birds of Cornwall, Devon and then the whole of England were joined together in one united chorus. Lucy listened intently, seeing if she could hear the blackbird that she'd heard singing outside the cottage the day before. Try as she might though, she just couldn't detect it.

It always amazed Lucy that in day to day life, you could hear the sound of birds singing around you, but not truly hear them. You just had to focus. After a while Lucy dozed off again.

'Wake up Luce' called Dad upstairs from the tiny kitchen of the holiday cottage. 'I've got your chocolate milk ready!' Lucy awoke with a start. She glanced at her watch. 'Ten to nine already?' she

198

thought to herself. She stretched for a moment and then tumbled out of bed and padded downstairs. Dad was sitting at the tiny kitchen table, nursing a mug in his hands.

'Hey pyjama girl!' he greeted her. 'How did you sleep?' Lucy mumbled something about not having slept so well and then took her mug of chocolate milk and sipped it, still sleepy and bleary eyed.

'I saw Bethany drive off up the lane in her Land Rover a bit earlier' said Dad conversationally. 'She's up with the lark, that one.' Lucy smiled.

'Actually she's not very good at getting up early at all' she replied.

'It's so lovely down here among the fields and the lanes and the sea. I've only been here a day and already I feel so much more calm and relaxed than when I'm back home' Dad continued. 'I feel like the peace and quiet is seeping into my bones.' Lucy smiled and Dad paused, collecting his thoughts.

'You know it's at times like this, when I feel more relaxed and happy, that it comes home to me that Mum isn't with us anymore. I feel bad that she isn't here to enjoy all this with us.' Lucy looked up at Dad. The emotion was written across his face.

'I know Dad' she said quietly. 'I feel the same too.'

'When I'm rushing around at work or doing chores at home I can block those thoughts out' he continued, quickly brushing his hand across his eyes as if to hide any trace of tears. 'Maybe that's why I haven't been there for you as much as I'd like Luce. But

199

that's going to change, starting with this holiday. You're growing up fast. Before I know it you'll be off to University. I don't want to find you've suddenly grown up without my noticing.'

Lucy felt for Dad but didn't know quite what to say, so she stretched out her hand instead and gave his a quick squeeze. She'd wished that he could have said something like that so much over the past few months. Now there was so much going on in her life, but she still didn't feel able to talk to Dad about it.

'I'm so glad to be down here and to be able to meet Spirit' she said, steeling herself against his response. Not so long ago he would have hit the roof if she'd started talking about dolphins with him. She still didn't fully understand why. She sensed Dad stiffening a little, though he tried hard not to show it.

'Yes I know you're going through this stage with dolphins' Dad replied. 'I dread to think what risks you've taken to see that friend of yours Spirit and what's her name, Dancer. But I suppose I'm glad you're able to while you can.' Lucy didn't know quite what he meant by that, but let the comment pass.

'You won't stop me seeing Spirit will you Dad, now that you're down here too?' Dad sighed and then forced a smile.

'I guess not Luce' he replied eventually. 'After all, we won't be here that long will we?'

'Can I go and see Spirit tomorrow morning?' she asked. Dad sighed again.

'I suppose so, but I'm coming too to make sure you're safe. Let's enjoy ourselves today though. There's this castle I thought we could go and see. They say you can see for miles and miles from the ramparts.' Lucy felt a knot of anxiety rising in her chest.

'But you know that boy Paul I told you about Dad' she said. 'There's something he needs to show me. It's… It's important.' She could see that Dad was hurt and didn't really understand.

'Can't you see that boy some other time Luce?' he asked. 'I really hoped that we could, well, hang out together.'

'Oh please Dad' she pleaded. He looked exasperated.

'I suppose so' he answered eventually. 'But we're going to the castle this morning. You can go and find this Paul boy this afternoon if it's so important. Now let's have breakfast. I've got bacon and eggs. Do you want your eggs fried or scrambled?'

Later that morning, they both stood on the castle ramparts, looking down at the fields below them. The castle keep was tall and stark. Its interior had long since been ruined, whether by some siege or other or simple neglect, but the outer walls and tight spiral staircases still remained and wooden gantries had been built so that the tourists wouldn't fall from the landings. Lucy loved castles and liked to picture in her minds eye what it must have been like all those years before, with peasants toiling in the fields and knights riding out to joust on their heavy chargers.

Lucy wandered along the ramparts, peering out of the arrow slits. Dad lingered behind her, reading a notice. From the west corner of the castle keep Lucy could just glimpse the sea. At that spot, carved into the stone work, was a creature leaping from the water. It looked to Lucy like a dolphin, though she couldn't be sure. She traced her fingers round the rough stone carving, wondering who it was that had put it there so many years before and why. She missed Spirit right now and wished that she could reach out to him, or swim with him again. She wondered where Paul might be right now and how she would find him. They had a leisurely lunch in the café next to the castle and then set off again. By this time Dad was happy to go back into Merwater again for an ice-cream and to wander round and this suited Lucy just fine. She would slip off for half an hour, find Paul and then... Well, she wasn't sure, but she'd figure something out.

Paul had been disappointed not to see the dolphin in the lagoon the day before and to compensate his mind raced with dramatic stories and adventures. He imagined evading the henchmen patrolling the grounds and climbing over the wall just in time while shots rang out behind him and bullets whizzed through the air inches from his head. He pretended that every car on the country lane he pedalled along back home was full of the bad guys searching for him and pictured himself hiding in the verge until they had passed. It was, he decided a criminal gang intent on training dolphins to smuggle drugs and he imagined how impressed the police would be when he helped them smash the operation. The day dream sustained him all the way home and he was still thinking about it the next day when his Mum sent him out to play in the recreation ground.

Afterwards, he couldn't remember quite what he had said at first, but he'd boasted to a younger kid that he knew where a criminal gang was operating from. Before he knew it a couple more kids joined them and started asking him more questions. As he tried to justify what he had just said, one of the children started jeering and that attracted a group of boys that had been playing football to come over. Then, as he knew they would, Baz and Mike appeared and he found that all the kids were jeering at him and calling him names, even children he used to play with a month or two before.

Then one of the gang of kids picked up a clump of earth and threw it at him. The hard dry earth stung where it hit his arm, but then another lump hit him and suddenly it seemed like half the children there were reaching down for bits of earth to throw at him while they encircled him and called out sneering insults. He tried to be tough, to show them he did not care, but then a pebble caught him on the neck. Paul seemed to fold in on himself and he started to cry quietly, his tears streaking the dusty earth that was stuck to his face; his hands at his sides, his head bent to deflect the worst of the blows.

After she left Dad down by the harbour, Lucy had taken the route up the walled stream bed which was the quickest way she knew to get up to the part of town where the recreation ground was. She had no idea if she'd find Paul, but it was the only place she could think of where he might be. She knew where his house was, but she was afraid of his mother and wouldn't dare knock on the door.

Then she heard the noise and the group of kids near some bushes on one side of the recreation ground and made her way over, curious about what was causing all the commotion. As she got nearer, she could hear that the atmosphere was nasty and threatening and Lucy started to run. The kids were so tightly packed in a circle, that at first it was impossible to see what was the object of their derision, but then at last she saw Paul, standing alone in the middle and in tears, while the children flung anything they could at him, no longer knowing or caring why.

One of the larger boys had just levered up a big clump of earth from a flower bed and was making a great play of getting ready to lob it at Paul. Fury overtook Lucy and she rushed at the boy, giving him an enormous shove between his shoulder blades and sending him sprawling at Paul's feet, his lump of earth dropped. Several of the other kids began to titter.

'Get off him you bully!' Lucy shouted angrily at Mike.

'Oi, who do you think you are coming here and spoiling our fun?' shouted Baz. Lucy turned on him furiously. She was shorter than the boy by a head and was much slighter than he was, but she detested bullies and was so angry that nothing was going to stop her. A few months ago Lucy's friend Amy had showed her some Ju Jitsu self defence moves and they'd spent the afternoon practicing them in the garden. Without thinking of how much bigger and heavier he was than her, she pulled him off balance and with an outstretched foot sent him crashing down too. Baz clutched his knee in pain and writhed on the ground.

The other kids were so surprised by what had just happened to the two biggest boys that they started to scatter.

'Clear off you cowards!' she yelled after them. Mike staggered to his feet and made to come towards her.

'Don't make me hurt you more than I've hurt him!' Lucy threatened, indicating towards Baz, who was still groaning on the ground. Mike started to back off too.

'Come on, let's get out of here' she said to Paul. Paul knew better than to argue with his deliverer and followed her as they marched off at a swift pace back across the recreation ground the way that Lucy had come.

As they walked Lucy still seethed with anger at how kids could pick on a lone boy like that, but as they strode along in silence, she became more aware of her heart racing. She'd never had to do anything like that before and now that they were out of danger, her legs felt as if they were turning to jelly. She thought that she might cry too, but she didn't want to show herself up in front of Paul.

They crossed the road and clambered across the broken down fence into the old orchard which the walled stream ran through.

'Lets sit down' she said and they both collapsed onto the grass verge. Paul was still crying and sniffed loudly as he wiped his eyes, streaking the mud on his face even more.

'You okay?' Lucy asked Paul, turning to look at him. He looked terrible, but she didn't feel that much better herself. He nodded silently and they sat there for a while, trying to compose themselves.

'What was that all about then?' she asked. Paul half shrugged.

'I, well I don't know' he stammered. 'They like make fun of what I say and...'

'What do you tell them?' Lucy was puzzled.

'Well, you know, just things I've seen. Like the lake and the house...'

'You didn't tell them about the dolphin did you?' she asked, suddenly worried.

'No, no' he replied truthfully enough. He hadn't got that far before they started jeering at him. 'It's just, you know, they say I make things up.' Paul sniffed again and wiped his eyes with his t-shirt.

'And do you?' Lucy asked. She suddenly felt a clutch of worry at the pit of her stomach. She'd had an uneasy feeling about Paul already. What if he'd made it all up and all the stuff he'd told her about dolphins was just a fantasy?

'Well, you know, sometimes, a bit' he sniffed.

'And did you make up your story to me about the dolphin?' Lucy asked sharply. Paul turned his head and looked her directly in the eye.

'No' he said firmly. 'I saw the dolphin in the lagoon. It's trapped there. They're keeping it there. I still don't know why. It's true that when I went back there yesterday after you didn't turn up I couldn't see it. But it's there. I know it is.' Paul sniffed again and half a sob caught at the back of his throat. He caught Lucy's eye for half a second more, then looked away down at the ground between his knees where he was sitting. Lucy knew instinctively that he was telling the truth.

'We've got to help that dolphin' said Lucy urgently. I keep dreaming about her like I did with Spirit before I knew how to reach out with my mind and speak to him. She's desperately alone and she needs her pod.' She turned to look at him again. 'We've got to save her.'

'Why didn't you come with me yesterday then, if she's so important to you? I waited for you for over an hour' Paul sniffed. It was Lucy's turn to hesitate now.

'I, I couldn't. My Dad came down to Cornwall earlier than we thought and he wouldn't let me.' Thinking of Dad, she glanced at her watch. She was already ten minutes late to get back to the car.

'What are we going to do then?'

'I, well, I don't know. Not today anyway' she replied, glancing at her watch again. They sat in silence for a bit longer.

'Why can't you just talk to the dolphin in the lake like you talk to Spirit?' asked Paul eventually.

'No it's only Spirit and Dancer...' Lucy started to answer before trailing off. Then she began to think. Why couldn't she speak to

207

the dolphin in the lake? If she could speak to Dancer when she wanted to, she could probably reach out to others as well.

'Maybe you're right. It's worth a try' she replied after a moment. But how? She had no idea where the lake was even, or what it looked like.

'You've got to tell me everything you know' she said urgently to Paul. 'You've got to describe to me in as much detail as you can exactly the route that you took to get there yesterday, so I can see it in my mind's eye!'

Lucy closed her eyes as Paul started to describe. At first he didn't have the words to tell her and she kept making him stop to describe things again more clearly, asking about this or that detail. Slowly, hesitantly, she started to visualise the squat church on Bussey Lane and then the route that Paul had cycled up the wooded hill out onto open fields, before he came to the raised embankment of the railway track.

Paul described how he continued on foot along the overgrown gravel of the disused railway track until he turned off and climbed up the tree so that he could get over the long stone wall, with ferns growing out of the top. Sometimes Lucy found it hard to visualise what Paul was telling her, but then it felt almost as if she were slipping into a trance and the picture came vividly into her mind's eye.

It was like tuning in to an obscure and distant radio station. Sometimes the signal came through clearly, before it was lost once more to static crackle. Paul continued to describe the leap from the stone wall and the walk through the pine trees until he came to the bank of rhododendron bushes. The image in Lucy's mind became weaker here and she had to get him to go over it again. Only when Paul told her how he had pretended that he was evading guards and snipers bullets, did the picture became vividly clear to Lucy again.

Then they came to the side of the lagoon and Paul described as clearly as he was able how it was really an inlet from the estuary river which had been blocked off at one end by a chain mail fence and had a house at the other end. With her eyes still closed, Lucy held the image as sharply and clearly as she could in her mind's eye, whilst at the same time trying to focus and then relax her thoughts, so that she could find the portal in the corner of her mind that would enable her to slip through.

It felt incredibly difficult and twice the image started to fade away, so Lucy had to get Paul to go back and describe it all afresh to her. Finally, her mental energy already running low, it was almost as if Lucy tripped by accident and fell through into the world beneath the waves.

The water was as muddy and murky as in her dream and the bed of the lagoon was shallow. Even at its deepest point it was barely more than two meters deep; certainly not enough for a fit and active dolphin. Little grew in the brackish water, as Lucy could see as she effortlessly glided along. Lucy thought that she could make out the flash of a dolphin's tail, but as she moved towards it, it seemed to disappear again into the murk.

'What if the dolphin is trying to get away from me?' wondered Lucy as she glided along. What if she's scared by the ghost of a human being in the water? Even though she could not yet see the dolphin, Lucy felt that she had to trust in her belief that it was actually there.

'I am your friend' she called out into the murk. 'I am a Dolphin-Child of the pod of Storm, Spirit, Dancer, Breeze, Chaser, Moonlight and Summer. I have come to help you!' Lucy stopped gliding forward and for a moment all was still. Then she sensed that something was approaching through the murk and for a second she was scared. Then she saw the dolphin. It approached her slowly and cautiously. The dolphin looked unhappy and its eyes were troubled.

'You know Spirit?' asked the dolphin incredulously.

'Yes, yes I do' replied Lucy hesitantly. 'What is your name?'

'My name is Star-Gazer' replied the dolphin sadly.

Chapter Fourteen:

It was growing dark and the dolphins idled in the water in the quiet of the late afternoon before night fell. It had been a busy day. Chaser and Breeze had ridden the bow of a fast sailing boat and were full of stories of their adventures. There were other sailing boats as well and they seemed to be engaged in some sort of a race. Chaser and Breeze had chosen the most beautiful and fastest of the vessels to accompany. They could easily have out-swum the boat if they had wanted to as it sliced through the water, but it was a pleasure to swim alongside the bow as though they were escorting it to the winning post.

Summer, Spirit and Dancer were making up stories. Dancer would start and tell the first bit. Then Summer would take over and make up a bit more. When it was Spirit's turn, he would try and give the story a twist and take it in a different direction to the story that Dancer had started. The story became more and more convoluted, but it was fun to tell and it set their imaginations on fire. Storm and Moonlight listened as they made their tale even more wild and improbable, laughing and commenting as it progressed.

Afterwards, they lazed together, staring up at the night sky which was particularly clear.

'Do you think there are dolphins living on the moon?' asked Dancer idly. They all looked up at the full moon high above them.

'I don't think there's much water up there to swim in' chuckled Storm.

'Maybe they don't need water' continued Dancer. 'Perhaps they can just float in the air.'

'You mean like birds do?' asked Chaser.

'Who knows?' said Dancer with a yawn. 'Anything might be possible on the moon!' Spirit smiled.

'Sometimes I dream that I swim straight out of the water and just keep swimming towards the clouds' he continued. 'In my dream I go higher than the birds, higher than the clouds even and when I look back down, the planet just looks so small and insignificant, I think I might as well keep swimming to the stars.

'That's a beautiful dream' said Summer, her young calf nuzzling at her side. 'It's the kind of thing that Star-Gazer would have dreamt about. What was it that she said that stars were made of?'

'Fireflies!' answered Breeze quickly and they all laughed. 'I swallowed one once by accident when was leaping from the water. I thought my insides would explode with light!'

'You know in the depths of the ocean there are strange fish that can generate their own light' said Storm conversationally. 'Angler fish they are called. It is so dark down there that they cannot see otherwise. Of course it is not possible for us dolphins to descend to such depths, but I have seen one or two that have come up to the surface. They use the light as bait to lure their victims to them. Strange ugly looking fish they are. They look like they might have come from outer space. I give them a wide berth.'

The dolphins chatted on for a while and then one by one they started to drift off into their waking sleep.

Just then Spirit felt a prickling sensation, like a wave of energy pass through his flank. He knew by now what this meant and swam a short distance from the others. A larger pulse of energy flowed through him a few moments later and then suddenly Lucy was there in the water next to him, her hair floating around her like tendrils of fine seaweed, her night dress billowing around her like a jelly fish.

'Lucy!' exclaimed Spirit keenly. 'Where have you been?' Even though he could not read the expressions on human faces in the way that other humans can, Spirit was able to sense immediately that there was something wrong. Lucy greeted him as warmly as ever, but then took a long time to compose herself.

'Spirit, there's something I need to tell you' she said. He waited expectantly for her to continue speaking.

'There's a narrow estuary along the coast, where a river flows into the sea. There are various inlets along it and one inlet is fenced off. In that fenced-off inlet or lagoon, there's …., well.' Lucy paused again before continuing. 'There's a dolphin kept there. It's your mother Star-Gazer.'

Spirit was dumb-struck and at first didn't know what to say or how to react. A whirl of thoughts passed through his brain.

'I...., you.., how do you know?'

'You know that boy Paul?' continued Lucy. 'The one who I introduced you to the other day and who swam with us? He told me that he'd seen a dolphin kept prisoner in a lake. I didn't know whether to believe him at first, but I kept dreaming about the dolphin and I started to wonder if it was linked to you in some way. I didn't want to say anything to you in case Paul was making it all up, or if I was entirely wrong. But I've been able to reach out to the dolphin, like I do with you. I've met her. It's Star-Gazer.'

It was almost all too much for Spirit to take in.

'Why would she be held prisoner like that? Why would humans do that to her?' asked Spirit, shaking his head in shock and confusion.

'I, I don't know Spirit' admitted Lucy. 'I haven't been able to find out yet.'

'Is she well? Is she safe?' asked Spirit anxiously.

'I think she's terribly unhappy' admitted Lucy. 'She's fed alright, but she hates being there. She's lonely and she misses you and the pod.'

'Humans!' exclaimed Spirit. 'Humans did this, like they hunt for pilot whales and catch us in their nets. Why can't they just leave

214

us alone?' Spirit pulled away slightly from Lucy. 'I love you Lucy, but I don't like humans. They do bad stuff to us.'

'I don't know what to say Spirit' she replied. 'But I won't rest until we've been able to rescue her.

'If it weren't for you Lucy, maybe I'd believe everything that Storm says about humans. But I know you and I know that humans can be good and loving. It just makes it harder to understand when they do something terrible like this. What can we do? How can we save Star-Gazer?' Spirit looked intently at Lucy, but already her image was starting to fade in the water. He could tell that she was starting to tire and that soon she would disappear altogether. They only had a few seconds left.

'If only she could jump over the fence, or find a gap at the edge of it and force her way through, then she would be able to swim down the estuary and back to the sea' replied Lucy. 'Otherwise we will have to set her free.' Lucy's image faded into the water like a drop of ink. She was gone.

Spirit was left with a great and overwhelming sense of relief at the knowledge that his mother was alive, but also a terrible anxiety at the thought of her lonely plight. He looked back at where the rest of the pod were resting. Storm and Dancer had awoken and were quietly looking his way, as though they already knew that something was wrong.

'Storm, Dancer!' whispered Spirit so as not to wake the others. 'I need your help.'

Dad had enjoyed the castle, with its views across the hills towards the sea. He was beginning to feel more relaxed now and some of the stresses of his working life were dropping away. He'd missed Lucy and worried about her, but when he saw her again in the farmyard the other day when he'd arrived she'd seemed so happy and alive, that he realised that he'd been right to give her the freedom she needed. 'You shouldn't deny Lucy her true self' Thelma had said a few months before. 'If you deny Lucy her true self now, she will never be complete. There will always be a ghost of what might have been. She will be restless and unhappy for all her days.'

Dad had thought about Thelma's words many times since he'd met her and he pondered them again as he walked along the High Street of Merwater after Lucy had gone to find that boy Paul. 'But a Dolphin-Child doesn't stay a child for long' she'd continued. 'Within a year her gift will leave her' she went on 'and she'll be just a regular girl again into pop music and whatnot'. Thelma's words had assured him. He hoped she was right. What Lucy had inherited from Megan was both a blessing and a curse. He was well aware that all Lucy could think about were the blessings. All Dad could think about was the danger and the curse. Every day he wished that Megan was alive and well still. Every day her loss ached within him.

Dad had spoken to Thelma on the phone once or twice in the intervening months and several times since Lucy had come down to stay this summer. He looked forward to seeing her soon, but today he hoped to find Mrs Penhaligon. He'd come across the business card she'd given to Lucy at the supermarket the other day and Lucy had mentioned that she was helping out her sister in the shop. The door-bell tinkled as he pushed open the door of the gift shop and walked in.

The shop was cramped and full of curios and knick-knacks. Dad was relieved to see Mrs Penhaligon working at the till, but there were several customers waiting to pay and she was obviously very busy. He browsed the shelves while she served them.

'Oh Mr Parr, how are you?' Mrs Penhaligon said, glancing up and seeing him once things had calmed down. Dad approached her to pay for the postcards that he'd selected. Dad chatted to Mrs Penhaligon for a minute or two and then got to the point.

'Can I talk to you about Lucy for a moment?' he asked. 'I'm a little concerned about her. She's got ....well a lot going on in her life at the moment.'

'I know it must have been terribly hard for you and Lucy after your wife died' Mrs Penhaligon answered sympathetically.

'I don't mean just that' replied Dad. 'There's other stuff going on as well. She's passionate about sea life and dolphins in particular'. Dad wanted to say 'she's a Dolphin-Child', but he couldn't bring himself to say the words. Fortunately he didn't need to.

'Yes, I am aware' said Mrs Penhaligon quietly. 'She is a Dolphin-Child.'

'So you know?' asked Dad, the surprise showing in his voice. She nodded silently.

'It's hard for you of course, but I hope you're giving her the freedom she needs to understand what she is. It's very important that you do.'

'Do you think she will grow out of it?' he asked anxiously. He needed to know that someone other than Thelma believed that would be the case and that he would not regret it if he did give her freedom now.

'From what I know of the folklore' Mrs Penhaligon replied, 'more often than not children will grow out of it by the age of thirteen or so. Children can feel a terrible loss when it happens though...'

'But it's for the best when it does' Dad broke in quickly.

'That's something I wonder about' replied Mrs Penhaligon frankly. 'She has a gift, a very special one.'

'And I want her to lose it and be a normal child again' replied Dad.

'You want her to suffer that loss too?' asked Mrs Penhaligon.

'I have my reasons' he replied. 'I intend to protect my daughter and make sure she has a long and safe life. If you learn something that I may need to know to ensure that, you will tell me won't you?' Dad urged her. Mrs Penhaligon thought for a moment and then eventually nodded again.

'Yes of course. I understand your concern. If I do become aware of anything, I will certainly tell you' she assured him. 'Lucy's safety will always be paramount as far as I am concerned.' Dad made sure that Mrs Penhaligon took his mobile telephone number and left the shop with his postcards. He glanced at his watch. Lucy would be already there, waiting for him at the car park. He hurried off.

'I can't believe that Star-Gazer is still alive!' exclaimed Dancer in amazement. 'Is Lucy sure?'

'Lucy has travelled there with her mind, like she does when she stretches out to talk to me or you' replied Spirit 'and this boy Paul has seen a dolphin trapped in this inlet from the estuary. We have to go there and find her.'

'It is very dangerous for us to swim into the mouth of an estuary' warned Storm. 'The waters are shallow and mud banks block the way. It is very easy to become stranded. What's more the rubbish that humans leave in the water can cut you open and there is not the space to avoid it. Boats may come and if you are not careful their propellers will slice you up the back' Storm continued. You might swim to your death if you try it.'

'How can I not try to find her?' asked Spirit passionately.

'At least because you are smaller like me, you'll be more agile and better able to slip through small gaps' commented Dancer. 'Me too for that matter. Maybe we can go together?'

'We will discuss it with the pod at first light tomorrow morning' said Storm. 'Only then will we decide if you should try to reach her. It is too important a decision to be taken without talking it through carefully with the others. Now both of you, go and eat. You need to keep your strength up for tomorrow.'

Dad sat in the car waiting. Lucy was definitely very late now. They'd agreed to meet there after half an hour. Dad himself arrived five minutes after he'd meant to. Lucy was by now twenty five minutes late and she still hadn't showed up. He tapped the steering wheel fretfully. He hoped she was okay. She said she'd gone to find this boy Paul. Maybe she'd got caught up in some game or other. Still, it annoyed him if she didn't come back when she'd agreed to. He'd have to have words with her.

Suddenly, there she was standing next to the car window, tapping on the glass. She'd appeared from a direction that he did not expect. Next to her was a slightly built boy with curly hair. He looked a complete state. He seemed to be covered in a film of dry dusty mud and his face was streaked with marks where tears had partially washed the mud away. What's more a couple of bruises had appeared on his arms. Dad got out and quizzed them on what had happened. Lucy quickly told him that Paul was being bullied by a group of kids and that she had stepped in and got him out of there.

'You did the right thing Luce' Dad assured her. 'And you Paul. Are you feeling better now?' Paul nodded, still sniffing back his tears as he did so and Dad could tell that he wasn't really feeling that much better at all.

'We'd better get you home to your mum' he said. 'She needs to know what's happened so that she can do something about it. This is serious. You can't fight these battles on your own.' Paul sniffed again, as though the tears were just about to well up.

'Can I go and wash my face?' he asked, pointing to the public toilets at the corner of the car park.

'Of course' said Dad. 'You clean yourself up and then I'll drive you over to your mum's house.'

'Dad, Paul's Mum doesn't like me' said Lucy, as they waited for Paul to come back. 'It's because I'm,... well..... And I'm a bit afraid of her as well.'

'Don't worry Lucy' replied Dad. 'You can stay in the car if you like while I go and speak to Paul's mum. I'm really proud of you for helping Paul like that. You remind me so much of Megan, I mean Mum when she was younger.'

Lucy felt emotionally drained. It was so good to know that Dad was there to take control of things, talk to Mrs Treddinick and help Paul. She wished that she could just tell him about what Star-Gazer had said to Lucy when she'd reached out to her, so sad and alone there in that muddy inlet. If only Dad could just sort that out as well. She wanted to be able to tell him, but she knew that she could not. That was something that she and Spirit would have to sort out on their own.

Paul came back and Lucy and Dad drove him home, with Paul giving directions as they went. When they got there Lucy stayed in the car while Dad walked Paul up to the front door. She shrank

221

into her seat in case Mrs Treddinick spotted her. Instead Paul's mum ushered them both into the house and Lucy waited for what seemed like a very long time before Dad finally emerged again. As Dad walked back to the car, Lucy glanced up at the box room window over the front door. Paul was up there. He held up his palm to the glass of the window, as if to say goodbye. Dad climbed back into the car.

'Mrs Treddinick was very grateful to you for helping Paul. She's very concerned and she's going to have a word with some of the local parents.' He paused. 'She's a bit prickly, that lady. I hope they can sort their troubles out between them.' He started the engine.

'Come on, let's get home to the cottage. Bethany promised that she'd cook for us this evening. Something with lentils I think she said.'

All Spirit could dream about that night was his mother, alone in the muddy waters of the lagoon, sad and unhappy. He woke as soon as the rays of light broke over the horizon and started circling restlessly while the others roused themselves from sleep. As soon as Dancer awoke, she soon brought the others to order.

'It's amazing that Star-Gazer is still alive' exclaimed Summer when she heard, as her calf No-Name nudged her playfully.

'And it was your human Lucy who found this out?' asked Chaser thoughtfully. 'Maybe that's the reason you are a Child-

222

Seer; not to find us fish but help protect us when we are in danger.'

'The point is that we must do something to help Star-Gazer' said Storm. 'But she is trapped behind some sort of steel netting up the estuary. It is perilously dangerous to venture up there. It would be a tragedy to lose another one of us in an attempt to save Star-Gazer.'

'Can't the human child save Star-Gazer?' asked Moonlight. 'Surely we should just leave it up to her?'

'No!' Spirit almost shouted. 'I know that Lucy will do everything that she can to save Star-Gazer. She is human but in her soul she is one of us. But it was humans that took my mother. We dolphins should first do everything in our power to help ourselves. I know we can do it.' The other dolphins pondered this for a few moments.

'Then Breeze and I should go and save Star-Gazer' said Chaser. 'We are the strongest and the fastest swimmers.'

'But you are also fully grown' replied Summer. 'How will you get up narrow channels and past the mud-banks?'

'That's true' said Moonlight. 'Spirit and Dancer are both much lighter than you. Spirit especially.'

'And she's my mother after all. It should be me that finds her.'

'Isn't Spirit too young for such an escapade?' asked Breeze. 'He may have taken his coming of age swim, but he almost died in the process and he still has much to learn.' There were murmurs of agreement.

'I agree with Summer' said Storm eventually. He looked serious and thoughtful. 'Spirit is the lightest and smallest of all of us. He stands the best chance of getting through. He has learnt much in the last few months and is a much wiser dolphin than he was. Also he has Lucy on his side and that is an advantage that cannot be underestimated'. The dolphins of the pod continued to discuss the subject. Eventually it was agreed one by one that Spirit and Dancer should go, but come back immediately if things got difficult.

'And remember', Storm continued 'it will be high tide half way through the morning, but then the tide will drop back rapidly. You do not have much time in the estuary. You must get there quickly if you are to come back to us safely. Dancer, it's your job to make sure Spirit doesn't get too carried away. You must be the voice of reason. Spirit, you must listen and obey Dancer if she orders you to turn back.

Normally Spirit would have swum to Old Man's Cove in the hope that Lucy would be there, but this morning such thoughts were forgotten. The whole pod swam with Dancer and Spirit to within a couple of hundred meters of the mouth of the estuary. The silt laden waters were discoloured and cloudy. Fresh water mingled with salt and tasted completely different to the familiar sea water that Spirit was used to. The tide was reaching its highest point and Spirit and Dancer swam off with a sense of urgency and danger.

'Are we mad to do this?' asked Spirit, suddenly anxious and doubtful.

'You know that until Star-Gazer is safely back with the rest of the pod, none of us will rest' Dancer assured him. 'This is absolutely the right thing to do, even if it is dangerous and ….exciting.' Dancer shot Spirit a bright look. 'Come on, we've got work to do.'

At first the swimming was easy. The estuary wasn't particularly wide, but at high tide it was quite deep enough for them to be able to navigate the waters without difficulty. Every so often they looked nervously over the surface of the water. Densely wooded slopes rose off to each side of the estuary, interspersed with the occasional isolated house. 'So those are the boxes that humans live in' thought Spirit to himself. 'I don't know how they manage it.'

The visibility was poor, but they were able to compensate by using their clicking as sonar to detect underwater obstacles. They spotted a couple of mooring ropes stretched tight across their path and swum around them just in time. They each took particular care to sense the waters, so that as soon as the tide began to turn and to flow out again, they would know and be prepared to get out.

Suddenly the deep channel that they had been swimming up appeared to finish. Instead, in front of them was a submerged mud-bank, with three distinct streams of water flowing in, each with a different taste and character. There was much less clearance between them and the mud below them now and suddenly they both became aware of the risk they were taking by going any further.

'Which way shall we go then?' asked Dancer uncertainly. Spirit had little more idea than she did, but he knew that the human town called Merwater lay to the left of them and he guessed that it was more likely to be in that direction than the other.

'This way' he said as he swam into the narrower channel. Dancer followed him, but she was bigger than Spirit and was feeling increasingly vulnerable and uneasy. It got narrower and narrower and at the same time the taste of the water seemed to become fresher. They both realised that this was some tiny stream feeding into the estuary waters and they only just had enough room to turn in to go back.

'I suppose we'd better try the next channel' said Spirit, once they were back in the deeper water.

'We don't have much time' warned Dancer anxiously. 'Remember we've got to do this before the tide turns, or we'll be stuck here'. The two dolphins headed up the next channel, which became deeper and broader again reassuringly quickly. It was still hard to see though and the soft mud seemed to absorb their echo location clicks. It became much harder to ascertain where the edge was. Spirit broke the surface of the water to look and was alarmed to see the silhouettes of two humans looming above him. They seemed to have long rods in their hands. They stumbled back in surprise at seeing two dolphins in such shallow water. Spirit and Dancer flicked their tails to head on past the two fishermen on the bank. After a minute or so they slowed down again and Dancer paused to sense the water.

'I think the tide is turning Spirit' she said, 'we should turn back now.'

'No, just a bit further' exclaimed Spirit. Suddenly, they both heard something.

'Is it? … It's the sound of a dolphin isn't it?' asked Dancer. Spirit let off a burst of whistles and clicks and then paused to listen for a reply. Nothing. He tried again. This time they heard a feint sound in response.

'Come on!' Spirit exclaimed, 'let's get closer.' They pushed forward and beyond them was something that looked like it might be a closed-link fence stretched across the channel. But the silt had settled there and as the two dolphins progressed, it boiled up into their eyes and face and then became more solid. Even Spirit could sense now that the waters of the tide were beginning to turn and retreat. The water level would soon drop and with it any chance they might have of escape.

'It's me! Spirit!' called Spirit with all his might. 'We're going to save you Star-Gazer! We're going to get you out of here!' They stopped and listened. Suddenly they heard a reply, the sound muffled by the mud and silt around them.

'I love you Spirit, but get out of the estuary now. Come back after the rains have come! They wash the channels clean of mud! Go!'

'I love you Star-Gazer! We will come back!' shouted Spirit, but still he lingered there hoping that there was something, anything that he could do to set his mother free.

'Spirit we must go now!' commanded Dancer urgently. Reluctantly, Spirit turned to follow his friend. They were so close, but the water level had already dropped. It was not safe to stay.

On the other side of the mud and the fence, Star-Gazer was elated that she had suddenly heard the voice of her son, but was scared for him in equal measure. The inlet where she was trapped was deeper than the channel on the other side and she raced round it in agitation, trying to leap from the water. When she had first been trapped there, she had tried many times to leap the closed link fence, but it was no good. She did not have enough clearance to make a really good leap and there was also a submerged cable stretched a couple of meters in front of the fence which made a good jump impossible.

Her heart raced and her thoughts burst with a thousand ideas. Meanwhile Spirit and Dancer struggled to get back to deeper water.

They seemed to be slithering over mud all the time now and Spirit could tell from her movements that Dancer was starting to get panicky.

'Don't worry Dancer' we're almost there now he tried to reassure her. They shot past the two humans who seemed to want to wade into the water to greet them and swam quickly on until the channel merged with the deeper water of the estuary.

'Wow, that was scarily close!' exclaimed Dancer, breathing a sigh of relief. They made their way back to the open sea to tell the rest of the pod what had happened. There was only one thought going through Spirit's head though. 'Star-Gazer's alive. She's alive!'

Chapter Fifteen:

Lucy had had an exhausting, emotional day. Not only had she used all the powers of her mind to find and talk to Star-Gazer, but she had summoned up enough energy to speak to Spirit too. She felt drained and weary. Despite her tiredness though, Lucy's mind was racing as she lay in bed.

Lucy had been so happy to be able to tell Spirit that his mother was alive, yet her friend's reaction had in a way surprised her. Normally he seemed warm and happy to be around humans, but the thought that his mother had been captured by some human had made him steely and determined.

'I am so lonely here' Star-Gazer had told her. 'I miss Spirit, Summer and the others so much. Please help me if you can'.

Like Spirit, Lucy wondered what sort of a person would capture a wild creature such as Star-Gazer who had spent her life swimming the wide open sea and imprison her instead in a muddy lagoon. Perhaps Spirit was right to learn to fear humans she thought and the harm that they could bring. It would be safer for him that way, than if he thought everyone could be trusted like her.

Lucy's mind wandered on to Paul. He had seemed so small and abject as he stood there surrounded by those kids, throwing clumps of earth at him. She knew that dolphins could be mean too sometimes, but not like this. 'They're more civilized than people' she thought. Maybe she was romanticising the lives of dolphins. Perhaps they could be as cruel to each other as humans, but she didn't think so.

As they had walked down the bottom of the walled stream to where Dad was waiting in the car park and while Paul still shook with tears and shock, he'd said to her 'I want to be with Spirit. I want to be a Dolphin-Child like you. You've got to let me.'

Lucy had not known what to say. She didn't know how she'd become a Dolphin-Child, or why. All she knew was that for as long as she could remember she'd dreamt every night of dolphins; vivid dreams that had been almost as real to her as her waking moments. She hadn't even heard the term 'Dolphin-Child' until Paul had used it. She'd had no idea before her trip to the museum that someone like Susan Penhaligon had once lived, or that there had been other children like her over the generations. She didn't think you could choose to be a Dolphin-Child.

'It's not like there's a magic spell I can teach you to turn you into a Dolphin-Child' she said as they carefully stepped from stone to stone.

'You can show me' replied Paul. 'I can learn from you and copy you. I swum with Spirit didn't I? I can do that again. I'll learn' he continued earnestly. 'You'll see!' Lucy wasn't so sure. It was

231

something that had to come instinctively, from deep inside you. It wasn't a skill that you could learn, like riding a bike, or doing tricks on a skateboard.

'I can certainly let you swim with Spirit again' she reassured him, though really Lucy did not know exactly what to say to the small boy. It sounded as though he was still very close to tears and she did not want to upset him again. Paul nodded.

'I'd like to be a dolphin and swim away for ever' he said 'as far as I can get from this dump' he added. Lucy smiled despite herself, but at the same time she felt uneasy, though she couldn't say exactly why. Paul paused.

'Up here' he said. They had reached the point where the walled stream had passed under the High Street, but the tide was part way in and sea water had flooded up the stream from where it flowed into the harbour. There were hand and foot holds in the steep stone sides and Paul climbed up to the top of the wall with ease. Lucy followed him more slowly and cautiously, wary of slipping backwards. When she got to the top Paul pointed down a narrow alley.

'Car park's just down there' he said. 'We'll find your Dad's car in no time.' Lucy glanced at her watch. She was much later than she'd promised to be and she didn't like to think what Dad would say when she turned up with a strange boy all covered in mud and smeared tears. Still, she had to do something. Things had got too serious. A grown-up needed to know what was happening to Paul.

He obviously couldn't cope on his own anymore or… Well, she didn't like to imagine.

Once they'd driven back to the cottage, Lucy asked Dad if she could wander down to the farm and the studio. Dad said he'd be down in a few minutes and hoped that whatever Bethany had cooked was going to be good, because he was feeling hungry.

The late afternoon sun flooded the valley and swifts wheeled above her in the air catching midges and flies on the wing. There was a low hum of insects in the hedgerow. It felt strange not to be living with Bethany in the studio anymore. It was great being with Dad in the luxury of the holiday cottage, but it felt somehow as though she were missing out on the fun of Bethany's bohemian lifestyle.

As Lucy walked in from the lane into the farmyard, she saw Mary and Darren sitting on the doorstep of the farmhouse, each with a mug in their hands. Darren raised his hand in greeting.

'Hello there young Lucy!' he called in a friendly voice.

'Had any adventures today then Lucy?' said Mary. Lucy walked up to them, but hardly knew where to begin.

'I heard you helped out a young lad who was in a spot of bother' continued Mary before Lucy had a chance to reply. Lucy looked surprised.

'I know, I know. News travels fast round here' Mary said. 'I was in town and I couldn't help but over-hear while I was picking up a few things in the shop. Mrs Treddinick is very upset about what happened to her Paul.'

'Well, you know, I had to do something' was all that Lucy could think to say in reply.

'You were a brave girl and you did the right thing' added Darren. Lucy felt awkward and embarrassed. She changed the subject.

'Mary, Darren, do you know a big house with its own lagoon in the woods off the estuary?' she asked.

'Why let me see' said Darren thoughtfully. 'That would be the Penrose place wouldn't it?' Mary nodded. 'It was bought twenty years ago or more by Norman Penrose who if memory serves was some fellow that had made it big in banking in London. Came down here to retire with his wife. Do you know anything about that place Mary love?' he asked, looking at his wife.

'Oh I think he was into sailing boats. Had one moored by the mouth of the river and liked to race. Don't know what's happened to him. It's gone quiet down there recently.' They chatted a bit more.

'You go and find Bethany' said Mary. 'A very tasty smell has been wafting out of the kitchen of the studio this last hour or so. I think you and your Dad are in for a treat this evening.'

Lucy gave them a little wave and strolled on round the corner to the studio. There was a small patch of grass between it and the hedge of the field and Bethany had set up a trestle table and brought the kitchen chairs outside. Crockery and glasses were set on the table. Lucy walked into the studio and was confronted by a warm and savoury smell from the oven. Bethany looked up from her cooking and gave her a brief affectionate hug.

'I thought we could all eat outside this evening and enjoy the late afternoon sunshine'.

'Lentils?' asked Lucy, inspecting a pot. Bethany laughed.

'No I just told your Dad that to wind him up' she explained. 'I've made two types of quiche, got new potatoes with mint, salad and freshly cooked bread. There's even a splash of wine for us grown-ups. Not a lentil in sight'.

'Mm! Sounds good' replied Lucy. Bethany busied herself with the finishing touches to the salad and Lucy wandered back into the work area where Bethany's oil paints and canvasses were arranged.

Recently Bethany had done some sketches of Lucy. One was of Lucy sitting on a large rock at the edge of the sea, her legs folded beneath her, looking back over her shoulder towards the lapping waves. Lucy had felt self-conscious posing for Bethany while her aunt sketched with rapid strokes of her pencil. Yet she was pleased with the result and Dad had asked whether he might have a copy when he had seen it. The sketch was pinned to a piece of board now leaning against the wall.

Next to it was a sketch of a woman in the same pose, seated upon the very same rock looking out to sea. It was unmistakably a picture of her mother.

'I'm sorry Kiddo' said Bethany coming up behind her and laying a hand upon her shoulder. 'I should have put that one away. It's just that…when I look at you I can't help but think of Megan'.

Lucy didn't know what to say, but instead leant instinctively in towards her aunt and the comfort that her presence gave. Bethany gave her shoulder a squeeze. Being close to Bethany helped her feel close to the memory of Mum. Curious though the picture was, it felt good to think that Bethany was still thinking of Mum and that she wasn't just a faded photograph in an album.

They stood quietly for a moment. Lucy wished that she could walk down to the sea and find her mother on a rock, looking up at her with a smile and waving as though she had never been away. She wished with all her being that Mum could come back to her and for a moment she felt the pang of loss within her again. Then she thought of Spirit and a curious thought seized her that would not leave her.

Just then Dad walked in through the open door of the studio. Bethany stirred herself into life and quickly covered the picture of Megan before Dad spotted it. Dad was wearing his shorts again but his legs had by now lost the worst of their pallor.

Dad was full of the news of the day and before long, they were sitting at the trestle table with the food spread in front of them, eating and chatting. Bethany had not yet heard about Paul and the gang of children, but she knew what Lucy had told her. Some local families distrusted Dolphin-Children because of what Susan

Penhaligon had done so many years before. Bethany looked at Lucy with quiet, insightful eyes.

'So what happened when you took Paul to the door?' she asked Dad, turning her attention back to him.

'She turned a bit funny when I said I was Lucy's dad' he explained, a forkful of food half way to his mouth. 'I don't know why, but she appeared to shrink away from me as though I had some disease. Like you say Luce, she doesn't seem to like you does she?' he said matter-of-factly.

'I don't think so' Lucy answered cautiously. She was reluctant to start explaining why.

'Apparently Mrs Treddinick has had her own troubles recently' Bethany broke in, before Dad could ask any more difficult questions of Lucy. 'I think she's a bit off with everyone really.'

'Oh well maybe that explains it' said Dad through a mouthful of food. 'She said something about 'you people' and looked at me as though I'd just beamed down from Mars or something' he continued. 'Anyway I told her what had happened and she looked set to blow a gasket. At the end though she did say how grateful she was to Lucy. It's a good thing his mother knows, kids can't cope with that kind of bullying on their own.'

They chatted on about Paul, where to go in Cornwall, the farm and all manner of other things. The only thing they didn't really talk about was Lucy's connection to dolphins and the time that she had spent with Spirit since getting there. She certainly couldn't tell them both about reaching out to Star-Gazer that afternoon. Lucy could tell that Dad didn't really want to talk about it and Bethany was wary of raising the subject in his presence too. She and Dad had reached an uneasy truce on the subject. Bethany brought out summer pudding and ice cream and they feasted on it greedily. All the while the thought that had struck Lucy before dinner kept running through her head so powerfully, that in the end she was hardly aware of what Dad and Bethany were saying at all.

'Are you alright Kiddo?' asked Bethany. It took Lucy a moment to realise that she was being spoken to.

'Oh yes, I'm fine' she answered eventually. The sun had dipped below the hills and it was practically dark. The candle that Bethany had put on the trestle table was burning low. A couple of moths buzzed around it whilst above them the pipistrelle bats swooped low over their heads.

'I suppose we should be heading on back to the cottage now' said Dad, glancing at his watch. 'It's been a delicious meal, but I for one am exhausted.'

'Oh!' said Lucy suddenly feeling anxious. 'I must help Bethany with the washing up'. She shot her aunt an imploring glance which Bethany seemed to understand.

'It's alright John, I'll walk Lucy up to the cottage as soon as we've finished drying up.' Dad strolled off up the lane and Bethany and Lucy carried the chairs and plates back to the studio kitchen. Lucy picked up a tea towel.

'Forget the washing up' commanded Bethany, 'I can do that in the morning. Sit down and tell me what's on your mind.'

Lucy poured out how with Paul's help she'd been able to focus her mind, find the murky lagoon and speak to Star-Gazer there.

'So you want to help Spirit's mother then?' said Bethany thoughtfully.

'I have to. She's suffering Bethany! She's so alone and sad, I don't think she'll hold out much longer otherwise.'

'You've got to find the place for real first. And you can't just knock on the door and say let my dolphin go.'

'Paul can show me' replied Lucy, 'and Darren says it's the old Penrose Place on the estuary'.

'I can see you've been doing your research' nodded Bethany approvingly. She paused and looked intently at her niece. 'But..., I can tell that's not all that's troubling you.' Lucy looked back at Bethany and as she did so a sob caught painfully in her throat and her eyes welled up with tears. She couldn't help herself and she cried for everything that had happened over the last year or so and for everything that might have been.

'There there' said Bethany, rocking Lucy gently in her arms. 'It's okay now.' After a few minutes Lucy was able to compose herself and wiped her eyes. Bethany smiled gently.

'What's up Kiddo?'

'It's just that... Well. I feel that Spirit is part of me and that I am part of him. He lost his mother and now he's found her again. But I....' Lucy broke down in tears again.

'... But you have not been able to find yours' said Bethany, finally finishing the sentence for her. Lucy nodded sadly. 'Listen

239

Lucy' whispered Bethany quietly, stroking her hair. 'There is a symmetry between your life and Spirit's, but it does not go that far. It cannot. Mum is gone. We buried her together. It was the saddest day of our lives, but we cannot bring her back with prayers and wishes, no matter how much we try. There are certain things we cannot change and that we just have to accept, no matter how painful they are.'

'But it's so unfair!' wept Lucy into her aunt's arms.

Presently, when Lucy had recovered sufficiently, washed her face and blown her nose, Bethany walked Lucy up the lane to the cottage. Dad had been reading in bed and padded down in his pyjamas to let Lucy in. As she climbed the stairs she heard Bethany murmur something to him about Lucy having had a long and emotional day. In the privacy of her own little room in the cottage, she sat cross legged on the bed and stretched out with her mind to Spirit and broke the news to him that his mother was alive. Her own sense of loss seemed less acute now and Spirit's happiness and determination were overwhelming. She had to put aside her own pain and focus on saving Star-Gazer.

So there Lucy lay, her mind racing, in her little bed in the cottage under the wide starry night. She imagined that somewhere far above, one star was sparkling down on her more than the rest. The thought comforted her and eventually she was able to slip into a dreamless sleep.

The next morning Dad awoke with a start. There was noise in the kitchen and his immediate thought was that there were burglars in the cottage.

'Who's there?' he called warily as he came down the stairs.

'Dad, the milks gone off' Lucy replied.

'Goodness Lucy, it's six o'clock in the morning!' exclaimed Dad. 'You should be snoozing in bed'.

'But we're going out' Lucy replied matter of factly.

'Out?'

'I have to see Spirit' she replied. 'You promised. Either let me go alone or come with me, but you said…' Dad put up his hand and nodded, still bleary eyed. It wasn't what he wanted to hear, but he knew that it was an inevitable part of being down here.

'Okay, okay' he replied, 'let me get my jeans and a t-shirt on.' Lucy wanted to cycle up to the cove and assured him that there were two bikes at the farm they could borrow. Mary was already up and doing her rounds of the farm as they tumbled out of the cottage and walked the short distance to the farmyard where the bicycles were kept in one of the sheds. She waved cheerily at them.

Dad, still half asleep, wondered what he was doing there and why they couldn't just drive up the lane like any sane person at six fifteen in the morning. Instead he soon found himself peddling up the lane next to Lucy on a bicycle that was way too small for him. He hadn't cycled for what seemed like years and his legs felt like lead. Still, it felt strangely exhilarating to be up so early in the morning and to see the day stirring.

Dad had never actually met Spirit and he had to admit that he was curious. Of course they were beautiful animals and if he hadn't been so worried about the danger they represented to Lucy, he'd have been thrilled to see them. As it was, he was there only grudgingly and against his better nature to try to protect his daughter until all of this was over and she could be normal again. He hoped it would be soon.

They came up to the main coast road and cycled along it for a short distance before Lucy pulled off by the gate with the stile and sign to the path. They hoisted their bikes over and leant them out of sight against the hedge on the other side. Lucy clearly knew the path well and Dad followed her, still stifling the occasional yawn.

Dad slipped and slithered his way down the steep path leading to Old Man's Cove, while Lucy bounded down it in front of him. He felt like he'd done a day's work already and when they finally got to the bottom, he planted himself on a boulder to recover. It was a lovely little spot he thought, just the place for a picnic and a paddle. Dad looked out to sea, irresistibly drawn to the far horizon and the prospect of being able to see a dolphin break the surface of the sea. He thought he saw one, but it was just a wave.

In the meantime, out of sight, Lucy had squeezed herself into her wetsuit and pulling up the zip at the back, she walked over the pebbles on her bare feet. Then she made her way down to the shoreline and stood with her feet in the water, staring intently out to sea. Dad was struck at how focused and alert his daughter was and how…., well how much like Megan she was in the early days of their marriage. All he wanted to do was to protect Lucy from all this, he thought to himself. All this danger in beauty. Was he right to trust Thelma Merryweather so much?

He thought about dragging Lucy away, up the path, into the car and back home as far away as they could possibly get from the coast. Yet at the same time Dad knew that it was futile and that the force that exerted itself on Lucy would still apply wherever he took her. He could never stop her reaching out to Spirit and the other dolphins with her mind if she wanted. It was no good; he knew he could not protect his little girl in the way that he would like. 'Ride the wave, ride the wave' he murmured to himself. 'Time will do its work and she will be a normal girl again.' Lucy glanced back at Dad.

'I'm sure he will come to us soon' she called with a smile. She turned back to look at the sea. Minutes past and Dad could see that Lucy started to shift restlessly as she waited. He decided to slip off his shoes and socks, roll up his jeans and wade out into the shallows to where Lucy was waiting.

'What's up then Luce?' he asked conversationally. Lucy shook her head.

'I have an idea…but…' she replied, trailing off. Dad could tell that she was reluctant to tell him and he didn't press the issue. It was natural enough that she would not want to tell him everything that was going on, after all the resistance that he had put up to this dolphin business in the past.

More time slipped by and from the expression on Lucy's face, it was obvious that she no longer thought that Spirit would be coming.

'Don't worry' he said, 'I'm sure he'll come some other day'. Inside though, Dad was secretly pleased. Was this a tell tale sign that the bonds between girl and dolphin were already weakening? He hoped so, though he could tell that Lucy was a little upset.

'I have to reach out to him' Lucy replied simply. 'With my mind I mean.' Dad watched as Lucy walked over to a boulder and settled down to focus herself and attain the mental state necessary to reach out to Spirit. Despite the fact that Lucy was his daughter and that they shared the same house, Dad had never actually seen Lucy do this before. He felt like an interloper, rudely intruding on this private moment. He'd heard a little about it, but even Thelma Merryweather didn't know exactly how it happened. It seemed to be a mystery to all but Lucy herself.

Dad watched curiously. There was not much to see, but after a while it seemed as though Lucy had become completely disconnected from her immediate surroundings and that her mind was somewhere else entirely. Dad started to look around distractedly. With a start that made him half jump with surprise, Lucy came to herself again and sprung up from the boulder where she had been sitting. She walked up to him and looked at him urgently.

'Dad' she said. 'I know you're not going to like this, but there are some things that I have to do today …. alone.' Dad looked back at her, puzzled and surprised. 'I'd like to tell you but, … well I don't know how to. Please let me do this thing!' she implored him. 'I promise I'll keep safe and that I won't do anything stupid.' Dad thought for a moment.

'Do I have a choice?' he asked sadly and quietly. Lucy gave the slightest of shakes of her head. He hated this, he really hated it. All Dad's instincts told him to tell her that no, she was his child, that he would protect her and that she must stay with him. Yet, as he looked into her eyes, he knew that it was pointless to say so.

'Go on then' he said eventually, giving her hand a little squeeze. 'But I want you back safe and sound by two' he added 'or I'll be coming to find you'. She squeezed his hand in return and then without a moment's hesitation Lucy turned and started to clamber up the steep path out of the cove.

Chapter Sixteen:

'Well, what happened?' asked Chaser expectantly as Spirit and Dancer swum up to the mouth of the estuary. Dancer caught his gaze, then looked away with a pained look in her eyes.

'So you couldn't free her then?' he asked.

'We found her' replied Spirit defiantly. 'We spoke to her. We weren't close enough to see her and we weren't able to save her there and then. But we're going to' he added. 'We'll figure out a way, somehow.'

They swam on with Chaser until they joined the rest of the pod. A light breeze had picked up. It whisked up the water into small waves, carrying fine sea spray into the warm air. Sea gulls wheeled lazily on the current and nearby a sailing boat was making its way towards the mouth of the estuary, its sails taut against the wind. Once they had found the rest of the pod, they all turned and swum back towards the open seas again, talking as they swam with the rhythmic undulating beats of their tail flukes.

'Star-Gazer's okay then is she?' asked Summer anxiously. 'She's well?'

'We didn't manage to speak properly' Spirit replied. 'It was barely more than a few words really. But no, I don't think she's well. She's trapped and unhappy and she needs our help.'

Dancer quickly explained how they had approached the inlet where Star-Gazer was being held, but that as the tide turned the level of the water started to drop and they were afraid of finding themselves stranded on the mud.

'So the inlet where Star-Gazer is held is behind a metal fence like a stiff fishing net that is stretched across the opening?' asked Storm once they had explained everything that had happened. It was Storm's habit to repeat back what he had just been told, so that he was sure that he understood it clearly. 'Star-Gazer would have leapt the fence already if she could' he went on thoughtfully. 'Is there anything else that you learned that might help?'

'Well' replied Spirit. 'It is the silt that stops us getting close to the metal net thing. It seems to have accumulated around the fence, perhaps because the metal slows the current there and allows it to settle. But Star-Gazer said that when the rains come, the silt will be washed away. Then we might be able to get near enough to it to find a way of getting through.'

'But why have they imprisoned her there?' asked Moonlight. ''What do they want with her? Why don't they just set her free?'

'I, I don't know' replied Spirit sadly.

'Who knows why humans do the things that they do?' said Chaser. 'We could study them for a hundred years and they would still be a mystery to us. Humans say that they like us, then they trap us. They are not to be trusted.'

Spirit would have liked to speak up for humans at that moment, except that he himself was having doubts. He cared deeply for Lucy and when he had been trapped the human from the fishing boat had come and cut him free. But now that he knew that humans had trapped Star-Gazer, he wasn't so sure.

Storm seemed to sense his doubt and questioning. He himself was wary of humans and had often warned Spirit and the other dolphins against them, but this time he did not agree with Chaser as he might have on other occasions.

'You have both done well young Spirit and young Dancer' Storm said as they all swam out into deeper waters. 'You may not yet have managed to free Star-Gazer, but you have learned more than you knew before and knowledge is power. We can use it when the time is right. What more can you discover about the humans that have taken her prisoner?' he asked.

Spirit knew what Storm wanted to say. He wanted to say 'Speak to Lucy. Find out what she knows'. It was the obvious thing to do. Yet strangely, though he felt as close to Lucy as any other living being, he felt reluctant to do so. He wanted to be an equal to Lucy. She had saved his life once and he owed everything to her. But that was all the more reason not to rush to her now, but instead to try to figure out an answer to their problems himself.

'I, well…. I want to prove to Lucy that we dolphins can look after ourselves' he replied eventually. Storm stopped swimming and so all of the rest of the pod paused in the water to rest a while. Storm took a long calm look deep into Spirit's eyes.

'It is good that you are proud young Spirit and that you want to find your own answers alone and without assistance. Yet now is the time that you should make use of all of the gifts that you have at your disposal. Star-Gazer is in trouble. Your special connection to Lucy might enable us to save her.'

'That's right' added Summer, while No-name snuggled into his mothers flank. 'There was a time that we thought that you were a Child-Seer in order to help us find fish. Now I'm starting to think that you have been chosen as a Child-Seer for a much more important reason. Perhaps your destiny is to save Star-Gazer and other fellow dolphins who may be in trouble.'

'I agree' said Storm. 'Star-Gazer needs Lucy right now just as much as she needs you. Star-Gazer's fate is tangled up with the humans that caught her. We need a human to guide us through the world above water where we cannot go.' Spirit looked from Storm, to Summer and then to Dancer.

'But I can't rely on Lucy to help every time we are in trouble' replied Spirit in a small voice.

'Listen to me Spirit' said Storm seriously. 'You have an extraordinary ability, one which no other dolphin that I know shares. You are more closely bound to Lucy than we can understand. She is almost part of you. To ignore the knowledge that she can share with you is like ignoring the evidence of your own eyes.'

249

Spirit let Storm and Summer's words sink in. He knew that what they were telling him was true. He had to stretch out to Lucy and speak to her.

Spirit settled down and tried to focus his mind on his task. It was difficult and he hardly knew where to start. He could not appear to Lucy as she could appear to him. He had to somehow summon her to him. It had come naturally and easily to him that time with the little girl on the rock. This time he wasn't so sure.

All that he had learned was that he had to create a sense of urgency in his own mind which he could then project into hers, so that she knew that something was wrong and would come to him. He had only tried this once or twice and it was still a new experience for him. He felt the others all watching him, wondering what he was going to do. That made him feel self-conscious and it became harder than ever for him to focus his mind in the way that he knew he had to. He tried turning away from the others so that he could not see them, but they simply swam round him, curious to know what he was doing. Exasperated, Spirit realised that it was not going to work. He felt as angry with himself as he did with the others. With a flick of his tail flukes he propelled himself away from them. Fortunately they hung back and did not follow. He needed to compose his mind before he tried again.

Suddenly though, the shape of Lucy seemed to swim into focus in front of his eyes. There she was, her hair billowing out around her in the water like the tentacles of a sea anemone.

'Lucy!' he exclaimed, surprised at her appearance. 'I've been trying to reach you, but I didn't think it was working. How did you know I needed to see you?' Lucy pulled the corners of her mouth up into what Spirit now knew was called a smile.

'I didn't' she said. 'I thought that you would meet me at the cove this morning. I've been waiting there for you but you didn't come. I thought that it was because I was with my Dad and that he had frightened you away.'

'No' he said. 'I didn't know about your father. I would have come to you but, well I went to see if I could find Star-Gazer.' Spirit quickly explained all that had happened.

'So we've both found her in our different ways' said Lucy when Spirit had finished his story. 'She must be glad to know that she has not been forgotten. But she is unhappy and unwell and we still have to do something to help her. Somehow we've got to save her.'

'I know' replied Spirit. 'Storm and Summer believe that the reason I am a Child-Seer is so that you can help us save Star-Gazer and other dolphins like her. Do you think that's true?'

'I, I don't know' replied Lucy hesitantly. 'You know what Spirit? Sometimes when I look at people walking down the street, I half close my eyes and imagine what it must be like to look at them through a dolphin's eyes. I imagine that I am a dolphin disguised as a human and walking on dry land. Normal life seems so strange and weird when I do. Who needs cars and houses when you can glide effortlessly through the water? If it weren't for Dad

251

and Bethany and my friend Amy back home, I think I'd rather spend my life living in the sea with you.' Lucy paused and looked directly at Spirit as she floated there, suspended in the water.

'What I mean is that I can't say why you and I have been given this gift. The most important thing for me though is that we are joined together somehow. I will do everything I can to save Star-Gazer. All I want is that we stay linked to each other for all our lives. That's all that I ask for. It's more important than anything.' Lucy stretched out her hand to Spirit and though she could not physically touch him when she came to him as a vision, he could feel the tingle of energy pass from her ghostly hand to his flank.

'What will you do now?' asked Spirit simply. Lucy shook her head.

'Well I've got to go and find a way to help Star-Gazer of course. Somehow I'll get away from Dad and then I'll go and find Star-Gazer for real this time' she said. I'll find the people who took her. And then....'

As Spirit looked on, Lucy started to fade away into the water. He realised that her energy had run out. A moment later she was gone.

'Take care Lucy!' he murmured quietly to himself as her shadow melted into the water around him.

By the time Lucy had scrambled to the top of the path from the cove where she had left Dad standing, she was completely out of breath. It was only once she got to the top that she realised that she was still wearing her wet-suit. Fortunately she had slung her bag with her normal clothes over her shoulder. There was no one else around except for a couple of disinterested-looking sheep and so she changed quickly there in the middle of the field while she recovered her breath.

She wondered whether Dad would appear at the top of the cliff telling her that he had changed his mind and that she must come back to the cottage with him, but he didn't. Once she had changed she quickly found her bike and heaved it over the gate. She got on.

'What now?' she asked herself. There was only one thing for it. She had to find Paul and get him to take her to the Penrose place, as Darren and Mary had called it. She wondered what the house was really like and whether the people there would be friendly or hostile.

It was true that Paul had helped her visualise the path he had taken that had enabled Lucy to reach out to Star-Gazer, but she did not think she could find the route in real life on her own. She needed help, but the idea of knocking on Paul's front door and speaking to Mrs Treddinick just made her feel anxious in the pit of her stomach. Paul's mother was scary and clearly didn't like her at all. There was nothing for it though. Lucy started pedalling.

When she got there Lucy was out of breath again and felt hot and sweaty. It was still relatively early and she wondered if Paul would be up or whether he would still be sleeping. She got off the bike and leant it against the wall in front of Paul's house. The front garden was overgrown and she could see that the paintwork of the living room windowsill at the front of the house was old and peeling. After Dad had taken Paul home the other day while Lucy had waited in the car, Paul had appeared in the window above the front door. She hoped that that was his bedroom window.

In films people would always throw a pebble up at windows. The little stone would clatter on the glass and then the boy or girl inside would look outside to see who had thrown it. She looked around for a pebble, but she could not see one at first and then the only one she could find was incredibly small. She flung it up at the window pane but the pebble was so tiny she could not even tell whether she hit the glass or not. In any case it made no sound.

Lucy looked for another pebble in Mrs Treddinick's front garden and this time found one that was so large it would be more likely to crack the glass instead. Lucy picked it up and looked at it uncertainly.

'I think we've had enough of kids chucking stuff at Paul.' The words made Lucy start with fright. She looked up and saw Mrs Treddinick standing in her dressing gown at the open front door with a milk bottle in her hand. She looked tired and drawn. 'But it's not you I've got to worry about on that score' she sighed. 'I suppose you'd better come in.'

Lucy felt desperately uncomfortable under Mrs Treddinick's unsympathetic gaze, but she had no choice. She followed Paul's Mum into the house.

'Paul!' called Mrs Treddinick. 'Your friend's here.' Paul and his sister had been eating their breakfast in the kitchen and he was startled to see Lucy standing there when he came into the hallway.

'What are you doing here?' he asked, Lucy tried to play it cool.

'Wanna go out on your bike?' she asked. Paul glanced warily at his Mum to see how she would react. His mother seemed to have relaxed a little in her opposition to Lucy, but she was still hardly friendly.

'I suppose it's better her than the kids in the playground' she said with a disapproving look. 'But no funny business okay? I don't want you two going down to the sea or along the cliffs together you hear me? And I don't want any talk about you-know-what.' Paul and Lucy eyed each other.

'I promise we won't go to the sea' said Lucy. She didn't like to lie to Mrs Treddinick, but thought it wasn't exactly telling a fib if she left certain details out. Lucy just hoped she wouldn't ask any more awkward questions.

'I'll get my bike out from round the back' Paul said.

'You remember what I told you!' called out Mrs Treddinick behind them, as they cycled up the street together a couple of minutes later.

'So where are we going?' Paul asked as they rounded the corner.

'You're going to take me to see the dolphin in the inlet' she replied.

255

'But you said……'

'I said we wouldn't go to the sea and we aren't. I never told your Mum we wouldn't talk about dolphins, or go and see one did I?'

The country lanes that Paul led Lucy down seemed strangely familiar, though it was the first time she had been down them. Then she realised that Paul had helped her visualise them just the other day.

They cycled on between green hedgerows and overhanging trees. They free-wheeled down the hill and over the little bridge before pedalling laboriously up the other side. The lane levelled out and eventually they came to the railway embankment and dismounted, leaving their bikes hidden behind a bush. They crunched along the overgrown gravel bed of the disused railway track. Again Lucy experienced a strange sense of déjà vu.

'So you'll teach me how to be a Dolphin-Child won't you? Like you are?' Paul asked as they made their way along the path.

'Listen Paul' replied Lucy, 'it doesn't work like that. It's not that easy. I can't just teach you.'

'Yes you can' answered Paul testily. 'You can if you want to. I want to be free like you are. I want to swim with dolphins like you do.' Lucy shook her head.

'I don't even know how I do it, let alone tell you how to do it' she replied.

'I'll teach myself if I have to' he answered defiantly.

'I'll do what I can' she said. 'I never give promises unless I'm sure I can keep them. Besides, I don't think you're such a great swimmer. It's dangerous in open water unless you know what you're doing.'

As they clambered up the tree to climb over the stone wall, Paul's attitude seemed to change. He started to look around him as though he expected someone to take them by surprise and stopped talking about becoming a Dolphin-Child.

'Watch out and keep your eyes peeled' he told Lucy warily. Lucy thought he was being a bit silly, but didn't like to say anything. As they dropped down between the pine trees, Paul seemed to be behaving like he was a soldier in a war movie and he ran from tree to tree, as though someone was going to try to shoot him.

'Don't be daft' Lucy muttered as they moved through the trees. Lucy was surprised to see the immense wall of green where the mass of rhododendron bushes had grown up. Paul plunged into the dense tangle of branches and leaves, whilst Lucy followed in his wake. They clambered up, over and through the rhododendrons until at last they saw the glint of blue water of the lagoon. Lucy immediately forgot about anything else and rushed the last few metres to get to the water's edge.

'Watch out soldier!' Paul called under his breath, but by this time Lucy was out of ear-shot. She stood by the lapping water on grass cropped close by wild rabbits and looked around her. To her left low bushes and small trees hemmed in the inlet up to the point where the big house stood. It looked a little forlorn and rundown to Lucy and she wondered if anyone actually lived there. On the other side of the inlet taller trees crowded down the hill to the water's edge. To her right Lucy could see the closed link fence that had been erected across the water to separate the inlet from the rest of the estuary beyond.

Lucy started to scan the water, searching for the distinctive sign of a dorsal fin breaking the water's surface. Just then Paul came up to her side.

'Keep out of sight, or we'll get in trouble' he whispered hoarsely. 'We're, like trespassing here you know.' Lucy continued to scan the water.

'I don't care' she replied. Just then there was a ripple on the surface of the water and they both stared intently at the spot. For a moment Lucy thought her eyes were deceiving her but then she saw it again. The tip of a fin slowly cruised along slicing through the water for a moment before disappearing again.

Without thinking what she was doing, Lucy just stepped off the grassy bank and into the water. She didn't care about the trainers, shorts or tee-shirt that she was wearing. The water was shallow here and she started wading out determinedly through the briny water, with mud and silt boiling up around her legs.

'Stop!' hissed Paul anxiously, looking from left to right as though he expected to see guards running. 'You'll get us in trouble!'

Lucy didn't even answer. She could see the faint ripples where the dolphin had been cruising through the water. Lucy had waded up to her chest now and started to swim. In her haste she'd forgotten that she was still wearing her trainers, but she could still swim well enough in them even though she knew it was better not to. She ducked her head under the water to look but it was too murky to see anything. 'Just like it was in my dreams' she thought to herself. She sensed that Paul was going frantic on the bank, but she didn't look back and kept on swimming.

Just then there was a swell of water in front of her and Star-Gazer curved round her, brushing her upper arms and shoulder as she did so. Lucy gasped.

'It's me Lucy' she whispered though she knew the dolphin could not understand her. 'I've come to help you Star-Gazer.' The water was still just shallow enough for Lucy to stand with her feet oozing into the mud and silt at the bottom. She stretched out with her arms to gently touch the dolphin's flank, face and beak. Star-Gazer hung in the water and looked up at her with big, sad eyes. Lucy embraced her with both her arms and pressed her head to the dolphin's side. Lucy could feel the life-force emanating from Star-Gazer through her finger tips and body, but it was a weak energy, sickly and disturbed. Star-Gazer had evidently lost a lot of her strength and Lucy feared that she would not last that much longer unless they did something to help her soon.

Lucy stood there in the water for a long time holding Star-Gazer to her side. She wished that she could speak to the dolphin then, but she was unable to do so. She felt anger growing deep within her at the thought of this beautiful dolphin being trapped in this tight, muddy inlet far from the wide sea and her own family.

Eventually Star-Gazer began to move and she guessed that she wanted to pull Lucy along through the water. Lucy held on to her dorsal fin and Star-Gazer propelled Lucy along, slowly and mournfully. They swam up as far as they could get to the closed link fence that cut her off from freedom.

Lucy slipped off Star-Gazer back into the water and waded up to the fence and shook it. It seemed to be firmly fastened. She wondered if there were any gaps below it and she ran her trainer along the bottom under the water. It was fixed to the bottom there too so that there was no way that a dolphin could slip underneath. Lucy felt exasperated and looked back down the length of the lagoon towards the house.

To her left she could see Paul. He had waded a short distance after her and was standing with water up to his knees, uncertain about what to do next. He was looking their way with an anxious and imploring look on his face. Lucy glanced beyond Paul to where the house was. To her surprise she could see a tall thin figure standing on the small landing stage, staring down the length of the inlet towards her. Star-Gazer nudged Lucy again and then slowly pulled her along through the water towards the figure that stood there so silently, watching her.

As they grew nearer, Lucy could see that it was an old woman who stood tall and thin, silhouetted against the house behind her.

Her grey hair was cut in a neat, short style and she seemed well dressed in long flannel trousers and a cardigan. She wore a string of pearls around her throat that looked expensive.

Lucy felt incensed at the elderly woman for taking Star-Gazer hostage and was determined to confront her there and then. She gave Star-Gazer one tender stroke to the dome of her head and then slid off and started wading through the muddy shallows out of the water and towards the woman. Lucy's clothes were soaked and covered with mud as she emerged from the water.

'Let this dolphin go!' she shouted angrily at the woman.

Chapter Seventeen:

It had been against all John Parr's instincts to let Lucy go like that. He watched her bound up the steep path from the cove, still wearing her wetsuit but with her bag with its change of clothes slung over one shoulder. She seemed so full of purpose and energy. Lucy hadn't told him what she needed to do, but he had a pretty good idea it was to do with her worrying obsession with dolphins.

Dad shuddered at the thought of the danger that she might be putting herself in. Yet wasn't this a phase that she would grow out of? By giving her the freedom now, wasn't he saving her from danger later? Dad wanted to believe that was the case, but really he didn't know. He thought about running up the path behind her and telling her that he'd changed his mind. It was too late now though. Lucy was faster than him on the steep track and by the time he got to the top, puffing and panting, she'd have disappeared down the country lanes, but where to he had no idea.

As well as feeling worried about Lucy's safety, he felt lonely and a little lost now that she'd gone. He'd just been starting to get used to hanging out with her again. He'd spent far too little time with Lucy over the past year. He'd been hoping to make up for his neglect during this holiday. Yet here he was standing alone on a thin crescent of beach at a ridiculously early time of the day. Dad sighed and started to trudge up the path back to the top of the cliff, while the sea frothed over the pebbles below him.

Dad reached the top and retrieved his bike. He was about to make his way back down to the cottage when he paused, lost in thought. Then he turned the handle-bars of the bike to face the other direction and started pedalling purposefully in the direction of Merwater.

Although it was fortunate that he remembered the name of road that Thelma Merryweather lived in, he could not bring to mind the house number. In any case he didn't even know where the road was and after he'd asked three different people without success, he decided that the only thing to do was to buy a map of the town from the tourist office. The map led him up the steep hill out to the edge of town. Dad hadn't cycled for years and knew that he'd never pedal all the way up there. He began to walk. Once he got to Thelma's road he reckoned he'd ask again and then someone would be able to tell him where she lived. Just as he turned into Crab-Apple Lane though, he saw the short, plump figure of Thelma Merryweather bustling towards him, with shopping bags in one hand and her handbag in the other.

'Mrs Merryweather!' he exclaimed in surprise. 'It's you!' Thelma glanced up and smiled.

'John Parr' she replied, 'father of young Lucy. What brings you to this neck of the woods then?'

'Well, I was looking for you actually' he answered.

'As it happens I'm off out' Thelma said, 'but if it's young Lucy you want to talk about, I can make time of course.'

'I don't want to put you out' replied Dad politely. 'If it's not an imposition, I can talk to you as we walk.'

'That will do very nicely', Thelma replied as they started making their way back down the hill that Dad had just come up, the bike at his side. 'Are you and Lucy having a nice holiday?' Dad didn't want to get caught up in polite chitchat though.

'I'm worried about Lucy' he said, 'very worried. 'I've given her the freedom to spend time down here with Bethany and these dolphins of hers despite all my misgivings. I've tried to understand her obsession. This morning I went with Lucy down to the beach to meet this dolphin friend of hers, but when he didn't show up she begged me to allow her to disappear off on her own and do something she thought was important.'

'And did you?' Thelma asked quietly.

'Yes, yes I did' he replied. 'I was left standing there on the beach of that cove while she cycled off to goodness knows where. 'Now all I can do is worry and hope that she comes back safe and sound. But all the time I know that association with dolphins can be … fatal.'

Thelma stopped for a moment and looked up at Dad, a sympathetic expression on her face.

'John Parr, I know now that you have reason for that fear. Your life has been struck by tragedy and you don't want anything bad to

264

happen to young Lucy because she's your only daughter and all that you have left.' Dad nodded.

'And a few months ago I told you that Lucy would outgrow all this dolphin malarkey soon enough and will get into what all the normal kids of her age like doing.' Dad nodded again.

'Let me tell you a little story' continued Thelma as they started walking again in the direction of the hill into town.

'In all my life I've only known two Dolphin-Children before your Lucy came along. As you know in any generation here in Merwater, there will generally be at least one Dolphin-Child. This young girl that I knew was fascinated by dolphins and the sea and spent all her spare time up on the cliffs or down at the harbour trying to persuade the fishermen to take her out with them in their boats. In primary school her exercise books were full of drawings of dolphins' Thelma adjusted the bag she was carrying before she continued.

'At first no one realised that she was a Dolphin-Child, though she showed all the tell-tale signs. She didn't tell anyone you see, not even her sister who she was really close to. Then one morning she was gone from her bed and their mum thought something terrible must have happened.'

'What did happen?' asked Dad.

'It was their father who found her' Thelma continued. 'He was a fisherman too like many folk round here in those days. He'd left before dawn to put out to sea and didn't know his daughter had gone missing, but he must have had a feeling in his bones. He thought he saw a pod of dolphins in the distance and as they sometimes show where the shoals of fish are, he put his eye-glass up to his face. There was a girl riding on the back of one of them beasts and although he couldn't see from that distance, he had a horrid feeling that it was one his own little girls that he'd thought he'd left tucked up safe and sound in bed.'

Thelma paid attention to the traffic for a moment while she and Dad crossed a road and started down the hill.

'The girl's father turned his boat around and followed the pod of dolphins. They weren't far from the shoreline and as he watched, dolphins brought her in uncommonly close and the girl swam back to the beach. He was unable to get his boat that close but he could see that it really was his very own little girl.'

Dad glanced at Thelma as they walked. He could see that she had a faraway look in her eyes as she remembered.

'Well that girl's mother and father were mighty worried when they found out that she was a full blown Dolphin-Child.'

'So what happened then?' asked Dad curiously. Thelma smiled.

'Well they just let her be' she said. 'They let it run its course like you might with a fever. She was like that for a year or two, you know swimming with her dolphins and whatnot. Then one morning she found that she couldn't speak with those dolphins using her mind anymore. Then her dolphin dreams lost their colour and she stopped having those too. She was growing up see?' Dad nodded.

266

'And how did the girl cope with it?' he asked. Thelma sighed.

'Well as you can well imagine, she felt she'd lost her closest friends. She was distraught. For a while she used to go out with her father on his boat and search for those dolphins and would weep buckets when she couldn't find them. Then her dad banned that, saying it wasn't good for her. She got over it in the end, but it took a while. She moved on. She's all right now you know. She's got kids of her own and they're all grown up and left home too.'

'This girl' said Dad. 'It wasn't you by any chance was it?' Thelma smiled sadly.

'No, no it wasn't. It was my sister. But I almost wished it had been me you know. When I was young I was quite envious of her. It must have been great...'

'Does she live locally? Can I go and speak to her?' asked Dad.

'Oh she moved away.' Thelma sighed again, shaking her head. 'She doesn't like to talk about those things now. I think she still feels the loss. She lives in a big town up north, a long way from the sea.'

'Is she happy?'

'Happy enough I reckon' replied Thelma. 'I don't speak to her that much now save for Christmas and birthdays. Our lives went in different directions I suppose. I stayed here and married Nate and she moved far away.'

By now Dad and Thelma had walked all the way down the hill and were close to the harbour. They paused and Thelma gestured for them to sit down and continue their conversation on a bench.

'And does it pass down the generations, from mother to daughter?' asked Dad. Thelma smiled again.

'I know why you're asking that John Parr' she replied. 'It can do, like with your Megan and your Lucy. But mostly it doesn't. It's not just girls that become Dolphin-Children you know' Thelma added. 'The other one I knew was a boy. But that's another story.'

'Is that why the town's called Merwater?' asked Dad curiously. 'I mean, is there a link between Dolphin-Children and well, mermaids?' Thelma nodded in the direction of the small town museum just across the road next to the public toilets.

'If you pop your head in over there, there're all sorts of stories about the name of the town, but I reckon you might be onto something.

'Is there more stuff about Dolphin-Children in there?' asked Dad, glancing in the direction of the museum.

'Well there's the tale of that sad girl Susan Penhaligon. But she must have lived a couple of hundred years ago now I reckon. There've been no stories like that about Dolphin-Children since then that I know of, not in modern times at least. They mostly all grow out of it by their early teens.' Dad looked down.

'I know of one girl that didn't' he said quietly. 'It cost her her life. I can't take that risk with Lucy.' For a moment Thelma thought he was going to be overcome with emotion and she briefly grasped his hand to comfort him.

'Let nature take its course' she assured him. 'It won't be like with your Megan. Not this time. Things will work out for the best,

268

you mark my words.' Just then they heard shouting across the street.

'Oh it's that pair Baz and Mike again' exclaimed Thelma disapprovingly. 'I really don't like those two boys.'

'Who?' asked Dad.

'Oh you know' replied Thelma. 'They're the two that have been ganging up on Paul, that friend of young Lucy. I don't trust them further than I can throw them. I wonder what they're doing hanging around here.' They watched for a few moments before the two boys suddenly turned and ran off up the street.

They chatted for a while longer and then Thelma apologised saying that she really must get off to her appointment in town. They went their separate ways and as Thelma bustled off, Dad pushed his bike across the road and walked up to the entrance of the small museum, lost in thought.

The bow of the Lady Thelma broke through low choppy waves. A wind had picked up and Nate could feel the small trawler rise and fall with the sea as they ploughed on. Bob was repairing a lobster pot at the back.

'Wind's rising!' Nate called to him from the cramped cabin.

'You heard the weather forecast?' Bob called back.

'I thought it was going to be clear for this morning' Nate replied. 'But it looks to me like the weather's on the change.' He thought about raising the Coast Guard on the radio to get a weather update, but he didn't like to bother them unless it was really necessary. They were heading back to port anyway and they'd be there long before the sea got rough enough to worry about. A while later Nate glanced over his shoulder. The sky was clear and the sun bright, but on the horizon a wall of grey blue cloud seemed to be rolling in towards them.

The pod rested in deeper waters a couple of miles off the coast. Wind picked the sea into tongues that flicked spray up into the air. A cloud of jelly fish drifted glumly into view but the dolphins ignored them disdainfully. Storm took a low leap and surveyed the conditions above the surface of the water.

'We will have rain before tonight and lots of it' he said. Spirit had been floating idly in the water, lost in thought.

'Rain?' he asked, suddenly paying attention.

'A summer storm' continued Storm. 'The clouds are piling up over there and they are heavy and dark. There will be lightning too. It should be quite a show.'

'You know what Star-Gazer said?' Dancer asked. Spirit caught her eye.

'Yes, she said that if there is rain, then the silt around the fence to the entrance of the lagoon will be washed away. Then there may be a chance of finding a way through. We might find some way to set her free.' They both turned to look at Storm. The others were all looking in their direction and listening too. He swam a long slow circle while he thought it over.

'That might just work' he said quietly, almost to himself.

270

Bethany strolled out of the studio and across the farmyard. She had been working hard on a painting and needed to go outside, breath in some fresh air and look at the view. She leant on a gate and stared out across the field to where the cows stood meditatively chewing the cud. Mary came up and leant companionably against the gate beside her.

'Handsome beasts aren't they' she said, 'and good milkers too'. Bethany nodded absently. 'What's on your mind then Beth?' Mary asked.

'Oh I was just thinking about Lucy and John' Bethany replied.

'Anything in particular?'

'I'll really miss Lucy when she goes back home and starts school again. But in the meantime I'm worried about her.

'This dolphin business?'

'That's right' replied Bethany. 'The dolphin she has this connection with, Spirit his name is. Well his mother has been lost but now they think that they've found her in an inlet off the estuary by a big house.'

'That would be the old Penrose place that Darren was talking to Lucy about?'

'Exactly' Bethany replied, 'have you been there?'

'Actually I have' said Mary. 'Norman Penrose was one of those financial wizards who made a lot of money in the City and then came down here with all his money to live in the lap of luxury. He and his wife were really into sailing in regattas and that kind of thing. They used to have a big party in the summer at their house. Lovely place it is. It looks down an inlet from the estuary. The house has got massive grounds and woods on both sides. They'd invite anyone and everyone to their summer parties and that's how I wangled an invite. I had a great time sipping their champagne and nibbling their canapés. Kept thinking I'd get slung out though.' Mary paused.

'Don't know what's happened to them actually. Haven't heard a peep about them for ages. I guess they just got old and quietened down. So you think this dolphin's mother might be stuck there. That's a bit rum isn't it?'

'I know' replied Bethany, 'and Lucy's still not really over the death of her own mother. She's been through so much in the last year or so and I'm afraid that she's going to feel even more hurt now, whether that dolphin trapped there is Spirit's mother or not.'

'Do you really believe all this stuff about dolphins?' asked Mary. 'I mean, they're just another animal aren't they? Don't get me wrong. I think dolphins are lovely, but I work with animals every day and I've learned not to be so sentimental about them. Maybe Lucy's imagination has got the better of her.'

'Well Lucy doesn't think so and neither do I' replied Bethany, feeling a little defensive.

'But what is it about dolphins that sets them apart?' asked Mary. Bethany could tell from her expression that she was genuinely curious. Bethany thought for a few moments. It wasn't an easy question to answer.

'It's not just the intelligence you see in their eyes when you look at them' Bethany answered eventually. 'It's more than that. Since the time of the ancient Greeks there have been stories of dolphins saving people in trouble at sea. They show empathy and compassion which is uncannily like our own.' Mary frowned a little.

'When I went down sick with the flu last winter, my dog Pip wouldn't leave me. She kept licking me and nuzzling in to me until I got better again. What's the difference between my Pip and the compassion which you say that dolphins show.'

'Yes of course dogs are loyal to their master and mistresses, but the remarkable thing about dolphins is that they are wild and free. They owe no allegiance to any human being. But time and time again they have come and helped us humans in trouble for no other reason than that they wanted to. I don't think that dogs are like that, do you?'

'No, I suppose not' replied Mary thoughtfully as she leant on the fence. 'But are they really that smart? Pip is a clever dog, but I know she's not going to start opening her mouth and talk to me.'

'Dolphins spend more of their time in social interaction than they do in searching for food' replied Bethany, warming to her subject. 'They use complex whistles and clicks to communicate with each other which we humans have yet to understand.'

'That's just meaningless noise isn't it? Like a bird singing in a tree.'

'A dolphin's brain is pretty much the same size as our own' continued Bethany. 'Scientists haven't been able to crack the code of what they are saying to each other, but we know they cooperate in complex social groups. They wouldn't need a brain that size if they weren't interacting with each other in a sophisticated way. It's a bit like with Egyptian hieroglyphics. For a long time scholars had no idea what they meant. Then they found the Rosetta Stone and that meant they were able to crack the code and figure out what it all meant. With dolphins, we just haven't found a Rosetta Stone yet.'

'No I see what you mean, really I do. But as you know, it's my Darren who's the local boy. I'm not from these parts. I don't have this thing with dolphins like some of the local people round here do. But what I don't reckon on is how Lucy could speak to dolphins somehow. That's just beyond me.'

'I don't know either' replied Bethany, 'but somehow it happens. How else could Lucy have known about that little girl trapped on the rock. If it weren't for her ability to communicate with dolphins, who knows what might have happened to that girl.'

'That's true enough' replied Mary. 'The coastguard were amazed when I rang up from the farm and said there was a girl stuck on a rock just off the beach. I could hardly believe it myself when I phoned up. I suppose there are just some things that can't be readily explained.'

'I guess not' sighed Bethany. 'But still, I worry about Lucy.' Mary glanced up at the sky.

'Weather's on the turn' she said. 'There's a storm forecast'. I'd better press on and get a few things sorted out round here before the rains reach us. Catch up with you later Bethany!'

With that, Mary strode off purposefully in the direction of the top field. Bethany stayed leaning on the fence for a few minutes more, studying the placid cows, before she too went inside to resume her work. She wondered where Lucy was now.

When Lucy had turned up at his house and asked him to show her the lagoon where the dolphin was trapped, Paul felt something inside that he hadn't expected. It wasn't just that he felt needed, or that now he had a friend who was actually seeking him out. It was that he was proud that in some way he could help. He didn't know what was going to happen, but at least he could guide her to the big house by the lagoon. They were a team.

As they cycled along, Paul wanted to tell Lucy all about his daydreams of guards running around the grounds with guns and mantraps, but he realised that it would be silly to do so and in any case, it all seemed less important now.

To be a Dolphin-Child seemed to Paul to be an amazing thing. His mum had told him that Dolphin-Children were dangerous and that generations ago a Dolphin-Child called Susan Penhaligon had led their ancestors to a watery grave. She warned him against Lucy and told him to stay away from her. Yet Lucy had been the only one to stand up against his bullies and tormentors. Even his mum seemed to recognise now that Lucy was a good person. Why else would she have let him cycle off up the road with her?

The time that he had swum in the sea with Lucy and her dolphin friend had been magical and electrifying. He could still barely believe it, but it felt as though it were the most important thing that had ever happened to him.

Paul glanced at Lucy as they cycled. She seemed so confident and self-possessed. He was convinced that she didn't need any other human being because she had her dolphin friends instead. Who needed people anyway? After the last few days, he knew that he didn't. If Lucy could be a Dolphin-Child, why couldn't he? It had to be possible, it just had to be.

Paul felt nervous as he showed Lucy the route over the wall to take her into the Penrose estate. He was still half convinced that they would have to dodge bullets on the other side. When they clambered through the rhododendron thicket and came out at the waters edge, Paul could see Lucy focus on the water of the inlet, scanning it for life. Covertly, he tried to do the same too, but was startled when Lucy had strode out from the bank, wading out into the briny water.

Paul didn't know what to do except just stand there, hoping that in some way Lucy would include him too. Instead she forgot everything else but the sight of the dolphin trapped in the muddy lagoon. Lucy looked and touched the dolphin in a way that showed a level of understanding between girl and creature that Paul could only imagine. He ached to be able to do the same.

In the end he ineffectually waded out a few yards into the water, his feet sinking down into the soft mud as he did so. He didn't quite know why he did it; he just wanted to be involved in some way. Instead the dolphin pulled Lucy along the length of the inlet all the way up to the closed-link fence that blocked it off from the rest of the estuary and kept the creature trapped.

As they turned, Paul became aware of the tall figure of the old woman standing watching them from the landing stage in front of the big house. He half expected guards to creep up behind him and seize him there and then. He was ready to turn and run, but instead of turning away, he couldn't believe that Lucy would confront the woman instead.

When she shouted 'Let this dolphin go!', it felt like an electric shock running through his entire body. He looked with a mixture of awe and fear from Lucy to the severe-looking woman, wondering what was going to happen next.

Chapter Eighteen:

'You'd better come in' the woman said curtly. 'You can't walk around in those wet things, even on a summer's day like this' she continued, looking disdainfully at Lucy's wet and muddy clothes. 'It's overcast and I think it's going to rain.' She glanced in Paul's direction where he was now standing thigh deep in the water. 'That goes for your friend there too.'

'But I said…' started Lucy, already feeling a little deflated. The woman cut in.

'I know what you said young lady and when you're clean and dry I will talk to you, not before then.' The woman spoke authoritatively and Lucy felt compelled to comply. She glanced down at herself. She did look a state and the mud she was covered in smelled unpleasantly. She looked back at Star-Gazer, but the dolphin had disappeared temporarily from view. Reluctantly, Lucy gestured to Paul to follow her and the woman into the house. They waited for Paul to wade round the edge of the lake to reach them and then both children squelched behind her round to the door at the side.

They entered a general utility and storage room which opened off the kitchen.

'Wait here' the woman said. 'I can't let you into the rest of the house in this state. I'll get you both something to wear and then you can get out of those clothes. Young lady, you will need a shower. Fortunately I have some of my granddaughter's things that I think might fit you while I give your own clothes a quick spin in the washing machine. Young man, it's only your jeans that are dirty and wet, but I don't have anything your size for you to wear so I'll have to put you in some old jogging trousers until your own are clean and dry.'

The woman was so commanding and business-like that it felt as though they were being told off by a head teacher. Both children fell silent as they waited for her to return. When she came back, Lucy made Paul turn the other way while she changed and she did the same while Paul took off his wet trousers and put on the jogging bottoms. The woman bundled their clothes into a washing basket and disappeared into the kitchen to put them in the machine.

'What now?' asked Paul. Lucy was still very angry with the woman for imprisoning Star-Gazer, but she had an instinct that the woman wasn't a bad person and she was so used to being polite to grown-ups that she was prepared to wait.

'Let's hang on a bit' she replied. 'Then I'll talk to the lady.' To their surprise another woman appeared who seemed to be wearing a sort of nurse's uniform and ushered Lucy silently to a downstairs shower room. A shapeless dress and a pair of underwear had been left for her to change into. Lucy showered quickly and then pulled the dress over her head. Lucy hardly ever wore dresses and it felt strange to put one on like this.

Paul had got muddier than it initially appeared and it was his turn to shower next. There were no spare clothes for him to change into though and he had to wrap himself up in the bathrobe afterwards until his clothes were washed and dry.

Without speaking, the nurse showed them back to the kitchen and indicated that they should sit down at the table in the large and well appointed room.

Lucy peered through the window, but it looked out of the side of the house and she couldn't see the lagoon or Star-Gazer. She felt anxious about her. It was evident that Star-Gazer was sickening. Lucy could tell from the touch and colour of her skin and the energy that she gave off. Compared to the other dolphins in the pod in the sea, she was very weak. Lucy feared that she couldn't last much longer at all. When Lucy had reached out to Star-Gazer with her mind, she had pleaded with Lucy to help release her. Lucy was determined that she would.

The two children heard footsteps approaching and the door opened and the woman came back into the room. She looked disapprovingly at them before pulling up a chair and sitting down opposite them.

'So what do you two think you're doing trespassing on private land then?' the woman asked sharply. Lucy wasn't going to take this without a fight.

'We've come to save Star-Gazer. You've no right to keep her trapped here in that lagoon.'

'Star-Gazer? I think you mean Flipper' the woman answered. 'We'll talk about the dolphin in a minute. Do your parents know you're here?' Lucy paused before replying. She didn't know whether it was better to pretend that her dad did know where they were, or to admit that he didn't.

'Our parents trust us to do the right thing' said Lucy defiantly.

'Well you did the wrong thing by breaking into private property' the woman replied tartly.

'It's only because you've got something to hide that you care' replied Lucy, her hackles rising. Paul seemed to have shrunk back into his chair and was silently following the exchange between Lucy and the woman. The woman glared at Lucy.

'I do not care for the way you are speaking to me young lady' she answered, 'and I'll thank you to address me more courteously. I care about two children trespassing onto private land without their parents knowledge and then swimming out into treacherous water where they could easily have got into trouble and drowned.'

'Star-Gazer would never have let that happen' replied Lucy defensively. 'I know what I'm doing.'

'Do you? Does he?' the woman replied, nodding towards Paul. Lucy blanched slightly. She had been so focussed on Star-Gazer that she had not realised that Paul had waded out into the water. The mud was so thick and glutinous that it would have been easy for him to get stuck there. He was the younger kid and she knew that it was up to her to look after him. Lucy glanced down guiltily.

'You've got to let Star-Gazer go' Lucy said again, more quietly this time but still defiantly.

'Why do you persist in calling him Star-Gazer?' the woman asked.

'Coz that's her name. She's a she, not a he. Lucy's a Dolphin-Child see?' said Paul. The woman stared at Paul and then at Lucy.

'I have no idea what that's supposed to mean young man' the woman answered eventually. She sighed and as she did so she seemed to soften. 'I'm going to make you both a hot chocolate drink to warm you up and then I'm going to tell you a story.'

As they watched the woman go to the fridge and then get a pan out to warm up the milk in, Lucy could see that she was old and tired. Her hands shook slightly as she poured the milk into the saucepan and sprinkled in the chocolate powder. It felt hard for Lucy to answer back to a woman like this but keeping Star-Gazer prisoner was wrong and if she didn't tell the woman, who would?

The woman brought the steaming mugs of chocolate milk to them and Lucy and Paul sipped them gratefully. The woman sat down.

'My name is Annabel Penrose' she said. 'And you are...?' The children mumbled their names in reply. 'Well Lucy Parr and Paul Treddinick. Let me tell you my story. My husband Norman and I came down here to retire some twenty years ago. We were both passionate sailors and our yacht, the Lady Jane, was moored down near the entrance to the estuary. We have sailed all around the coast of Cornwall and the Scilly Isles from here and a more beautiful place I have never known'. She glanced down at her hands for a moment before continuing.

'Right from the beginning, the dolphins were our friends. They have always sought out our yacht and swum alongside us at the bow, or greeted us with a jump out of the water. Other sailors that we spoke to said that they hardly ever saw dolphins, but we never missed them when we went out sailing. We even learned to recognise several of them by sight, from the scars and wounds on their dorsal fins and we studied them closely. I've got books and books about dolphins in the living room. We loved the dolphins and our life here felt complete.'

Lucy frowned into her chocolate milk. That didn't give her the right to trap one of them, she thought. She should know better than to take one of them from the wild. Lucy remained silent though and let the lady continue.

'About a year ago we had just put out from the mouth of the estuary in the Lady Jane. A scientific vessel was sailing down the coast and conducting some sort of survey of the underwater landscape. We raised it on the radio and had a brief chat with its skipper. It was using an experimental type of sonar. We hoped the dolphins wouldn't be affected by it but we couldn't see them so we thought it would be okay and expected them to be too far out to be affected. Then a squall blew up unexpectedly and we decided not to sail out into the open sea after all.' Lucy could see the woman's expression change as she remembered the events.

'The squall died down almost as quickly as it had blown up. Then we saw a dolphin lying listlessly on his side on the surface of the water, his blow hole nearly submerged. We guessed that the sonar had disorientated him and that he must have banged his head on a rock or something. There was blood coming from a gash on his head. If he rolled in the water anymore he would drown. From the markings on his dorsal fin we recognised him as the one we called Flipper.'

'It's Star-Gazer' Lucy thought to herself, but she still didn't say anything. She wondered what would happen next in the story and let the lady continue instead.

'My husband Norman was well over seventy at this point. He jumped into the rubber dinghy that we always had behind the Lady Jane and with a lot of effort, he was able to lash Flipper with some spare rope into an upright position between the yacht and the dinghy, so that we could head back into the estuary using the out-board motor. Flipper was badly injured and we were really worried that he would bleed to death before we got there. We didn't know what to do with him once we got back, but then Norman hit upon the idea of keeping him in the lagoon at the front of our house while he recovered.' Lucy couldn't contain herself any more.

'But why is Star-Gazer still trapped here?' she asked. Mrs Penrose's expression clouded.

'We had to cordon off the lagoon until Flipper had recovered' she continued as though Lucy had not said anything. 'We used the closed link fence to block off the exit to the rest of the estuary.' She paused. 'Norman was exhausted by the effort of saving Flipper' she continued in a quieter voice. 'I think the strain of it all was too much for him. About a week later my poor Norman suffered a massive stroke.' She remained silent for a few moments and pain from the memory showed in her face. 'Do you know what a stroke is?' Paul shook his head and Lucy wasn't sure, so she didn't say anything.

'It's when there is a blood clot in one of your veins and it blocks the blood flowing to your brain. It happens in older people sometimes. Your brain is starved of oxygen and it gets damaged. That's what happened to Norman. He's paralysed now on one side and he cannot speak. But …'

'But what?' asked Lucy. Mrs Penrose took an intake of breath.

'But he can still write on a pad and communicate with me even if he cannot talk. He tells me that he feels, no he knows that he and Flipper are connected somehow. I believe him. Flipper will help Norman get better. I'm sure of it.'

'That's not true!' Lucy blurted out impulsively. 'They're not connected in the way that you say. Star-Gazer would have told me if they were.'

'And he has been making progress, just as Flipper has been getting better' Mrs Penrose continued. 'Norman's regained some movement in his paralysed arm. The Doctor says its almost a miracle.' Mrs Penrose's face lit up in hope again. 'And its all down to Flipper. It's taken time for both of them but we're getting there. I'm sure we are'. Mrs Penrose paused and sniffed.

'The nurse that you saw helps me care for Norman and I've been caring for Flipper too, feeding him fish every day and seeing that he gets strong again. Of course Flipper is able to move around well enough, but he still swims lopsidedly sometimes. It makes me think of Norman being lopsided because he's paralysed. I don't think that Flipper's ready to go back to the sea, not yet. In any case, Norman needs him. Sometimes Norman comes out in his wheelchair to see Flipper and it always makes him feel better. I can see it in his face.'

'No no' exclaimed Lucy with rising anxiety. 'You're wrong!' Mrs Penrose fixed Lucy with a stare.

'Just because you hitched a ride on Flippers back a short while ago, doesn't mean that you know all there is to know about dolphins. Norman and I have been studying them for years. I think we know a little more than you young lady.'

'You may have helped Star-Gazer originally' replied Lucy passionately, 'but now you're killing her. Dolphins are meant to swim in the sea with their own kind. They are intelligent and sociable. Just imagine if you were locked up on your own for a year without anyone to keep you company. You'd go mad. That's what it's like for Star-Gazer. You may be feeding her fish, but the loneliness is killing her'.

Lucy hoped that her words were having their effect on Mrs Penrose and that the old lady had accepted that imprisoning a dolphin was wrong. She could see a cloud pass across Mrs Penrose's face as she absorbed Lucy's words. Then she shook her head, as if to dispel the negative thoughts.

'I still don't know why you keep calling him Star-Gazer' Mrs Penrose replied with a hint of irritation in her voice, 'but you are clearly a girl whose head is full of quite fanciful ideas. Flipper is not lonely, he sees Norman or myself every day and he gets more fish than he could dream of. He has plenty of water to swim in too. He comes to us when we walk down to the landing stage and he allows us to pet him. We look after him well and when he and Norman are well enough, we will let him choose whether to remain with us or to return to the sea. Not before. Only when the time is right.'

Lucy was so astounded by the idea that anyone could think it was right to keep a dolphin prisoner like this, that for a few moments she was lost for words. Then she had a flash of inspiration.

'You can't just keep a dolphin. It's not allowed. You need a licence or something.' Lucy could tell immediately that she had hit a nerve and that the woman didn't have permission to keep a dolphin. A look of fear seemed to pass across her features, but then she seemed to harden again.

'Norman and I saved Flipper's life. Norman would be distraught if Flipper left us. It's the only thing that keeps him going. It'd be the death of him if Flipper goes. I can't do that to Norman. You can't do that to him either. Not if you've any heart.'

'What if Star-Gazer dies of loneliness. How will you and your husband feel then?' Lucy asked. She almost felt like crying.

'It's not going to happen. I won't let it happen' Mrs Penrose replied quietly but defiantly. Just then the washing machine juddered to the end of its drying cycle. Mrs Penrose glanced at her watch. She stood up. 'I must be going. I have errands to attend to. I'll get Mathew our handyman to run you into Merwater once you're back in your dry clothes. I'm not having you traipsing through the woods and clambering over walls.'

She left and a few seconds later the nurse appeared and pulled out their clothes which were now crumpled but at least dry and ready to put back on. Lucy realised that she'd been out-manoeuvred. She could report Mrs Penrose to the authorities, but if she did and if her husband got sicker, then how would she feel then? Besides, it might take weeks for the authorities to do anything about it. By then it might be too late for Star-Gazer.

As she and Paul sat in the back of Mathew's car and rattled up the pot-holed drive from Mrs Penrose's house a few minutes later, Lucy stretched out with her mind to reach Star-Gazer. All that the sad and lonely dolphin was able to say was 'Don't leave me, don't leave me. You've got to get me out of this horrible place.' Lucy was quickly jolted out of her trance when they bumped through a particularly bad pot-hole before she had barely had a chance to say anything comforting to Star-Gazer. She had to speak to Spirit as soon as possible. Maybe he had some idea about what to do next.

They persuaded Mathew to drop them off by the railway embankment close to where they had hidden their bikes.

'What now then?' Paul asked gloomily as soon as they were alone. Lucy had so hoped that Mrs Penrose would relinquish and simply agree to let Star-Gazer go, that now she felt drained and empty. Paul seemed disappointed too. They had achieved nothing.

'I, I don't know' she replied flatly. 'But I'll think of something' she added with more resolve. She looked at her watch. 'I'd better get going or my Dad is going to kill me. But I'll get away again and come back and see you. Look outside at six o'clock. If there's a pebble on your gate post, it means I'm waiting for you in the recreation ground. I don't want to knock on your door again. Your mum still doesn't trust me.'

They cycled along some way together, but then they parted at a fork in the road.

'See you later' said Paul doubtfully. He didn't see what Lucy could do now. He really wondered if Lucy would be there at six pm as she said she would be. As he pedalled along, Paul imagined swimming with a whole pod of dolphins, free and happy at last. When he got near home though, he saw two familiar figures on the pavement.

'Where's your girlfriend Paulie?!' shouted Baz.

'What, isn't she with you to wipe your nose and keep you out of trouble?' jeered Mike. Paul kept going, trying not to take any notice of them.

'Go on back home, you mummies boy!' sneered Baz. 'We'll catch up with you soon enough' he added menacingly. Paul shuddered inside. He couldn't take much more of this. He just couldn't. He got home and wheeled his bike through to the back yard. He glanced up at the sky as he put it in the shed. It was dark and brooding and it looked like rain.

Lucy got back to the cottage. Dad was in the pocket-handkerchief sized garden at the back, which looked onto the fields beyond. He was sitting on a garden chair in his shorts and t-shirt reading a book, but the sun had gone in and he was beginning to feel cold. He glanced up as she approached him.

'Hey Luce' he smiled. 'I was beginning to wonder if you were going to come back. You're only twenty minutes late though' he added, glancing at his watch.

'You want to tell me what you've been up to this morning?' he asked. Lucy shrugged shyly. She didn't really.

'Oh you know, just dolphin stuff with my friend Paul' she replied noncommittally. She wanted to reach out to Spirit straight away and tell him what had happened, but Dad insisted on spending time with her and she didn't have the chance.

'I've spoken to Mary and she's agreed that we can help her out on the farm this afternoon' he said. It should be fun. We can pretend to be farmers. What do you say?' Lucy smiled weakly.

'Sounds good Dad' she replied.

By the end of the afternoon they had shifted hay about, filled water-troughs and mended holes in the hedges with bail wire. Normally it was fun to help out on the farm with Mary, but she was eaten up with worry about what to do to help Star-Gazer, her thoughts gnawing her inside.

As soon as they finished and went back to the cottage to freshen up, Lucy went up to her room. She settled down cross-legged on the floor and the strained her thoughts before relaxing them again in the way that she had learnt to help her slip from the world above water and into the watery world below. Before long she found the gap between the two states of consciousness and tumbled through.

The dolphins were all gathered in a loose circle, engrossed in conversation. It was Dancer who first noticed Lucy and called to Spirit. Lucy told Spirit and Dancer as quickly and concisely as she could what had happened that morning at the Penrose place. She was tired and knew she could not sustain the energy she needed to stay with Spirit for very long.

'It's okay!' said Spirit excitedly. 'We're going to save Star-Gazer. There's going to be a heavy storm tonight. Fresh water will flood down from the land. It will wash away all the silt from the inlet and around the fence. We'll find a way through the fence, or we'll get Star-Gazer to jump over it. She'll follow us down to the sea and she'll be free! It's all been decided.'

As Lucy's tiredness overcame her and she was pulled back to the world of dry land, she knew that she was going to be there to help them.

Chapter Nineteen:

'Would you like a snack Luce?' Dad called up the stairs of the cottage. Lucy became slowly aware of the room around her again.

'Not at the moment' she called back down the stairs. Lucy got up and looked out of the window. The air had become cloying and muggy, as though it were heavy with moisture and she could see that great black clouds had boiled across the sky. It looked like there was going to be a storm but Lucy didn't care. She wanted, no she needed to be there with Spirit. She just had to get back to the lagoon.

Lucy padded downstairs, unsure about what to do or say next. Dad was in the kitchen making himself a sandwich.

'There's going to be a good old thunderstorm' said Dad from the other side of the doorway. 'You can almost feel the electricity in the air. I'm just glad I'm not a sheep or a cow out there in the rain and wind, that's all I can say' he continued conversationally. Just then there was a spattering of light rain against the window, the precursor of worse weather to follow.

Lucy stood there in the small dining area of the cottage, tense and uncertain. Dad was just through the doorway. She knew that she should walk through and tell him that she had to do something, something important and that he had to let her go to do alone. She just couldn't bring herself to do it though.

Lucy had already been amazed that Dad had let her go off on her own that morning. Six months ago he wouldn't even have let her come down to the coast at all. He'd changed so much and she was beginning to feel so much closer to him and yet there were still things that she was simply unable to speak to him about. She was reluctant to tell him more than she needed to about the world of dolphins that was so important to her.

If Lucy went through the door now to tell him what she wanted to do, she knew he'd forbid it. There was no way he'd allow her to walk out into that dark and brooding storm. Even Bethany would have said no, she realised.

'I'm just popping over to the studio to talk to Bethany' Lucy called back to Dad through the doorway. 'I expect I'll be a while' she added.

'No worries' Dad answered trustingly. 'I'll have dinner on the table by about seven, so if you're not back by then I'll come over and get you. Take your coat now' he added 'We don't want you getting a soaking now do we?'

'See you later then Dad' Lucy replied, slipping out of the cottage. She felt terrible about lying, but by the time Dad bothered walking down to the studio to find out where his daughter had got to, she'd be long gone. It was the only way she could think of to get away. Heaven knows what Dad would do or say when he caught up with her, but she'd worry about that later.

Lucy slipped on her rain coat and ran down to the farmyard where the bikes were stored. Fortunately no one else was around so she pulled out the bike, jumped on it and started peddling off up the lane again.

The blackness of the clouds made it much darker than it normally would be for that time of day. Despite the rain that had begun to fall, the air still felt sticky and close and Lucy quickly started to sweat as she pedalled up the lane. The weather had brought out the snails, that trailed up plant stems in search of dinner. Lucy couldn't quite believe she was doing what she was doing and for the second time that day she half expected Dad to come chasing after her and tell her to come back to the cottage.

Just as Lucy turned out from the end of the lane onto the main road, the rain that was falling from the slate-grey clouds became heavier and Lucy could feel the drops of rain from her hair trickle down her back. Lucy realised that she had a choice. Turning right would be the quicker route out to the Penrose place. On the other hand if she turned left and decided to go and try and find Paul, she'd be going in the opposite direction and it would take much longer.

Lucy leant on the handle bars of the bike with one foot on the ground while she thought. Then impulsively she turned left in the direction of Merwater and Paul's house. She didn't know how Paul might help and in some ways she thought that she'd be better on her own. Paul was part of all of this now though. He had a right to be there with her.

It was raining steadily by the time that Lucy got to Paul's house and she was already wet through. Her rain coat was only designed for light showers and by now it was thoroughly waterlogged. Lucy glanced at her watch. It was already twenty past six and maybe Paul had given up waiting to see if she'd put a pebble on the gate post. Still, it was worth a try. She certainly didn't want to risk knocking on the door and dealing with Mrs Treddinick again. She'd never let Paul go out in the rain. Besides, Dad may have realised she was gone and already spoken to Mrs Treddinick on the phone. She daren't risk it.

Lucy took the pebble out of her rain coat pocket that she'd picked up from the beach and placed it on the fence post. She went back across the road and into the recreation ground opposite, where she looked back at the house from the protection of the straggly hedge.

The minutes ticked by. First Lucy promised herself that she would just wait five minutes and then go if Paul did not appear. Then she added another minute and then another but still he did not come. In the meantime Lucy was acutely aware that all the time she waited here was time she could be spending getting to the lagoon. More rain trickled down her neck as she stood there. It might not be cold rain, but it still felt uncomfortable.

After nine minutes, Lucy decided that Paul either hadn't seen the pebble, didn't care, or wasn't allowed to go out in the rain at this time. She sighed and pushed her bike back onto the street to leave, but just then Paul appeared pushing his own bike up the side of the house from the shed. He gave Lucy a shy grin.

'Let's get out of here' she said, relieved that he was there. He mounted his bike and then both of them went off up the rain-swept and deserted street together. Soon they had left Merwater and the houses gave way to hedgerows on either side. The wind had picked up and the rain was falling as fat heavy drops, each smacking into them with what felt like the force of small canon fire.

'What's the plan then?' Paul asked eventually. Neither of them had said much at all until they were clear of the town. Lucy glanced over at him. Paul was already almost as wet-through as she was.

'The rain will wash away the silt round that fence barrier thing' Lucy answered between pants as they pedalled up an incline. 'Star-Gazer will be able to jump over the fence or something. Then she'll be free.'

'Is that it?' asked Paul sceptically.

'That's it' replied Lucy. Something will happen. Something's got to.'

The sky was so dark that they could hardly see the hedgerows on each side of them as they pedalled along. The rain was coming down harder and it almost hurt the skin of Lucy's legs under her sodden shorts. The feeling of oppression and closeness intensified.

Suddenly there was a crackle of electricity in the air and in a blinding flash of lightning the whole countryside around them was briefly illuminated. The lightning struck a dead tree in the field to their left. Before they could adjust their eyes to the brightness it was gone again, but immediately the ear-splitting crack of thunder followed. The storm was immediately above them now. Lucy could hear the shattered tree topple over in the field.

'Go faster!' yelled Paul, putting on a spurt of speed on the pedals, desperate to get away.

'No stop!' Lucy hollered back at him urgently. 'Get off your bike NOW! They're metal and metal attracts lightning.'

Paul did as he was told and they both threw down their bikes into the ditch and continued on foot. Thankfully they were not far from the old railway embankment and the path that took them to the wall of the Penrose estate.

Just then another bolt of lightning hit the ground so close to them that Lucy almost felt that she could stretch out and touch it. The thunder struck in the same instant with a crash that left her ears ringing. The two children hurried on, fear crackling in their veins, not daring to turn and enjoy the strangeness of the scene around them. Lucy could hear a cow lowing in a nearby field and she wondered what it must be like to be a farm animal caught in an exposed field in a storm like this. Then she thought of Star-Gazer and pressed on again.

At the foot of the railway embankment a torrent of water was pouring out onto the road from the slope. They made their way up and were soon running along the overgrown path of the abandoned railway track, gravel crunching underfoot as they went.

They were both out of breath when they reached the base of the high stone wall separating them from the woods and the lagoon beyond. Paul started to climb the tree in order to scramble over the top of the wall and drop down on the other side.

'Wait' said Lucy, leaning against the wall. 'I need to focus.'

'You what?'

'I need to reach out to Star-Gazer and tell her that we are coming.' Another crack of lightning came down close by and moments later the thunder burst above them making them jump in alarm. Strangely the noise and the confusion of the storm around her made it easier to focus and before she knew it she was gliding through the dark waters of the lagoon to where Star-Gazer was circling nervously.

'Star-Gazer!' Lucy whispered so as not to alarm her by her arrival. 'It's me, Lucy, Spirit's friend.' Rain pounded the surface of the water just above their heads. The dolphin turned to face her. 'It's just like you told Spirit, the storm will wash away the silt. In a few minutes I'll be there with my friend Paul. Somehow we will set you free' Lucy continued.

'That sounds great Lucy' replied Star-Gazer, but in a way that made Lucy think that she didn't quite believe her. Lucy could sense that the dolphin was so sad that her spirit was almost entirely crushed. Lucy guessed that she was near the end.

'And Spirit's coming up the estuary too' she added. Immediately Lucy could see Star-Gazer's eyes light up again. 'Just hang on in there.' Lucy was about to return to her physical self when she turned back.

'You know the old man in the house, Norman Penrose. Is it true that you have some sort of a link with him?' asked Lucy.

'What, the man human pushed on wheels? We used to swim alongside their boat sometimes. Then the man and the woman saved me when I was in trouble. But now they just keep me here. I don't know why. They throw dead fish to me every day but that's no way to live. I want to look up at the stars again from the wide open sea, not here in this terrible place. No, there is no special link with him, not like you have with Spirit. None at all.' Lucy's mind came back to where she was standing with Paul.

'We're coming!' she assured Star-Gazer, as her silhouette dissolved back into the dark water.

Back under the wall, Lucy came to and looked up at Paul, half way up the small tree next to her.

'Let's get going again' she told him. Paul quickly disappeared over the wall and she heard a wet thud as he landed on the other side. Lucy clambered up behind him. She leapt down from the wall but instead of landing on her feet, she slipped on the sodden muddy earth at the base of the wall on the other side, tumbling over. She was unhurt and stood up again quickly, but mud was streaked all the way up her legs, rain coat and one side of her face.

Paul and Lucy ran on through the trees, muddy pools forming at their roots and then battled through the rhododendron bushes to get to the side of the lagoon. The eye of the storm had moved on a little now and although the rain was still intense, it did not feel as dark and oppressive as it did before.

Both Lucy and Paul were completely bedraggled, their wet hair plastered down flat over their skulls, with mud splattered up all over them.

'My mum would say we'll catch our death of cold' smiled Paul. They'd reachedthe edge of the lagoon. With a flash of lightning the scene was brightly illuminated again. Star-Gazer was racing agitatedly from one end of the inlet to the other. The water was too shallow to leap, but she was trying to do so anyway. With convulsive flicks of her tail flukes Star-Gazer repeatedly tried to jump. It was a desperate, heart-wrenching spectacle to watch.

Lights flicked on in the big house at the end of the inlet as someone evidently had noticed Star-Gazer's distress. A door clattered open at the side somewhere and then Mrs Penrose appeared, holding an umbrella ineffectually over her head. It promptly blew inside out and she let it drop to the ground.

'What's the matter Flipper? It's only a storm' Lucy could make out Mrs Penrose saying over the wind and driving rain. She could see that Star-Gazer was desperate to escape. Mrs Penrose's voice became more plaintiff.

'You can't leave us Flipper. Norman needs you! Stay with us!' she cried out as another flash of lightning illuminated the sky. Star-Gazer paid no heed though, as she continued her compulsive flailing to and fro in the water. Lucy could see Mrs Penrose go down onto the small landing stage and kneeling down, it seemed as though she were trying to offer Star-Gazer something, though Lucy could not make out what. Just then Paul nudged Lucy with his elbow.

'This is weird' he exclaimed.

'You're right' replied Lucy, pulling herself together. 'We've got work to do.' They made their way along the bank towards the closed-link fence that separated Star-Gazer from Spirit and the wide open sea beyond the estuary. Lucy didn't care about Mrs Penrose now. It was probably too dark for her to see them and even if she did, in the midst of the storm it felt as though different rules applied.

The storm was so heavy and so much water had fallen so quickly that great rivulets of fresh water were running into the inlet now. It seemed as though half a dozen streams had appeared from nowhere. Lucy and Paul splashed through them as they made their way to the fence. It didn't matter if their shoes got wet, they were soaked already.

When they got to the fence Lucy could see that Star-Gazer had been right. The storm had succeeded in washing away much of the silt that had accumulated around it. The channel on the other side down to the sea was free now.

'Spirit!' she cried, splashing down into the water to greet him. Dancer was there again too. Paul followed her and they both embraced the two dolphins briefly. Spirit and Dancer started to let out a succession of clicking and whistling sounds to alert Star-Gazer to their arrival.

Star-Gazer immediately gave up her flailing and approached the fence. Spirit was there on the other side, looking through it at her. It was the first time that they had actually seen each over for other a year and for a few moments they seemed lost in each others gaze. Lucy could only guess at what was going through both of their minds at that moment.

Despite being so close to Spirit on the other side of the fence, Star-Gazer was still not free. She swam around in a circle and then tried to jump again, but there was a wire submerged just below the surface of the water and there was still not enough depth to enable her to jump high enough to clear the fence. On the other side Spirit and Dancer started ramming the fence, trying to dislodge it at the bottom and make a gap big enough for a dolphin to swim through. It was no good though; the fence had been fixed in place well and though it bent when they rammed it, it did not break or dislodge. Lucy produced her penknife from her pocket.

'Let's help them' she said to Paul, wading into the water. The penknife had a saw blade and after a couple of minutes she was able to cut through the submerged wire. It wasn't enough to enable Star-Gazer to jump the fence though and she started hacking at the fence links. Paul tried pulling it up at the base while the dolphins continued to ram in. The worst of the storm had passed and though there was still thunder and lightning, it was not overhead now. The rain continued to sheer down and twilight was descending. It would soon be dark.

'This is like, impossible' panted Paul. 'It's going to take forever to cut through the wire with that penknife of yours and we're not going to be able to open up a hole at the bottom, that's for sure.'

'You'll be needing a pair of these' a voice suddenly sounded behind them. Both children whipped round in surprise, Paul nearly slipping into the water as he did so. Mrs Penrose was standing behind them on the bank. She looked gaunt and severe and almost as soaked as they were. Lucy made an involuntary gasp. What did she want? Would she insist that they stopped, or would she even call the police?

'You'll be needing a pair of these' she repeated again, holding out something in her hand. Lucy couldn't make out what it was at first in the deep gloom. 'They're wire-cutters' she added, her voice choked with emotion. Lucy looked up into her eyes in wonder. Another flash of lightning illuminated the scene momentarily and Lucy wondered whether it was rain or tears streaming down the old lady's face.

'You were right' she continued. 'Flipper, Star-Gazer or whatever you call him needs to be free. I can see that now. I think Norman can too.' She held out the wire cutters again in her hand. 'Take them!'

Lucy needed no further invitation. She scrambled up the slippery bank, took the wire-cutters from the old lady's outstretched hand and slid back down into the water. She threw her penknife to one side and started clipping through the wire as quickly as she could. One by one she sheared through the links and after a couple of minutes the fence was sagging low.

Star-Gazer circled again and as Lucy continued to clip, she sailed through the air over the sagging fence, so close to Lucy that she could almost feel it. Star-Gazer splashed into the channel on the other side next to Spirit and Dancer. She was free!

A great feeling of joy surged through Lucy and she hugged Paul briefly. She turned and looked up at Mrs Penrose.

'Thank you' she said simply. Mrs Penrose smiled, wiping her eyes as she did so. Then Lucy waded back into the water to where the three dolphins were clicking excitedly in the small channel. Paul followed.

Lucy hugged Star-Gazer and Dancer in turn and shyly, Paul followed suit. Then she stood for a moment and looked deeply into Spirit's eyes, before climbing on to his back.

'Children, come back out of the water, it's not safe. You'll drown!' called Mrs Penrose behind them. Lucy was completely absorbed by the three dolphins. She pulled herself up onto Spirit's back and the two of them started to make their way off down the channel towards the sea. Paul followed suit and mounted Dancer's back, holding on fast to her dorsal fin.

'What are you?' called Mrs Penrose in exasperation and wonder. Paul looked back at her.

'I told you, she's a Dolphin-Child' he replied. 'I'm a Dolphin-Child too now' he added, as if the thought had just come to him. He and Dancer started swimming behind the other two.

Star-Gazer looked up out of the water at Mrs Penrose standing there on the muddy bank in the rain. She regarded the old lady with kindly eyes before swimming off behind the other two dolphins to freedom.

It was exhilarating to hitch a ride on the backs of dolphins in the middle of a thunderstorm in the encroaching darkness. The rain still beat down and the occasional flashes of lightning revealed the stark silhouettes of trees on either side of them as they swum down the estuary towards the sea. Lucy began to feel really cold now and glancing at Paul, she could see that he was shivering convulsively in his sodden tee-shirt as he clung on to Dancer.

As the estuary widened they could hear the creaking of the yachts and boats moored in the shallow water and the crack of wires against the aluminium boat masts. Beyond them was the dull roar of the stormy sea.

At the mouth of the estuary, looking out to sea was a pub, the 'Man Overboard' built at the top of stone steps that led down to a short sandy beach. The bright lights from inside the pub shone out into the darkness of the stormy night.

It was the lights of the Man Overboard that Lucy saw as the three dolphins swam towards the sea. Beyond the estuary Lucy could tell that the sea was rough and choppy. There was no way that the children could venture out on the dolphins backs into all that, especially not in the dark. Spirit, Dancer and Star-Gazer seemed to be aware of this too and they made for the small strip of beach just below the pub. They got as far into the shallows as they could without risking grounding themselves and Lucy climbed off. She leant over and hugged Spirit tightly before wading up out of the water. It was just a few short steps to get to the warmth and safety of the pub. It had been wonderful to stay with the dolphins after helping to liberate Star-Gazer, but Lucy knew that now was the time to leave them. She turned to wave them farewell.

Following suit, Paul slid off Dancer's back as well, but he stood there uncertainly up to his waist in the cold salt water.

'What's going on?' he asked, sounding confused.

'We've got to leave them now Paul and come ashore' Lucy replied.

'Why can't we just swim out to sea with them?' he asked plaintively. 'We can stay with them in the ocean.'

'Don't be daft Paul' said Lucy. She was tired and cold and wanted to get on dry land as quickly as possible. 'It's freezing out here.'

'But we're Dolphin-Children now. We don't have to come back to land anymore. We can just swim out to sea if we want to.' Lucy didn't know what to say to him. People had said that she was a

Dolphin-Child but she still didn't really know what that meant. She certainly didn't think that Paul was one too. She wondered if the cold had made him delirious somehow.

'Look we can't stand here waist deep in the freezing water. Come ashore and we can talk about it then.' Lucy could see Paul shiver again convulsively, but he still would not come onto dry land. Dancer started to move off and Paul turned round in a panic.

If only Lucy had known everything that was going through Paul's head she could have said something to reassure him, but she had no idea. In Paul's mind though all he could see were the taunts and threats of Baz, Mike and the other kids. He thought of the mud that they had thrown at him and the feeling of loneliness now that his best friend had moved away. He thought of his mother, depressed and distant, and of his father who hadn't even called him for months. Then he thought of the sense of belonging and intimacy he had felt in the presence of Spirit and Dancer, of how they had needed his help and how he needed theirs.

He thought of the story of Susan Penhaligon and how many people in Merwater still believed that the children who had swum out to sea with her had really turned into dolphins. His mum was wrong about dolphins, he knew she was. It would be better to be a dolphin than to be a miserable and unhappy human he thought. He imagined his arms transforming into flippers, his legs turning into tail flukes. He would be free in the wide seas and every day would be happy. All he needed to do was to welcome the water and let it happen, he thought.

'No' he answered in a cracked and anguished voice. 'I'm not going back. You can't make me! I'm going with them.' He turned and started swimming out to sea. Dancer had already disappeared into the black, choppy water but he was determined to catch up.

'Paul, you're crazy, come here now!' Lucy cried in what she hoped was a commanding voice, but Paul took no notice and Lucy was overwhelmed by a sense of growing panic. 'You'll get yourself killed!'

Lucy started swimming desperately after Paul, but it was dark now and she could hardly see where Paul was going. She couldn't even hear him over the roar of the sea. She'd already seen that he was a weak swimmer and she knew that he wouldn't last long in conditions like this. It was so dark now that he could slip under the water a metre from her and she wouldn't even know it. Cramp and tiredness could easily overcome him. He'd go down like a stone.

Even though Lucy was a strong swimmer, she wasn't used to conditions like these either. She wished with all her heart that Spirit and Dancer would come back, but they would have no idea about what was going on now. There was no time to reach out to them with her mind. Everything was spiralling horribly out of control and Lucy knew that in as little as a minute Paul could die, his lungs choked with water, the life squeezed out of his slight body.

Just as Lucy thought it was all going to be too late, a bright spotlight suddenly clicked on and illuminated the water in front of Lucy. There was Paul, clearly struggling in the water, but still with his head above the surface. Just in front of them was the familiar yellow of the Merwater Lifeboat. It was coming in from the direction of the sea and Lucy became aware of voices calling out to Paul and Lucy, though she couldn't make out what any of them were saying. A figure in a yellow outfit jumped from the lifeboat into the water attached to a rope and struck out to where Paul was flailing. The experienced hands of the lifeboat-man quickly secured Paul and they pulled him in up onto the deck.

Lucy trod water with difficulty and was dazzled when the light of the lifeboat picked her out. There were more cries from the deck and another figure plunged into the water. Even before they reached her, she felt a sense of relief that help was at hand roll over her. Lucy didn't quite know how she found herself on the deck of the lifeboat. Then a familiar face appeared in front of her as other hands busied themselves to cover her up and restore some warmth to her chilled body.

'Hullo there Lucy' smiled Nate Merryweather. 'Thought I'd hitch a ride on this tub for old time's sake and who should they pull out of the water but young Paul Treddinick and young Lucy Parr. Now however did they come to be out here on a wet and stormy night I wonder?' He smiled. 'Well I'm right glad we found you both. And in the nick of time too I reckon.'

The lifeboat came ashore on the beach under the Man Overboard, where the flashing light of an ambulance was waiting for them. Lucy leant back and gave a silent prayer of thanks that they were both alright.

Chapter Twenty: Epilogue

It was a hospital bed that Lucy woke up in the next morning. They'd been scared that she and Paul would suffer from hypothermia and the doctors had decided to keep them both in overnight under observation at the local cottage hospital. Lucy had felt utterly exhausted and had slept deeply through the long hours of darkness after the storm.

When she awoke bleary eyed the next morning, Dad and Bethany were sitting by her bed. It looked as though they'd been dozing in their chairs and they both looked tired and drawn.

'Hello Dad', Lucy said in a small voice. She didn't like to think what he might say to her.

'Hey Luce' he whispered, giving her hand a squeeze. She couldn't tell if he was angry with her or just glad she was okay. He was about to say something when a male nurse appeared at her bedside. The nurse busied himself with taking Lucy's temperature, checking her heart rate and updating the chart at the foot of her bed. He turned to Dad and Bethany and smiled brightly.

'Well the doctor will have to come round later, but I think she'll give Lucy the all clear. She's been stable all night and there's been no sign of exposure developing. Lucy had a very lucky escape.'

'Please, what about Paul?' asked Lucy, struggling to sit upright.

'You lie down now Lucy' replied the nurse.

'He's okay Kiddo' Bethany broke in. 'He's just down the corridor. It looks like he'll be fine too. I was chatting to his mother a bit earlier. They were a bit worried about his vital signs over night, but he stabilised an hour or two ago.' The memory of last night came back vividly to Lucy.

'I, I didn't mean it to happen like this' she stammered. 'He got it into his head that he could actually turn into a dolphin or something. He started swimming out after Dancer. I tried to reach him, really I did. But if it hadn't been for.....' she trailed off as she thought of the lifeboat. Another minute and it might have been too late, she thought. Lucy could see Dad's face clouding again but Bethany spoke before he could.

'It's alright, we know' Bethany reassured her. 'Nate went with Paul in the second ambulance. Paul was quite upset but he told Nate about the bullying and then wanting to turn into a dolphin like those children who swam out with that Susan Penhaligon all those years ago. You couldn't have known Kiddo, really you couldn't.'

You should never have been there in the first place, neither of you' muttered Dad darkly. Lucy didn't seem to hear though.

'What was Nate doing there anyway?' she asked.

'You know he used to be a lifeboat volunteer himself for many years' Bethany continued. 'Well he was having a chat with one of

313

his life-boat pals when the call came through. He hitched a lift when he heard you and Paul mentioned. Paul's Dad used to be a lifeboat volunteer too so he knows the Treddinick family quite well. It was Mrs Penrose who raised the alarm when you both disappeared down the estuary on the dolphin's backs.'

'Just as well too' said Dad, frowning. 'Your Aunt and I nearly went spare when we realised you'd given me the slip and ran off like that into the storm. You must have been mad. I must have been mad to ever think about letting you come down here in the first place'.

'I'm so sorry Dad, really I am. I know what I did was wrong but....'

'But nothing' broke in Dad, his anger getting the better of him. 'It's not going to happen again. We're going home tomorrow far from the sea where you'll be safe. You'll be waking up one morning soon and you'll realise that you can't communicate with your precious dolphins anymore. That's what Thelma says. That's what your Mrs Penhaligon from school says. That's what happens with all these Dolphin-Children. It will all just fade away. Then I can have my daughter back again. It's not going to be like it was with Megan. You'll just grow out of it. It'll be over at last.'

Lucy looked from Dad to Bethany and back again.

'That, that can't be true!' she exclaimed. Dad looked angry and Bethany had a pained sympathetic expression on her face. The thought of not having Spirit in her life felt like having her heart torn out.

314

'That's not what happened to Mum is it?' she asked. Dad leant forward hotly and seized both her arms as though he was going to shake her. He looked passionately and angrily into her eyes.

'Your Mum would be here today if it weren't for all of this......' He gestured around him as though he meant Merwater, the sea, dolphins and everything else. Lucy knew what he meant. He expected her to just forget about dolphins and to live an empty grey life instead.

'NO!' cried Lucy full of anguish 'I can't lose Spirit. I won't. I'm not going to let it happen!

****

'Midnight Dolphin'. What is the secret of Lucy's mother's death? What are 'The Three Sisters'? What links three generations of children and their dolphins? Read the third book of the trilogy and find out the answers to these questions.

Printed in Great Britain
by Amazon